Adam

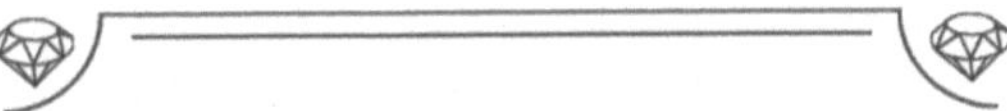

Diamonds of the First Water
Book Three

SYDNEY JANE BAILY

cat whisker press

Boston

Second Paperback Edition, 2024
ISBN: 978-1-957421-56-8

Published by Cat Whisker Press

Cover: Dar Albert, Wicked Smart Designs
Book Design: Cat Whisker Studio
Editor: Chris Hall

DIAMONDS OF THE FIRST WATER

A Diamond for Christmas

Clarity

Purity

Adam

Radiance

Brilliance

OTHER WORKS

The RAKES ON THE RUN Series
Last Dance in London
Pursued in Paris
Banished to Brighton
Gretna Green by Sunset
The Lady Who Stole Christmas

The RARE CONFECTIONERY Series
The Duchess of Chocolate
The Toffee Heiress
My Lady Marzipan
The Gingerbread Lady

The DEFIANT HEARTS Series
An Improper Situation
An Irresistible Temptation
An Inescapable Attraction
An Inconceivable Deception
An Intriguing Proposition
An Impassioned Redemption

The BEASTLY LORDS Series
Lord Despair
Lord Anguish
Lord Vile
Lord Darkness
Lord Misery
Lord Wrath
Lord Corsair
Eleanor

PRESENTING LADY GUS

THE BLACK KNIGHT'S REWARD
with Marliss Melton

DEDICATION

To all those who see beyond
the shields we "wear" in one form or another

You know it is what's inside that matters.

INTRODUCTION TO
DIAMONDS OF THE FIRST WATER

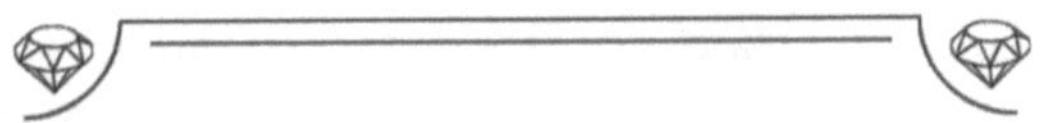

Once upon a time, an Irish family by the name of O'Diamáin emigrated to England from the north of Ireland, from County Doire to be specific. You may know the area as Derry or even Londonderry if you are thinking of it after King James I granted the city a royal charter.

Felim O'Diamáin, who was the youngest son, sailed across the Irish Sea to make his fortune, bringing his pretty wife and two young children with him. As the story goes, they stopped on the Isle of Man for a perfectly peaceful night before landing at Ravenglass the next day and traipsing through the Lake District.

Another version swears they took the shorter but far more dangerous route north across the sea to Portpatrick, finding themselves in the southernmost part of Scotland. From there, if they indeed came that way, they headed east toward Gretna Green. Not for any quick anvil marriage, mind you, but to traverse the border to England.

No one knows for sure the veracity of either tale, nor particularly cares. Once they arrived in England, Felim did very well for himself, as did his descendants.

At some point during the twelve-year reign of George I, another O'Diamáin by the name of Liam was made an earl for his devoted service to the Crown. During those years in the early eighteenth century, King George also created a few dukes, at least one marquess, some barons, a single viscount, and other earls. But we're not interested in any of them, although some may have helped to quell the riots that ensued when Hanoverian George outmaneuvered any pesky residual Stuarts hoping to claim the English throne.

Nevertheless, our interest lies with Liam. With his new earldom came much wealth and land, specifically in Derbyshire. And naturally, a title. However, George I, being of Germanic descent, didn't find the Celtic name of O'Diamáin tripped easily off his tongue. Neither did he master Gaelic or Manx, for that matter. In any case, with a little persuasion and an extra thousand acres, Liam became William, the Earl Diamond, as his male descendants have been known ever since.

Over the years, the earls have enlarged the original house to be an impressive manor, always named Oak Grove Hall, which is the translation of their long-ago home of County *Doire*.

Generations later, while inheriting the earldom and all its assets, Geoffrey, Lord Diamond and his beloved wife, Caroline, have wealth of a different nature as well—five healthy children: Clarity, Purity, Adam, Radiance, and Brilliance. They are known as the Diamonds of the First Water, at least by their parents.

This is Adam's story . . .

PROLOGUE

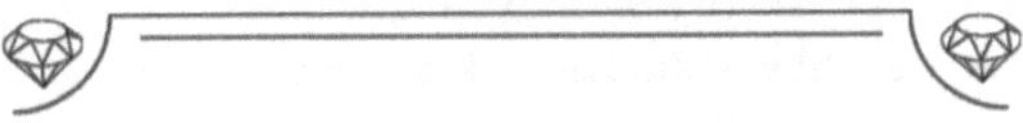

Bath, England, 1851

Adam saw the small package slip from the grasp of the lady ahead of him. He might not have noticed, except he had been watching the pleasant sway of her hips as she strolled along Great Pulteney Street. Despite the attractive Palladian architecture rising up on either side of him, the honey-haired beauty had all his attention.

When the package slipped from amongst the others she carried, he darted forward, wondering why her maid who walked beside her wasn't carrying more.

"My lady, a moment," he said to catch her attention and get her to halt. He knew her to be one not only because her gown was well-made of a pretty summer cream-and-lavender cotton, but also because she had a lady's maid beside her in the plainer clothing of her class.

At his words, however, she kept walking.

"My lady," he tried again, feeling a little awkward as he dogged her steps, until the maid glanced over her shoulder before tugging on her lady's arm.

At last, she stopped and turned.

Adam had been right to think her a lady. A patrician nose, amethyst earbobs, and an intelligent silvery-green gaze with which she took his measure confirmed his assumption.

"Have we been introduced?" she asked, as any upper-class female would when accosted in public.

"No," he confessed. "And I never would be so presumptuous as to approach an unfamiliar lady upon the street except you dropped this."

Holding out her package, he felt like a supplicant. Her generous mouth suddenly opened in an *O* of surprise. Then she nodded, but she didn't move forward to retrieve it, remaining motionless as she stared at him.

Instead, her maid finally took the paper-wrapped item, which had felt like something light and frivolous. Perhaps lace gloves for a ball.

Glancing at her hands, they were ensconced in gloves that weren't nearly as fine as the ones he'd imagined but perfectly clean.

"Thank you, my lord," she said when she found her voice, wresting his attention back to her stunning face. "I would have been sorely disgruntled to arrive home and find I had lost my purchase."

"Indeed," he said, for he could think of nothing else to say, no way to keep her talking. Yet Adam couldn't help wishing propriety allowed him to ask her name or introduce himself. But that would be too forward. On the other hand, he could let her know of his interest.

"I hope I shall see you again, my lady. Perhaps at an assembly one evening."

She paled. "Unlikely, my lord. Again, my gratitude. Good day."

Then she turned and walked away.

CHAPTER ONE

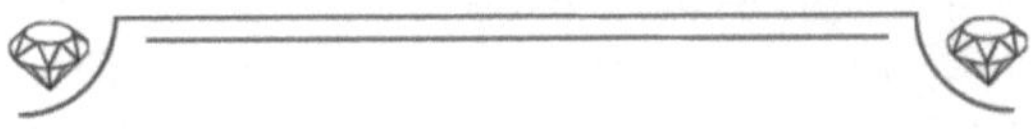

"Upstairs," Alice ordered the two young ladies in her charge. They were spoiled by their mother. But they were also smart and eager to learn whatever Alice could teach them. They rarely talked back, nor complained when made to conjugate French verbs or practice the violin.

Today was going to be a geography lesson followed by a discussion in French, and as their governess of the past two years, Alice was proud of the girls' progress. Their education had been less than satisfactorily handled by the ones who came before her. And their eldest sister, Susanne, who was now out in society and eager to marry, suffered from a distinct lack of learning.

Luckily, the young lady in question was also sweet and pretty, but Alice felt badly at how few significant thoughts Susanne had in her head. Moreover, she was unable to speak a second language, nor play an instrument. She was, in a word, uncivilized.

On the other hand, the eldest Beasley daughter had her entire life ahead, full of promise, with every door open and every opportunity still afforded her. Alice, taking her seat in the salon they used for lessons, had grown up with the best education money could buy, and her future had fallen like an unfortunate squirrel down a well. Despite being the only offspring of a depleted, nearly bankrupt earl—at *low tide*, as her mother called it—Alice's prospects were now limited to working as a governess for Lord and Lady Beasley's daughters until they outgrew her.

Then, with an ounce of luck, Alice hoped she would find another position equally fulfilling with younger children who would need her longer. Then she could settle into the next household, perhaps for a decade.

And after that? Maybe another situation of equal length before she could retire to the country in a small, tidy cottage.

It sounded pleasant. *Not the least bit dreadful, dreary, and tedious,* she promised herself. And after the drama of her own early twenties, she ought to be glad of a calm respite— for the rest of her life.

So why did she want to put her head into a pillow and scream, at least once every day?

"Mrs. Malcolm," Pauline got her attention. "Would you please speak to my mother about piano lessons again? I think I prefer the pianoforte to the violin."

Alice smiled to herself. What Pauline had liked about her previous lessons was how the teacher used to doze off and let her do nothing.

"Since I cannot play it well," Alice told her, "Lady Beasley would have to hire another teacher for your music lessons. If she is willing, then I will find a suitable piano instructor who will make you learn your scales and practice daily so you can become proficient."

"Oh," Pauline said before sniffing and sitting back in her chair, looking instantly disinterested. The girl wasn't lazy exactly, but she did like to take the easy way whenever possible. Sadly, she had no innate talent for a musical instrument.

"Well, I prefer Mrs. Malcolm," Pauline's sister, a year younger, declared. Leila had a better knack for the violin. However, her French accent was atrocious no matter how well she handled the grammar.

Alice only wished she could convince Lady Beasley to allow her to instruct Susanne on the rudimentary knowledge she ought to have learned. The last time they spoke about it, Lady Beasley had been adamant.

"Susanne is the prettiest of my three girls. Thus, she won't need the other skills necessary to capture a husband."

Skills like basic mathematics, knowing Spain from Germany, or being able to have an informed discussion about anything other than textiles. But Alice had been forced to give up.

As if she'd conjured the buffle-headed young lady whose only interest was in fashion and how attractive she looked, Susanne appeared at the door.

"Mother has a favor to ask you, Mrs. Malcolm," the brown-haired eldest Beasley daughter said.

Alice frowned. She was rarely summoned by Lady Beasley, who trusted Alice completely by this time with her younger daughters' education. Rising, she considered the best use of their time while alone.

"Come up with a discussion you might wish to have upon traveling to the Continent or meeting with a visitor from France."

"Is he a male visitor?" Pauline asked.

Alice, who knew how the mind of a female on the cusp of womanhood worked, nodded. "If you wish, then yes. Pretend you are the dining companion of a handsome man whom you wish to impress. Leila, you can be the gentleman. When I get back, you two shall present your dialogue to me."

"Like a play," Leila said with an enthusiastic clap, not minding being the male lead. "Bonjour, mademoiselle," she said to her sister.

Alice nodded and followed Susanne downstairs to Lady Beasley's private salon where she was writing her daily correspondence and taking tea.

"*Ah*, there you are, Mrs. Malcolm."

She said it as if Alice had been off gallivanting around instead of in her normal place upstairs, tutoring the girls.

"You wished to speak with me," Alice said, sitting without being asked. It was a nasty habit, but she had been born and raised as a titled lady. In her daily dealings with others, it was sometimes difficult to remember how far she had fallen in her station.

Lady Beasley briefly frowned at the governess taking a seat, but then she got to the point.

"I shall not be able to accompany Susanne to the ball."

"Which ball, my lady?" Alice wondered at her ladyship assuming she had any idea of the social schedule of Bath's finer people.

"Two nights from now at the assembly rooms."

"I see." Alice waited, wondering what it had to do with her.

"I would like you to be her chaperone."

Oh dear! Alice tamped down the instant apprehension. This was her life now, hardly above that of a servant. And as if she were an old married woman or someone's mother, she was being called upon to observe a young lady's manners and protect her virtue.

If only someone had done that for her!

She would refuse. It was not in her employment description, and it would cause her personal discomfort to be thrust into a situation that was as familiar as breathing, but in which she no longer belonged. Moreover, in such a situation, there was the danger of being recognized.

Susanne had stayed in the room to listen. Now she spoke up with genuine enthusiasm.

"How fun it will be for you, Mrs. Malcolm, to see all the lovely gowns and to listen to the music. I know how you love music."

"Nearly as much as you love gowns," Alice said to her without malice. "However, I do not believe I can attend."

"If additional pay is the issue," Lady Beasley began, causing Alice's cheeks to heat.

"No, my lady." Although she *would* accept any extra wages since she saved every penny. The sooner she had enough, the sooner she could retire to the country—in twenty years or so.

"I only ask because I will, in fact, pay you well to attend my Susanne. I trust you implicitly, Mrs. Malcolm, not to be foolish or flighty or let my daughter take the smallest of risks."

Alice tried to breathe steadily. Even if she could bear the reminder of her life that once was . . .

"I have nothing to wear to a ball," she pointed out. The two women in the room would be surprised to see the wardrobe she had owned merely two years earlier. *Gowns of satin and fine silk for dancing with dukes and dining with earls and even for falling prey to a debauched viscount.*

"We shall take care of that," Lady Beasley insisted. "If one of Susanne's dresses does not fit you, then we shall go to the dressmaker on Pulteney Bridge. She nearly always has something already sewn that can be tightened with a ribbon or two at the waist. Luckily, you are neither unusually short nor unbearably tall, but as perfectly proportioned as my own girls."

The comparison was *nearly* accurate except for two items. The Beasley females were on the daintier, less fulsome side of the scale, whereas Alice took after her own mother, who was exceedingly shapely when it came to her bosom.

In any case, at the mere thought of entering a ballroom, she was beginning to feel queasy.

"Is there not a close friend of yours, my lady, who would be more suitable, someone accustomed to the social life of Bath?"

"I wish there was, but on short notice, I can think of no one I can ask. Susanne could attend with a friend, but I do not trust that another girl's mother will look after her as her own. She might become distracted. Worse, I have heard of someone letting a young lady stray with the specific intent of her ruin."

Alice gasped as if she'd been found out. Susanne gasped at the awful notion.

"Mother!" she exclaimed. "Who would do such a thing on purpose?"

Lady Beasley sighed. "You are so lovely and naïve, dear girl. And you have a titled father and a large dowry. You can have any man in Bath or, next year, in London. Many others cannot say the same thing. Thus, your competition may try to get rid of you in any manner they can."

Alice could barely breathe. Then, all at once, she blurted, "I shall chaperone her!"

Indeed, she would. Lord and Lady Beasley had given her employment on the basis of a fraudulent letter of recommendation and treated her with kindness. What's more, Lady Susanne was all wide-eyed innocence. Alice would rather be flayed alive before she let the girl experience anything like what had happened to her.

The matter was settled. When she climbed the stairs to the salon, she could hardly credit she was going to attend a ball at her age, in her circumstances, as a chaperone!

ADAM ALIGHTED FROM A sedan chair in front of his mother's friend's townhouse on The Paragon, a street running parallel to the River Avon. He thought the river itself, one of five Avons in England, to be an interesting phenomenon, winding narrow and long for seventy-five miles, yet only traversing nineteen miles westward from its source to its mouth, all the way to Portishead. It spilled into the Severn Estuary and the Bristol Channel.

Adam considered life to be much like the River Avon, or at least he hoped it would be—taking him through many and varied places and, of course, being many long years, like his grandparents, all four of whom were still living.

In any case, he liked to try new things, such as the wretched sedan chair, a box suspended on two poles. His mother had told him the chair used to be much in fashion in Bath when she was a girl, not only for the infirm but as a for-hire conveyance. Its popularity was currently giving way to a wheeled version. Thus, the Countess Diamond had advised him to try it before it vanished forever like the unfortunate dodo bird.

"You will feel like a foreign emperor from India or China," she'd said.

He felt like a damn fool!

Arriving at Lord and Lady Beasley's home after a far shorter journey than the River Avon's, he vowed never to climb into such an embarrassing, uncomfortable contraption again. The two chairmen had been quick enough after he'd hailed them outside his residence on the Royal Crescent, but the journey made him shake like a dried pea inside a baby's rattle. Not only did his teeth clack together, but his head banged side to side every time the shorter chairmen took a step.

Besides, the whole experience of being carried by two other chaps—yelling to everyone to move aside with "Chair, ho!"—made him feel like a pompous arse the entire way.

At his mother's request, he had agreed to a visit with the Beasley family, and naturally, there were daughters involved. An honest woman, Countess Caroline Diamond had confessed her old friend had three of them, although only one of them was of marriageable age.

Lady Diamond's friend from her youth, Lady Beasley was attractive and intelligent, and his mother assumed the eldest daughter would have at least those traits. Thus, he had dropped off his calling card days earlier upon his arrival in Bath and been invited to tea.

A rap on the door gained him entrance by a short butler, who ushered him into the drawing room. His hostess would be with him shortly.

Adam surveyed the room, grandiose with robin's egg blue wallpaper and enough white painted molding to fell a forest. It looked rather like his own parents' house. Then he heard music, not the pianoforte that his sisters played but a richly resonant violin. A tad introspective and solemn, rather than bright and lively, however.

Unable to help himself, he followed the music through the doorway at the far end of the drawing room into a smaller salon set up for reading and then into another. The violinist had her back to him and was staring out the window, playing from memory.

Wishing he hadn't been so forward, since now he was alone with a female, Adam suddenly knew he'd seen her before. By her hair, he believed she was the lady from the street whose package he'd recovered. And at once, he also realized she must be the eldest daughter.

His mother had done him a good turn. He admired Lady Susanne already. Besides being lovely, she must be clever indeed to play so well.

Waiting silently while she finished, he was pleased to listen and to observe her. He'd experienced an instant attraction days earlier but feared he would have to wait until the first assembly to see her again. He had even returned each day to the same stretch of street, to no avail. Yet here she was.

As soon as the last notes died out, he spoke.

"Good day, my lady. I am sorry to intrude."

She whirled around to face him. The expressions flickering across her face were easy to decipher—alarm, confusion, and then recognition.

"How did you get in here?"

"I was invited," Adam said. "I am pleased to meet you. I am Lord Diamond."

Her eyes widened slightly, and then she offered a polite curtsy.

"I believe you have mistaken me, my lord."

"On the contrary. In fact, I have kept my eyes open for you while strolling Great Pulteney Street ever since our last encounter."

Before he could say more, footsteps and voices came behind him. He turned to see the woman who must be Lady Beasley and another of her daughters. They were alike as two peas, with brown hair, soft brown eyes, and round cheeks with pleasant smiles. Apparently, the eldest daughter with the violin took after her father, for she had lighter hair, different color eyes, and sculpted cheekbones.

"There you are, young Diamond," Lady Beasley said.

He bowed to her. "It was rude of me to have left the drawing room, and my mother would take me to task, but I heard your daughter's exemplary violin playing and followed it like a sheep to a shepherdess. I am enchanted."

The two females looked at one another, and then the younger one laughed while her mother shook her head.

"You mean Mrs. Malcolm," Lady Beasley said, gesturing with a wave of her hand. "She isn't my daughter. She is the governess to my two younger daughters."

The governess! He nearly winced at his mistake. Her bearing was not what he expected a governess to have. Moreover, on the day he'd seen her, she had appeared to be accompanied by a lady's maid when, really, she was one of two household staff out for a stroll.

What a dunce!

"You are correct, my lord," the daughter added. "Mrs. Malcolm plays heavenly. I love to listen, too."

"*This* is my daughter, Lady Susanne," Lady Beasley introduced her.

The young lady eyed him openly with her coffee-colored gaze.

"It is a pleasure to meet you," he said. Adam did not let his disappointment show, but she seemed like a child compared to the governess and no wonder. Mrs. Malcolm was a married woman!

"Let us retire to the drawing room," Lady Beasley said. "Tea will have been served by now."

She preceded her daughter, but Adam hung back. Turning around, he faced the woman who still stood there, having watched and listened and been ignored by her employer. She had not been invited to tea at any rate.

Mrs. Malcolm remained composed with a certain sophic air about her. Adam would say she had a worldly quality, as if older than her years. Not that he knew her years.

"You are staring, my lord." She said it as factual, not as a reprimand.

It was true.

"My apologies." He was merely rearranging his preconception of her from a lady of the household to an employee. "Again, I am sorry I intruded and for mistaking you to be a . . ."

He trailed off, stopping himself from saying she was not a lady but simply a regular woman. That definitely was not coming out well.

"A member of the family," he finished, watching her suck her cheeks in slightly, accentuating her cheekbones while appearing irritated.

"Your tea will be growing cold, my lord." She raised her violin once again to her shoulder and turned her back on him.

CHAPTER TWO

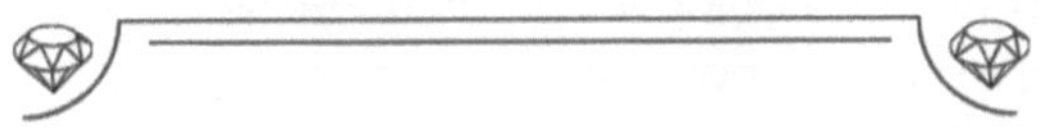

Adam grinned. Mrs. Malcolm reminded him of his feisty sister Radiance, putting him in his place.

"Good day," he said to her straight back. For answer, she began to play.

Time to visit with the Beasleys, he reminded himself and sprinted toward the drawing room, knowing he'd lingered too long with the governess.

Not good form, he muttered to himself.

In short order, he was seated opposite the two Beasley females, mother and daughter, drinking tea, eating biscuits, and enjoying the conversation, mostly because it had to do with Bath and his mother's youthful mischief.

"I was happy for Caroline making a love match, despite the small scandal that ensued," Lady Beasley said of the now Countess Diamond. "Unfortunately, she and your father made all our parents watch us far too closely."

Adam had heard about his parents' elopement. It took the pressure off the next generation of Diamonds to behave appropriately all the time since their parents had raced off to Gretna Green. Even his older sister Purity, whom they all considered the most proper primster, had eventually relaxed and fallen in love with a rakish baron.

"My parents are as much in love as ever. Mother says she will come visit you this fall if you wish," he told Lady Beasley.

"I would like that very much. I shall write to her directly. And I hope your father will come as well. They haven't been here together for years, and it would be such fun. The earl is rather a dash-fire man, as I recall."

Adam coughed, having no opinion upon his father's dash-fire. If it suited Geoffrey Diamond, then he would come. If not, he wouldn't—that was, unless his wife wanted him to, in which case, Adam knew his father would do whatever his mother asked.

For his own part, Adam was ready to fall in love and take a wife. His parents and his older sisters had set fine examples, showing him only the best of happy companionship. While having had his fair share of females around him, thanks to four sisters who all had acquaintances of the fair sex, as well as friends at university who introduced him to their sisters, none had made him yearn to ask for their hand. Nor had the bevy of young ladies from London's highest echelon, who were always happy to keep company with him because one day he would be the Earl Diamond.

That fact, although something for which he was immensely grateful, was the main reason he was temporarily residing in Bath. Too many females saw him as a title to be won. Sometimes, rather than deal with the fastidiously polite games of the sexes, he visited one of London's exclusive high fliers. Those females were beautiful, clean, doused in the most expensive perfume, and extraordinarily talented. From them, he'd learned a lot about pleasing women and hoped to apply his lessons to a wife someday soon.

Lady Susanne might be a potential mate. Seated beside her mother, her posture erect, her movements graceful, she nodded and smiled. She'd poured his tea and handed him the saucer. She'd reached out not too far, merely far enough to offer him the platter of biscuits. Obviously, she had trained to be the perfect hostess.

He hadn't thought too much about what it took to be the wife of a nobleman since all the women of his acquaintance had received similar training, but he imagined if he was with a female who wasn't born and bred to the lifestyle, he would find her lacking.

"Will you be attending the assembly tomorrow evening?" Lady Beasley asked.

Her daughter's gaze fixed upon Adam; her head tilted becomingly as they both awaited his response.

"I shall indeed," he said, although he'd been looking forward to finding the mysterious lady from the street, and now he knew he wouldn't see her there. "I have purchased a subscription for the Season and am looking forward to my first ball in Bath."

"Your first, is it?" Lady Susanne said. "How fun! If you allow, then we shall introduce you to many nice people we know."

"But none so nice nor so lovely as my Susanne," Lady Beasley added.

This was familiar territory, a mother promoting her daughter to him. However, Adam didn't mind in this case. After all, the family was known to his mother. They had welcomed him into their home. And Lady Susanne was, in fact, pretty and pleasant.

She was also offering to present him to others, an unusual offer. Most of the young ladies he met at assemblies became instantly proprietary. While they would chat with other females when alone, the moment he appeared, they pretended none of the others existed.

Lady Susanne even had the grace to blush at her mother's boast.

"There are plenty of attractive ladies in Bath," she went so far as to say. "My mother is biased for me and my sisters, and I love her dearly for that."

He was touched. The Beasleys truly were quality people, as his mother had indicated.

After a few more minutes of idle chatter, he took his leave with the understanding he would see Lady Susanne and her chaperone at the ball. Once in the front hall again, he cocked an ear to listen but could no longer hear Mrs. Malcolm's talented fingers.

A pity!

THE DAY HAD FLOWN BY, and Alice stood dressed in a new burgundy-colored ballgown, purchased for her by Lady Beasley. As her employer had hoped, the dressmaker produced a suitable article, already made, which had needed the barest of attention to make it fit. Last year's fashion, the woman had explained. It hadn't been picked up by its intended owner and was then passed over as out of style for the current Season by the new crop of young ladies who wanted only the latest.

Alice intended to give it back to Lady Beasley afterward. While she knew her employer wouldn't deduct the cost from her wages, she couldn't accept it as a gift. *Wherever would she wear it again?* Perhaps in a couple years, Lady Susanne might wish to wear it if the style came back around.

In any case, Alice was happy the color wasn't an insipid pastel since she was not a debutante by any stretch of the imagination. The only issue was the bodice, but there hadn't been time to let it out by adding a panel of fabric under each of her arms.

Examining herself in the oval handheld looking glass in her third-floor chamber, she thought she spilled over a little too generously. Unfortunately, with nowhere for her breasts to go, they were pushed up and nearly out.

For the sake of modesty, Lady Beasley leant her a finely woven silk shawl in a pretty gray and rose paisley. This, Alice snatched off her bed and draped around her shoulders, and she intended to keep it there throughout the evening.

Downstairs, she wished she had access to a glass of wine to calm herself. And then decided she would "borrow" a few mouthfuls of sherry from the sideboard while she waited for Susanne. Lord and Lady Beasley had already left, and as the adult and chaperone, she decided it was her right to have a tipple, especially when she was doing them all a favor.

Downing it in two gulps, she heard Susanne upon the stairs. As the young lady entered the room, Alice gasped. Something inside her, a memory of looking similarly fresh and radiant, pinched painfully.

"You are breathtaking," she told her. It wasn't flummery, either. Susanne wore a pale lavender gown that complemented her brown hair, making it an even richer tone.

"Thank you. And you look very pretty, too," Susanne returned.

Suddenly, however, Alice felt very old. Looking longingly at the sherry bottle, she wished she'd had a little more and now stood awkwardly with the glass in hand. Susanne's eyes fixed upon it. Alice knew she ought to take it to the kitchen, wash it off, and return it. Instead, she set it back on the little tray beside the decanter. For now, they must be off.

"Let's get you to the ball so you can dance the whole night through."

"Perhaps I shall catch the eye of a gentleman or two," Susanne said, turning before she noticed Alice squeeze her eyes shut a moment. That was the last thing Alice wished for the young lady. It was too easy to imagine this evening playing out as one fateful night had for her about four years earlier.

When they were settled in Lord Beasley's second-best carriage, Alice decided to counsel her charge.

"You are young. Try not to rush into an attachment despite your mother's wish for you to find a husband. Enjoy dancing and being adored. This is a wonderfully exciting time of your life, so I advise you not to do anything to hasten its end."

Susanne, who was all eyes and ears at this unexpectedly solemn discussion, asked, "How do you mean?"

Alice would not explain her own personal disaster. Instead, she sighed.

"Do not become seriously attached to any man until . . ."

"Until what?" Susanne leaned forward.

Indeed! "I was going to say until you are certain of his intent and his character. But I suppose it is easy enough to be fooled as to both. Perhaps the best path is, as I said, to do nothing in haste. The truth reveals itself in time."

Although Susanne nodded, Alice feared the young lady only thought her overly cautious and would pay her no heed.

The limestone, U-shaped building of the assembly rooms, located northeast of the famed residential Circus, between Bennett and Alfred Streets, were the main attraction in the fashionable, upper town. While the former lower assembly rooms had been beautiful for daily promenading on the stone walks and terraces and nightly dancing, most agreed the upper rooms to be superior. Still debated and discussed by the older generation, it was a moot point since the original lower rooms had burned thirty years earlier.

The Beasley family were already registered with the Master of Ceremonies, so Alice simply told them Lady Susanne had arrived, and they proceeded successfully into the main ballroom, easily one hundred feet from end to end.

Her charge clapped her hands once in excitement before visibly trying to comport herself with less enthusiasm and more aplomb. Alice hid a smile, letting Susanne lead the way. Her own task would be to remain close and take the measure of those who wished to dance with the lady, as well as keep track of whomsoever might wish to come calling in the days to come.

Her own mother had tackled a similar task when Alice flitted like a bee seeking nectar from flower to flower—and the flowers were dangerous gentlemen.

Not all of them, but the one who captured her certainly had been. And her mother had failed miserably in keeping her only daughter safe. Worse, she had contributed to her downfall, thinking it for her own good.

Alice shook her head, banishing thoughts of another time and place. Susanne was, in fact, practically buzzing as she strolled ahead, bathed in golden light under the five magnificent crystal chandeliers. She was like a bird, looking right to left until she spotted someone she knew. Two sisters from a neighboring household chatted with her briefly, then made it plain they wished for her to move on.

"They are usually so friendly," Susanne complained as they strolled farther into the room.

"Tonight, you are competition. And standing next to them, your shine dims their own."

Susanne's head swiveled back as if expecting to see light shining from her friends.

"Lady Susanne, well met." Lord Diamond was before them, appearing from a group of gentlemen standing separately, awaiting introductions.

They were like wolves in a pack, Alice thought bitterly. And this one was a particularly enticing wolf.

He appeared startled to see her. "Mrs. Malcolm," he greeted with a nod.

"She is my chaperone tonight," Susanne volunteered. "Wasn't that kind of her? We even bought her a new dress."

Alice cringed, feeling her cheeks warm. Susanne meant no harm, but it was mortifying nonetheless to sound like an employee, which she was, and a charity case, which she most definitely was not.

Lord Diamond's eyes flickered over her from head to toe, but thankfully, he made no comment. If he had, she might have growled with irritation.

"It sounds as though you are going above and beyond to ensure Lady Susanne has a successful evening," he said.

Alice thought that was well put, although she could have done without his impertinent perusal. In any case, it was time to do her duty.

"Do you wish to dance?" she asked him, and then remembered to add, "With Lady Susanne?"

He looked at Alice a long moment before turning his attention back to where it belonged.

"Indeed. May I have the honor of the next dance, my lady?"

Susanne's cheeks instantly went red and a wide smile pushed them out to double their size. She looked like a lovely chipmunk.

Alice wished the girl would tamp down her emotions, at least not be quite so blatantly enthusiastic.

"Thank you, my lord. I would be pleased to do so."

The evening was as long as Alice had assumed it would be, and Susanne was as successful as predicted. She was never in want of a partner. Moreover, Lord Diamond asked for and received a second dance. Perhaps she had already made a conquest.

Alice shivered at the notion of Susanne rushing into a marriage agreement. If Lord Diamond had tried for a third dance, Alice would have rebuffed him even though she and Susanne had assisted his entrance into Bath's society by taking him around and introducing him to Susanne's friends and acquaintances between dances.

Alice was proud of her, sure no other young lady would be so magnanimous.

Toward the end of the ball, in fact, Lord Diamond approached again despite Susanne being already partnered and waiting for the music to begin.

"You are too late," Alice said, oddly pleased to thwart him. He was a tad too cocksure of himself. *And why not?* Like everyone else, she had heard of the Diamond earldom with its long bloodline and the current large, happy family.

"I didn't come for Lady Susanne. I came to ask you if you wished to dance with me. I would be honored," he said politely.

Her breath caught, and her heart raced at the unexpected invitation.

"Chaperones don't dance," she said at last, barely getting the whispery words out upon a rush of air.

He smiled. "Some don't because they are ancient and incapable. You appear to be neither."

"I have a job to do," she reminded him a little sharply, having regained her poise and her tongue.

Glancing to where Susanne chatted with her partner, Lord Diamond shrugged.

"She will be safe enough on the dance floor. Even more so if you are dancing nearby."

With that, he held out his hand.

Unable to think of an excuse and starting to feel foolish for protesting so vehemently, she placed her hand in his, unprepared for the shocking tingling that went through her.

Attributing it to how long it had been since she'd been touched by a man, she squared her shoulders and let him lead her to the floor. Whether by design or as happenstance, he took a place that wasn't directly beside her charge. For that, she was grateful. Knowing Susanne's spiritedness, the young lady would mostly likely have exclaimed with delight that her chaperone was dancing and wearing her new dress.

Silently, Alice faced him and curtsied, receiving his bow as the music began.

She had to stop herself from being taken back to the last time she'd danced. Focusing upon Lord Diamond, she thought him too good looking, too tall, too assured, and an excellent dancer. *Perfect for Susanne if his nature matched his demeanor.*

The music's pace picked up. As they spun and turned together, Alice let a little ray of happiness seep between the cracks in her shell of disillusionment.

"You are an excellent dancer," Lord Diamond said when they were halfway through.

"I love to dance," Alice confessed, not knowing why she told him any such thing. It was true, though. She'd been the belle of many a London ball a few years back.

A question was in his eyes, and she knew what it was: *When do governesses have the opportunity to dance?*

Halfway through the polka, her foot caught on something. Shocked, she tripped and stumbled, having never done anything so mortifying upon the dance floor in her entire life.

"Your shawl," Lord Diamond said, bending to retrieve it. Gallantly, he stuffed as much as he could into his pocket, and they caught up their steps with the other dancers.

However, her gladness had vanished like morning mist. She'd made a mistake, appearing dreadfully clumsy. And she'd done it in front of the most attractive man she'd ever met.

"Don't worry about it, Mrs. Malcolm. No one even noticed," he lied.

Men lied easily enough, especially if they were interested in getting something—or someone. When next she faced him, it was impossible not to see his gaze dip to her low and revealing décolletage.

And just like that, the dance had gone on far too long. Despite whatever disruption would occur, Alice had the urge to run away. She didn't. Keeping her gaze fixed on a place over Lord Diamond's shoulder, she continued.

As soon as the last note sounded, she wrenched her grasp free, gave him a hurried curtsy, and rushed to where he'd found her. She even beat Susanne back to their spot by the windows.

Watching Lord Diamond stroll away, probably relieved he hadn't had to escort her any longer, Alice caught her breath and hopefully appeared composed when her charge rejoined her.

"Wasn't that lovely?" Susanne asked. "I saw you on the floor, too. That dress is much prettier without Mother's shawl. I don't know why you wore it in the first place."

The shawl! Lord Diamond was no longer in sight. He had probably forgotten it due to its lightweight silk weave. She had to retrieve it. Unlike the dress, she would undoubtedly be charged for the loss of the expensive item, brought all the way from India.

"Stay here, do not move. Do not speak with anyone. Do not dance either, unless you already know the gentleman." Alice reconsidered. "No, not even then. I shall return anon. Please, please, Susanne, do as I say and remain rooted to this spot."

"Of course. But where——?"

Alice dashed off into the throng in the direction he had taken.

CHAPTER THREE

Adam felt badly for how wooden Mrs. Malcolm had become after her shawl slipped. On the other hand, he didn't feel at all unhappy over what it had revealed. He'd tried not to stare, but in that dress, the fullness of her breasts was evident. He'd half expected to see a rosy nipple peek over the neckline.

Still, as gentlemanly as possible, he'd looked away and completed the dance. Strangely, he'd already been taken with her, even when she'd demurely put her gloved hand in his. The zing of excitement that ensued was unfamiliar. From the start, each and every pull of attraction he'd felt for her was, in fact, unusual.

Regardless, he had to set it aside. She was most definitely not a suitable candidate for becoming his wife. Even if she weren't married, a governess, no matter what airs she put on to seem like a lady, could not fit into his world, nor would he want her to. Amongst the *ton*, Mrs. Malcolm would be forever playing a part for which she was not destined. There would be mishaps, like tonight. No one danced while wearing a shawl and for good reason.

Pushing out of the warm assembly room, he strode out onto the back terrace and took his flask from his jacket pocket. Sipping the fine French brandy, he accepted there could be nothing between them except his ardent admiration for her hair, face, and figure.

Still, he couldn't deny the hope she would perform the role of chaperone again in the future. Elsewise, unless he happened upon her while visiting the Beasleys' home, this might have been the only time he would see her. Certainly, the singular time he would ever dance with her.

With that thought in mind—disturbing him more than it should—he was shocked to hear his name and turn to see her.

She rushed toward him across the darkened terrace.

"Did you not hear me calling you?"

"I confess, I did not." His heartbeat sped up at this strange turn of events. "Is something wrong?" She was breathing hard, and the view was magnificent. His mouth went suddenly dry, and his body sizzled as it had when he had first touched her hand.

How extraordinary!

Thinking her distraught, he reached out and took her hand again.

"What are you doing?" She stared at their joined hands, then back at his face.

"I have no idea," he said. He was the one who ought to ask her why she had followed him. Regardless, he thanked his good fortune.

Could it be she was tired of the husband at home, wherever home was? Maybe she wanted a quick dalliance behind the hedge. Maybe the unfamiliar excitement of attending a ball, something a governess probably never did, had left her over stimulated.

In any case, he felt an answering excitement at being near her, glad she had pursued him.

Taking her other hand, he drew her close. They were far enough from the lamps on the terrace that if anyone looked out, their identities would be concealed. She was trembling under his touch.

"Your eyes are pure silver in the moonlight," he told her. "And you are easily the most beautiful woman here."

"Am I?"

He couldn't discern from her husky tone what she was feeling. *Passion, perhaps?*

"Yes. And easily the most captivating." It was true. He'd known it from the moment he'd seen her in the rich wine-colored gown, making all those around her look washed out and wan. The ballroom's massive chandeliers had made her honey-colored hair glow with a golden halo.

Without asking for permission, he leaned toward her and kissed her. She was motionless, at least for a second, and then her lips moved on his.

Groaning at her acquiescence, Adam slanted his mouth against hers and licked the satin seam of her lips, ready to dive in and taste her sweetness. He felt a fist slam into his gut.

"*Ooph!*" He didn't double over, but he stood back in case her knee was coming next.

"How dare you!" she raged.

Was it possible both the trembling he'd felt and the passion in her voice had been from fury not desire?

"My apologies, Mrs. Malcolm. When you sought me out, running after me into the garden, I thought—"

He stopped and flinched when she reached forward. However, all she did was go for his pocket and snag the end of her shawl, entirely forgotten by him.

"Whatever you thought, you were wrong." Turning heel, she ran just as quickly back inside.

"Bloody hell!" Adam swore viciously at his own stupidity. He had cocked that up for certain.

ADAM SENT HIS CARD IN the morning via a footman, asking if he might come calling the following day. Then he waited on tenterhooks. If the answer was no, Mrs. Malcolm had told her employer of his despicable behavior. If it was yes, then at least he would get his foot in the door. He wanted to apologize in person to the governess, and that would be made difficult, especially if he was confined to the drawing room sipping tea.

Which was precisely where he found himself. In a repeat of the previous visit, he was seated opposite Lady Beasley and Lady Susanne.

"I wanted to thank you personally for introducing me to others at the assembly," he said to explain his visit.

"A pleasure, my lord. The entire evening was a delight, was it not?"

"Indeed," he said, hoping to hear the bright tone of Mrs. Malcolm's violin floating from the other room.

"I understand you danced together twice," Lady Beasley said. "And now, here you are."

He tugged at his cravat, which was suddenly choking him. She considered him to be a suitor, and in a way, he was. Lady Susanne was a solidly acceptable choice for a wife. He liked her company already both for her soft-spoken manner and her gentle ways. Moreover, she was a good dancer and smiled a great deal. She was pretty in a sweet, cherubic way, and he might become fond of her if he spent more time in her company.

What's more, his sisters would like her, and his mother would be especially pleased if he made a match with her friend's daughter.

However, that didn't change the fact that he'd kissed Mrs. Malcolm, nor how his thoughts were even then wandering to her silvery-green eyes and her full lips.

"The musicians were fine," he said, trying to come up with something to say, "and yes, I believe we did dance twice."

"And the supper was better than expected, Mother," Lady Susanne said. "The spread in the Tea Room contained everything from absolutely transparent broth to sandwiches to the most delicious little cake squares."

Lady Beasley nodded. "No thick, white pottage and stale bread?" she quipped.

Adam ignored their conversation and craned his head to see past them to where the door at the far end stood open. If only Mrs. Malcolm would come into view, then he would rise to his feet and, in some way, impart his apology even if only with his eyes.

A shadowy figure was down the other end, he thought, although it might be his dire imaginings.

"What did you think, my lord?" came Lady Beasley query.

Was she still talking about the food? "It was as good as any at a London ball, to be sure."

They stared at him.

"I asked if you had yet been to the Sydney Gardens."

"Did you?" *When had they stopped speaking about soup?* He chuckled lightly. "My mistake."

Lady Susanne joined him with a good-natured laugh. "It's no matter. I'm sure you have much on your mind. Mother explained you are in Bath to determine whether to sell your maternal grandparents' home. Your own mother lived there, did she not?"

"She did." He thought her a very amiable young lady. She was good fun, didn't put on airs, nor was she too silly. Truthfully, his grandparents' investment property was low on his list, far beneath enjoying the ladies of Bath to determine if one might be a suitable wife. "Would you have an opinion on the best course of action if I told you I have been charged with two options?"

Lady Beasley eyed her daughter, who shook her head.

"I am sure I know little about such things."

"But you must have an opinion," he pressed. "To sell, to keep closed up, or to keep and lease, risking damage by dissolute tenants."

"I suppose I do, but your opinion must be infinitely more informed and thus better."

Lady Beasley nodded with satisfaction at her daughter's neutral, even placating response.

Hearing footsteps, Adam peered between them but couldn't see anyone.

"Are you well, my lord?"

They were both staring at him in return.

"I wondered if Mrs. Malcolm were here."

"Our governess?" Lady Beasley asked with surprise.

"I think of her now as your chaperone. I didn't see her to say goodbye the other night, and that seemed dreadfully rude of me."

Lady Beasley blinked at him, and for a moment, Adam wondered if she suspected something.

However, Susanne smiled. "That's very kind of you. I believe she is teaching my sisters at present, but I'll tell her you asked after her. Will that suffice?"

"Perfectly," he said, feeling thwarted. Unless Mrs. Malcolm acted as chaperone again. To that end, he would invite Lady Susanne on an outing and try to make it happen.

"Would you like to take a walk through the Sydney Gardens? Perhaps tomorrow if the weather permits."

"That would be lovely," Lady Susanne said. "You are free to accompany us, aren't you, Mother?"

"Most certainly, I am," Lady Beasley answered, "and I shall."

Blast!

ALICE KNEW *HE* WAS IN the house that very minute. She'd overheard Lady Beasley mention his name to Lord Beasley before he'd escaped to the York Club on the exclusive and elevated terrace known as Edgar Buildings.

Her conflicted emotions had kept her awake the night of the ball into the wee hours. Since then, she had decided despite how attracted she was to Lord Diamond— uncomfortably so, in fact—he was to be avoided.

She had adored dancing with him until her misstep. And she had not struggled when he'd drawn her close. Most certainly, she had felt a sizzle of sensual satisfaction the instant his mouth claimed hers.

Then she'd recalled who she was and where she was, not to mention what had happened last time she'd been attracted to a man. Socking him in the stomach had seemed a natural reaction. Alice wished she'd done it to Richard when he'd first kissed her. If she had, she would still be a member of the *ton*, perhaps married by now to an upstanding gentleman.

And how upstanding could Lord Diamond be if he was supposedly interested in Susanne, an entirely appropriate match, yet willy-nilly kissed her, a woman of seemingly inappropriate status. Only men who took advantage of women would behave thusly.

After the first lessons of the day were finished and the girls were taking a break, Alice thought the safest place until she was sure Lord Diamond had left, short of staying cooped up in her room, would be the back garden. It was a generous sized space, not something one would find in the middle of London.

With the peonies in bloom, she promenaded around the perimeter, working off some pent-up energy before taking a seat in the shade. No book, no violin, nothing but her thoughts.

That was a mistake because they returned immediately to Lord Diamond. He was fine looking with very dark hair, cobalt blue eyes, a strong chin, and a tall muscular frame without a hint of sedentary, overindulgent paunch.

He was undoubtedly also a flash swell!

What's more, astonishingly enough, the man was walking directly toward her. She rose to her feet when he was two yards away.

"What are you doing here?" He was even bolder than Richard Fairclough had been. But this time, she was not a reckless debutante, eager to kiss and ready to be deceived.

"I was visiting Lady Susanne, but I had hoped to see you."

"A governess does not sit in the drawing room during a visit," she pointed out.

"I realize that. After I took my leave, I appreciated the benefit of a corner house and strolled along the hedgerow until I saw you."

She folded her arms, wanting to present him with a wall of strength.

"You cannot see me through the hedgerow. It is a privacy hedge of the thickest yews."

"Truthfully, I peered between the branches, hoping to get a glimpse. And when I saw you, I pushed my way in."

Her heart was beginning to pound. "You are a scoundrel, as I suspected."

"I assure you I am not." He looked amused, which was infuriating. "No one has ever said such a thing before."

"What do you call kissing me behind the ballroom?"

"Delightful," he said. "Until you punched me, that is. I thought women only slapped a man's face."

Ah-ha, Alice thought. He was a rascal. "You would know, I suppose."

"I have never been slapped, nor called a scoundrel before. And that is no lie," Lord Diamond vowed. "Nor have I ever kissed a woman who didn't wish to be kissed."

"Until now."

He cocked his head.

She wondered if he doubted her. Maybe he was so full of himself he imagined she'd wanted and enjoyed his kiss. In truth, she'd been so surprised by the swiftly unfolding events, when suddenly, he had drawn her close and kissed her, for a second—before she regained her senses—she had enjoyed it. Immensely. Her body had thrummed with pleasure, and she'd wanted to melt against him. He smelled good and kissed better than he smelled.

"Until now," he agreed finally. "Which is why I came here today. I wish to apologize. It seems I keep having to apologize to you."

That was probably a ruse. After all, he was compromising her at that moment by sneaking into the yard and being alone with her.

"You have said your apology. Thus, you may go, and we shall hopefully never see one another again."

A foolish statement since he was apparently in Bath for the small Season, and she was stuck here until the girls outgrew her in about four years.

"I have said my apology for my ill-advised, rash action, but have you accepted it? Perhaps if you do with the understanding the kiss was born of an impetuous nature, combined with your loveliness and my own mistaken notion you were chasing me..." He trailed off and rubbed a hand over his handsome chin.

"Chasing you?" she muttered into the pause, rolling her eyes.

The old Alice of four years ago might have done just that. She had, in fact, done something similar on a few occasions before the final ruinous event that had led to her demise and into a marriage of the utmost disappointment.

He cocked his head and appraised her.

"Well?" she prompted when he remained silent, her cheeks warming under his scrutiny.

He grinned suddenly, then shook his head. "I confess I have entirely forgotten where my meandering thoughts were going."

Alice felt a smile tug at her own lips, but she managed to restrain herself. Just because he had called her lovely and apologized profusely didn't mean he wasn't a cad.

"No wonder you have lost the message you intended to impart, after all that fluff. And if I accept your apology, then what? Does it make a bit of difference?"

"Ah, yes! That is what I was saying. You are very helpful, Mrs. Malcolm."

He was teasing her, and she was allowing him. She ought to turn heel and disappear into the house and let him retreat through the hedgerow.

"The difference is if you have forgiven me, then when we meet again, we can have a light and easy discourse, rather than any tension. At the very least, I can give you a friendly wave when I come to collect Lady Susanne."

The rogue! Just like that all her good feelings toward Lord Diamond dissipated. He was too worldly for the Beasleys' eldest daughter. And any man who kissed a chaperone and still wanted to escort her charge was assuredly a reprobate.

Despite knowing she should mind her own business, through gritted teeth, Alice asked, "Where are you escorting Lady Susanne?"

"We are going to Sydney Gardens to take a walk. I hear it is quite the place."

Hoping she didn't look like the disapproving scold she felt at that instant, she tried to keep her mouth from pursing.

"It *was* 'the place'," she corrected. "It has fallen out of fashion, and the Royal Victoria Park has become all the rage. Regardless, Lady Beasley prefers the former because of fond memories from childhood, hot air balloons and fireworks. That sort of thing."

"Not at the same time, I would hope," his lordship quipped. He was trying to be funny and charming but was not succeeding, not with her.

"Do you think it wise to court her?" Alice couldn't help asking.

"Wise?" he repeated, plainly befuddled. "Isn't she of marriageable age and of good character?"

"Yes," she bit out.

"Then I cannot see how it would be unwise."

Because you kissed me! she wanted to point out and emphatically, too, perhaps even raising her voice. However, she did not. Her lips pursed after all, which made her feel old, and then she managed to speak.

"Very well. If that is your decision."

She couldn't figure out how to make him leave her, and it would be detrimental for them to be found together.

"Good day, Lord Diamond." Alice walked away.

CHAPTER FOUR

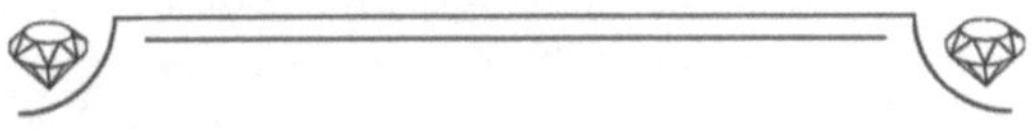

Although Mrs. Malcolm did not come along on their outing to the Sydney Gardens, Adam had a grand time, anyway. Lady Susanne and her mother were kind and amusing people. However, from the moment they left the carriage and entered through the gate beside the Sydney Hotel, each with a shilling ticket which Adam purchased, the daughter seemed as much a visitor as he was. She didn't even know why the pleasure gardens had their name.

Despite knowing the answer, he'd asked simply to let her show off her knowledge of her city of birth. Instead, she was perplexed.

"I could not tell you, my lord. It is a mystery."

That made him laugh. "Not really. The original designers named the gardens for Thomas Townshend, the first Viscount Sydney."

She looked at him blankly.

"He was a powerful politician at the end of the last century," he added, hoping she would show a spark of knowing. "Lord *Sydney*," he repeated the name, feeling frustrated as if he were speaking another language, "was and is extremely well-known. The colony in Australia? The East India Company?"

She shrugged, and he gave up asking anything and just told her.

"The gardens' planners hoped to gain his favor so he would fund some of the development or, at the very least, its upkeep."

"How clever of them," Lady Susanne said, "and of you, too, for knowing so much."

He glanced at Lady Beasley. She shrugged slightly.

"It is believed Lord Sydney never even bothered to come here," she disclosed, proving she was not as unfamiliar with Bath's history as her eldest daughter. "If I had been them," her ladyship continued, "I would have changed the name directly. He didn't deserve the recognition."

Adam had to stop himself running his hands through his hair and tugging on it. In the next instant, Lady Susanne exclaimed in delight over some beautiful flower she couldn't name, and he realized her lack of learning didn't matter so much because she was interested in hearing whatever information he could tell her. And her mother was able to answer any questions he had since she had lived in Bath all her life.

Thus, Adam's only dissatisfaction was in how little he could pull from Lady Susanne's thoughts as to *her* interests and likes. His parents led separate lives but were also extremely compatible on many aspects. How could he tell whether he and Lady Susanne could share marital happiness when she rarely responded to a question except to parrot it back at him?

"What is your favorite city?" he asked as they strode along the wide path of crushed yellow stone.

"Oh, I am sure they are all nice," she said blandly. "What is yours?"

When they passed by the entrance to the Labyrinth, reportedly twice as large as that at Hampton Court, he paused and asked her, "Do you think you might like a small domestic animal in the home, a dog, cat, or bird, perhaps?"

"They are all the same to me."

Her words stunned him to argue, "Surely a fluffy, soft cat is not like a sharp-beaked bird."

She blinked, then smiled. "You are teasing me, my lord. If I marry a man who likes dogs or cats or even monkeys, it is of no matter to me. Whatever he likes, I shall certainly accept."

She was either the most amiable female he had ever met, a bold-faced liar, or utterly disinterested in life, perhaps a simpleton at heart and head. To him, it was absurd not to care whether you had a monkey or a cat running around your home.

The moment two well-dressed ladies strolled by along the promenade, he watched Lady Susanne perk up.

"Mother, I have seen that dress in a fashion magazine at our modiste's. Not the one on Pulteney Bridge, mind you, but Madame Peridot's. I cannot believe someone is already wearing such a creation. Isn't it divine? Although I might have chosen a different color ribbon. I would love to stop at Madame Peridot's tomorrow and ask how soon she can whip up one for me."

"Of course," her mother said. "You would be lovely in it. Don't you think, my lord?"

Adam wished he knew which dress they were speaking of, for they all looked rather similar, and he couldn't detect which might be a new design. There was only one correct answer.

"Lady Susanne is lovely in what she is wearing now, and I have no doubt she would be lovely in anything she wore."

He felt a little insipid saying the words, but it earned him twin smiles of approval from mother and daughter.

Adam turned to her mother. "Do you wish to enter the maze?"

"It is dreadfully long, and we could be in there for hours."

Hours? Being trapped with Lady Susanne suddenly held no allure. Instead, the image of Mrs. Malcolm flashed before his eyes. He banished it, knowing he had no business thinking of her at all.

"These gardens are truly splendid at night, my lord," Lady Beasley said. "They rival Vauxhall, and we shall bring you back here soon to see the entertainment."

Thus, while he had some reservations, he didn't hesitate in agreeing to escort Lady Susanne to a concert in the Octagon Room at the same assembly rooms two nights later. And when she thanked him emphatically and blinked her deep brown eyes, he felt even better about it. She was a charming female.

As they arrived back at the Beasleys' home, Mrs. Malcom exited the front door. Adam wondered if the governess was going home to her husband, for he still didn't know if she was married, nor even if she lived with the Beasleys. He hadn't been able to ask his companions since his curiosity could have no reason beyond nosiness.

"Mrs. Malcolm," Lady Susanne called out in her usual good-natured way. "We went to the Sydney Gardens," she added as the governess came to a halt.

Adam jumped down and held his hand out to Lady Beasley and then to Lady Susanne. Then they all joined Mrs. Malcolm, who kept her gaze upon the females.

"Lord Diamond had never seen them," Lady Susanne continued. "Did you know they were named after a dead man who founded Australia?"

Mrs. Malcolm's expression was priceless, then her gaze flitted to Adam who bit back a laugh.

"I know of Lord Sydney," the governess said carefully, probably not wanting to disabuse the young lady in public of her skewed and incorrect facts. "You had fine weather for such an outing," she added.

"We did," Adam agreed.

Reluctantly, or so it seemed, Mrs. Malcolm turned her gray-green eyes upon him.

"Did *you* enjoy the gardens?" she asked, with a hint of tartness.

"I did," he said. And then the devil got into him and he added, "but not as much as the garden behind the assembly rooms."

She paled, and he instantly regretted his thoughtless remark.

"Why?" asked Lady Susanne. Her sweet open face was now frowning. "I don't recall anything special there."

He couldn't look at Lady Beasley. She was an astute woman and might see the truth.

"I was teasing," he said at once, "since the garden there was nothing more than a strip of lawn and a few shrubberies. Nothing in comparison. Merely a jest."

"I see," Lady Susanne said, but her tone declared she didn't.

"And not a funny one," he muttered.

"Where were you going?" Lady Beasley asked, and from that question, Adam learned a small kernel of information. Mrs. Malcolm lived with them, elsewise the question would be impertinent, even for an employer.

"To purchase a new string for my violin and more sheet music for Pauline."

"Truly? Has she mastered the last piece?"

"No, my lady. It was too difficult for her. I must find something more basic."

"*Tut-tut,*" Lady Beasley said. "Is she hopeless?"

"She had a late start is all," Mrs. Malcolm said. "That lazy piano teacher did none of your daughters any favors."

Lady Susanne laughed. "He was dreadful. His snoring was louder than the piano notes." Then she gasped. "You enjoy music, don't you?"

Mrs. Malcolm appeared startled. "Yes."

She said it as if she didn't wish to disclose anything personal, maybe not in front of him. Adam wondered what would be disclosed next.

Lady Susanne looked at her mother. "Please let Mrs. Malcolm come to the concert as my chaperone. She will so enjoy it, and she was such fun to be with the other night."

Lady Beasley raised a brow, and her daughter laughed.

"Not that *you* aren't fun, Mother, but Mrs. Malcolm is more like being with a friend."

Adam thought this conversation would have been better conducted indoors and in private. Moreover, he wondered if he should quickly bow and leave so they could continue. Yet he was decidedly curious as to how it would conclude, so he remained where he stood.

Mrs. Malcolm glanced at him again, and he was sure she would say no, which was a pity.

It wasn't that he wished to see Mrs. Malcolm dressed again in a form-fitting evening gown. Nor because he wished to have her seated close beside him, so he could catch the intoxicating scent of her perfume. Yet both were true. Her floral fragrance had warmed and caught in his clothing when they'd kissed, and now, he thought he could detect it once again on the slight breeze.

How had a governess got her hands on something that smelled expensive and French?

More than anything, he hoped she would accept the task of chaperone in order to hear a concert if music made her heart happy. For she seemed a rather serious young woman otherwise, and he would like to see her smile.

"I believe your mother would like to hear the concert as much as I would," Mrs. Malcolm said finally. "But I thank you for thinking of me."

Lady Susanne sighed her disappointment. And then Lady Beasley gave in and addressed the governess.

"We all know your love of music," she began. "I am sure you would enjoy it, and I have been to many concerts recently."

Adam didn't think Mrs. Malcolm looked particularly grateful, and he had a feeling it was because he was attending, too. But he couldn't simply change his mind, for then Lady Susanne wouldn't need the chaperone at all. They would all miss out.

Instead, he watched while the governess warred between wanting to hear the music and not wanting to be in his company.

"Please say yes," Lady Susanne said, and that tipped the decision in his favor.

"I shall be your chaperone," Mrs. Malcolm said, giving Adam the swiftest of wary looks, before turning to her employer. "I thank you for the opportunity to attend, my lady."

"But no new dress this time," Lady Beasley said, making Lady Susanne shake her head.

Mrs. Malcolm's nostrils flared slightly. "No, of course not. I didn't expect any such thing."

Adam hoped she wore the same one from the ball. It had been gloriously revealing.

EVERY TIME SHE WENT out in society, Alice was risking recognition, detection, and thereby utter humiliation. And worse. Yet, against her better judgment, she had agreed because listening to skilled musicians was a treat she greatly missed in her present station.

Regardless, Alice had hardly ever expected to find herself seated not only near Lord Diamond but beside him. Having arrived late due to Lady Susanne having a sudden fashion emergency, the three hurried to their seats, and her charge practically galloped to their appointed row, scooted in, and took the first of three seats.

When Alice went to sit, Lady Susanne said, "No, please, Mrs. Malcolm, allow his lordship to sit beside me."

The infuriating girl ought to have allowed Alice to sit first! When she tried to rearrange her, the manager hurried over and insisted they take their seats at once. The conductor was already facing the audience.

Lord Diamond quickly sat, and Alice had no choice but to do the same, and thus, he was between them. On the other hand, she enjoyed being on the center aisle with a much better view of what was going on up ahead. When the first pure notes carried her away, she cared not a whit for Susanne's virtue—*after all, what could happen in the Octagon Room?*

Yet try as she might, she could not forget the man beside her. Their upper arms were touching, and the warmth seeped through the sleeve of her second-best gown. Her vanity had refused to let her wear the same ballgown again so soon. This one, a dove-gray cotton with cream piping trim, fit her well and was more suitable to a governess. Compared to all the other ladies, however, she appeared drab and underdressed.

Regardless, no one else seemed to be distracted by an attractive man's shoulder, causing a fiery sensation to sizzle through her. Thus, Alice earnestly tried to ignore him and focus upon the musicians.

Impossible! Lord Diamond's right leg swayed along to some unfathomable part of the composition, but since she couldn't tell which, she half-wondered if he were tone deaf or devoid of any sense of rhythm.

When he next leaned his leg in her direction, touching her knee, she started to think he was doing it on purpose.

Startled, she moved away, pointing her toes toward the aisle.

"I apologize," he muttered. Leaning his mouth down to the shell of her ear, he made her shiver as he whispered, "I am enjoying it so much I—"

"*Shh,*" she admonished.

He ceased at once.

The remainder of the concert's first half passed without any further annoyances from Lord Diamond—except she was unable to cease her acute awareness of his closeness. Nor could she quell the tingling in her body. He was a nuisance.

When they arose to stretch their legs before the second half, Susanne was bubbling.

"How beautiful. Don't you think?" Her question was, as usual, doubtful of her own opinion.

"Indeed," Lord Diamond said, quickly glancing at Alice. "What did you think, Mrs. Malcolm? *You* are the expert."

Something about the way he said that rubbed her the wrong way, like stroking a cat from tail to head.

"I am sure these musicians are far more adept than I could hope to be. To think anything else would be presumptuous." However, she had noticed some *sour* notes, as her father might have labeled them, were they still speaking to one another.

"In that case, without giving offense, may I ask simply whether you enjoyed it?" he asked.

She was being unnecessarily peevish, which wasn't like her. She had accepted her lot in life after Richard's untimely yet welcome death. *So why was she now taking it out on the only man who had ever made her crackle with desire from head to toe?*

"Of course I did. Thank you for asking," she replied more softly, earning a raised eyebrow of recognition from him that she was, at least, trying to be polite. "I thought they—"

"There is Lady Francine," Susanne interrupted. "She wasn't at the ball, nor in Bath this past week. I must go speak with her at once and discover where she has been. Probably to get new gowns in London. I wish Mother would take me to do the same, but she always says we can get anything right here on Milsom Street." She was still talking about fashion as she wandered off.

"I suppose I should trail along behind her."

"I believe that's what chaperones do," Lord Diamond agreed. He turned and let his gaze follow Susanne's path. "Except she has stopped already. And since there isn't a man near her, I believe she is safe."

"Thank you for explaining my duty," Alice quipped, and the crabby tone had returned.

"Are you married?" he asked, obviously intending to catch her off guard.

And he had. She answered before she realized.

"Not any longer." Then she shut her mouth firmly. *Blasted nosy man!*

"I only asked because some missus, such as my parents' housekeeper, Mrs. Cumby, have never been a wife. Funny that, don't you think?"

"Funny," she muttered before raising her chin and looking him in the eye. "I am a widow," Alice added, in case he thought she was lying. Also, pride made her want him to know another man had asked her to marry him and made her his wife. *More was the pity!*

In any case, she wasn't merely someone's governess with whom he could dally.

His expression sobered instantly. "I am terribly sorry."

She had thrown Lord Diamond off his stride, and no mistaking it. But she didn't want his pity, nor did she wish for him to start sentimentalizing something that was possibly the least sentimental moment in her life.

Before she could say more, however, Susanne reappeared. Alice had nearly forgotten her existence.

"If I can convince Mother to take me to London, we shall also go to the Great Exhibition."

Alice felt a surge of envy. She would love to see the wondrous items and inventions that had been collected from all over the world. She recalled one in particular.

"Lord Diamond's namesake will be there," she quipped.

Lady Susanne looked blankly, but Lord Diamond nodded.

"The Koh-i-Noor," he said.

At Susanne's raised eyebrows, he expounded, telling her a little about the diamond's long history, and how it ended up being given to the Queen once she was made Empress of India.

"I would like to see it," Susanne said, "along with all the clothing on display."

Then they took their seats again, but this time, Lord Diamond gestured for her to go into the row first.

Apparently, learning she was a widow, he had decided to stop flirting with her. She took the farthest chair, with Susanne sitting beside her, and Lord Diamond taking the chair on the aisle.

When the music recommenced, Alice felt the loss of his warmth along her side at once. It was for the best, however. He was asking questions, and she was foolishly starting to answer them. Neither of which was a good idea.

Better she should ignore every tiny spark of interest that was flitting through her body and mind regarding Lord Diamond, each wicked thought of how magical his kiss had felt. Nothing repulsive or off-putting or even tawdry. It had been almost chaste and yet thrilling.

But she was no longer a part of his world. And she had best remember that! If she could be taken advantage of when she still had the trappings and the protection of being a lady, only imagine how much trouble she could get into if a titled lord set his sights on her as a lowly governess.

Thus, when she found herself alone with him again a few days later, Alice started to wonder if she had angered Lady Fortune in some fashion.

CHAPTER FIVE

"**P**lease come riding with us. It is so much more fun."

Susanne left hanging without speaking the implied words "than when I'm with my mother."

"Governesses don't ride," Alice informed her. "Not for pleasure anyway, only to get from one place to the other, and usually in a stuffy coach-for-hire or by second-class train carriage."

She ought to know. It was how she had fled her former life in an overly cramped train, clutching her ticket, only grateful she hadn't been condemned to a rooftop seat of a mail coach, exposed to the elements.

"Then you cannot ride a horse," Susanne said, sounding dejected, not to mention a little disappointed.

Alice's whole existence was a lie, but she didn't have to compound it with extra lies, so she replied honestly. "I can, in fact."

Was it her vanity again wanting this young lady not to see her as a lesser female?

Susanne clapped her hands. "You are *not* merely a governess, I know that. We all know that."

Alice swallowed a lump of fear.

"What do you mean?"

"Mother would not have let you be my chaperone if you weren't also a widow. Besides, my sisters and I have had other governesses. None of them were like you."

Alice decided not to ask the difference. She was doing the best she could to be subservient to Lady Beasley and her daughters while maintaining her dignity and giving them a decently broad education. She couldn't abide by the fluffy-headed females with wool for brains.

Unfortunately, Susanne was not her pupil, and she, more than the younger ones, could use some learning.

"If I agree, will you do me the honor of attending some of my lessons?"

"I am too old for that," Susanne scoffed. "I know all I need to know to run a household, or to direct a housekeeper and butler to run it. I must focus on finding a husband."

"But what will you discuss with him if you do not know a little history? If you don't learn a second language fluently, how can you travel together and not be a burden to him? What about going to a museum and speaking with him knowledgeably about art?"

Susanne shook her head. "Oh, Mrs. Malcolm. None of that is important to the gentlemen among whom I must find a husband. They can hire a translator when we travel and a guide for museums. He won't be impressed if I am spouting information. In fact, that might dissuade some nice viscount or earl who wants nothing more than a dutiful, obedient wife."

Alice wanted to shake her, but if Susanne truly had no interest in the outside world, then there wasn't any way to force facts into her brain.

"Please come riding as my chaperone," the young lady begged. "Just for the fun of it, without thinking of any of that knowledge stuff."

Alice cracked a smile. *That knowledge stuff.* Maybe Susanne was correct. In her case, she was adorable, kind, and had a large dowry promised to any man who married her. Perhaps anything else was superfluous.

Thus, wearing one of her full skirts and missing her favorite green riding habit, Alice found herself seated sidesaddle, reins in hand, and hat upon head. Beside her rode Susanne, and on the other side, Lord Diamond, who sat his horse very finely.

They agreed upon the Royal Victoria Park. At least Susanne could be certain for whom it was named, although she didn't know Victoria had officially opened the park when only a child of eleven.

After riding from Lord and Lady Beasley's stable behind their home on The Paragon, the three riders eventually entered the park on Royal Avenue.

Lord Diamond spoke up as they passed the Royal Crescent.

"I am staying there," he told them.

Of course he was! Where else would this perfect man reside but in one of thirty exclusive homes spanning five hundred feet of prime land overlooking the park?

Their three heads turned right to look up the slight incline across a stretch of green lawn where sheep had once grazed over the hidden ha-ha. Beyond it was a formal garden directly in front of the terraced townhouses. One hundred and fourteen Ionic columns greeted the eye, if Alice had counted correctly on one of her many walks.

"You are fortunate," Susanne said.

"Indeed. My grandparents own it, although they are of a mind to sell."

Alice would love to see inside one of the Palladian-style homes built by the same John Wood, the Younger, who had completed the celebrated Circus for his deceased father. However, she would never voice her desire. Next thing she knew, they would all be traipsing through a single gentleman's abode, and that could hardly be what Lady Beasley intended for her daughter and her chaperone.

The wide path led them to the Victoria Obelisk, which Susanne was also able to identify as named for their queen. They continued on the large circuitous path.

Having always loved riding in Hyde Park or Richmond Park, Alice considered the outing to be an unexpected treat. Ignoring the curious glances of Lord Diamond—or trying to—Alice patted the horse's neck and let herself become lost in the joy of being atop a gentle mount again.

"You ride well," he called out past Susanne, who also looked over at her.

"His lordship is correct," she said, sounding amused. "You appear like a lady and not at all like a governess."

Alice tilted her chin, annoyed that Lord Diamond would think her unable to ride. In the next moment, she cursed her own pride. She ought to seem inexperienced and timid, but that was a hard part to play.

"My father kept a horse," she said lamely. "I was merely lucky to get to learn… in my position, I mean."

"Very lucky," Susanne agreed.

Lord Diamond's gaze narrowed. Not caring for his scrutiny, Alice dropped back to let the courting couple ride together.

She had been in Susanne's situation many times before she'd made her fateful error. But she was there to make certain Susanne made no similar mistake. Therefore, Alice spent the rest of the ride watching the nearly hypnotizing view of horses' rumps sway and their tails flash, trying not to look at Lord Diamond's broad shoulders or his muscular thighs gripping his mount.

Seeing the two riders conversing, pointing out things, leaning over to talk, and laughing together, Alice tamped down the envy and bitterness she thought she'd outgrown and left behind.

That was *before* Lord Diamond kissed her and sparked to life a yearning for more.

When Susanne shrieked and the vignette suddenly changed, for a moment Alice did nothing, too shocked to react.

Something had spooked Susanne's gelding, making it rear and take off at a gallop.

Urging her mare forward with a flick of her crop, suddenly Alice with Lord Diamond beside her were giving chase.

"What happened?" she called to him.

"I know not."

It became plain at once that Susanne had dropped the reins and was hanging on to the horse's neck as best she could.

"Can she jump?" he asked.

His question made her blood chill.

"I don't know," Alice said. But without reins, it was desperately dangerous.

In a short while, they'd crossed the oval field, approaching the cart path which circled up the other side and, after it, the hedgerow that divided one area of the park from another.

Since Susanne's horse was racing full tilt toward it, they did, too. Luckily, the only carriages on the path were many yards away with no danger of collision.

"Veer off," Lord Diamond yelled to her, but Alice was entirely capable of jumping the hedge.

In fact, as if he'd ordered Susanne's gelding to do so, the horse swerved sideways a yard from the hedge, dumping its rider into the trimmed yews.

It was too late for Alice and Lord Diamond to do anything but keep going. Avoiding Susanne who luckily rolled over the top instead of sitting up, Alice jumped the hedgerow and cantered to a stop.

Lord Diamond came to a halt beside her and looked with astonishment.

"You are a *very* good rider," he declared.

She could practically hear him silently add, "Too good for a governess."

Without answer, she turned her horse around. Spying her charge on the ground, Alice dismounted unassisted and ran to Susanne.

"Are you unharmed?"

The young lady was already rising to her feet and brushing herself off, but her cheeks were pale from her ordeal.

"I believe I am." Her tone was slightly shaky.

"Is she injured?" Lord Diamond asked, approaching, still atop his horse.

"I don't believe so," Alice answered him.

"Then I shall go in pursuit of her horse before it causes an accident or gets itself injured."

After watching him leave, Alice turned her attention back to the young lady. Her eyes were large, and her lower lip was trembling.

"People fall off their horses all the time," Alice reminded her, hoping to tame any fears immediately so the incident wouldn't cause a lasting scar on Susanne's tender psyche. "And then, they get directly back on."

"I don't want to get back on," Susanne said. "Besides, I seem to have lost Rowan."

"I didn't know your horse's name," Alice said to keep her speaking and distract her from what had occurred, "but Lord Diamond has gone in pursuit."

"Your horse is Polly," Susanne added, and tears started to run down Susanne's cheeks.

Alice gathered her in a hug. "You came to no harm," she said, running her hands soothingly down the girl's back. "Just a nasty fright is all, but when Lord Diamond returns with your horse, you shall mount up, and we'll go home."

"No!" It was the firmest Alice could recall Susanne ever speaking. "Not today. There was a bee. I believe it stung Rowan. I won't get on him again."

An open-air barouche drew up beside the hedge. A lady and a gentleman were in it.

"Lady Susanne," greeted the woman. "We saw what happened. Are you injured?"

"No, I don't think so," she said meekly.

"May we give you a ride back to your residence?"

Susanne leaned away from Alice and blinked at her. "May I please go home with Lord and Lady Eldridge?"

"Of course," she said. "I shall bring Rowan back."

"There's a break in the hedge on the other side of the tree," the gentleman said, then directed his driver to move the carriage forward.

Holding her arm, Alice led Susanne around the tree and through the yews and let the Eldridges take her away. She hoped that was the correct thing for a chaperone to do, but she had little choice. She couldn't abandon the mare, nor had Lord and Lady Eldridge invited her along.

Even as the two carriage horses pulled away at a trot, Lord Diamond returned, leading Rowan.

"Lady Susanne has abandoned us," he said.

Thus, Alice tried to ignore him. "Luckily, some of her acquaintances came by."

"*Hm,*" he said, looking in the direction they went before glancing down at her. "She ought to have got back on her mount."

Alice nodded. "That's what I told her, but she adamantly refused."

"You know a lot about horses and riding."

Ignoring his questioning tone, she looked at Rowan's head. Sure enough, he had a swelling on his velvety nose.

"Lady Susanne was correct. He was stung."

Lord Diamond dismounted. "If you hold his head, I will see if a stinger remains."

"Very well."

And thus, Alice found herself in close proximity to the best smelling, most handsome man she'd ever met.

With a hand tucked around each of the lower cheek straps of Rowan's bridle, she did her best to hold the horse's head motionless.

Beside her, Lord Diamond looked at the small swollen bump.

"There is a stinger. Hold on." Yanking off his gloves, he pressed a finger to either side of the pink area to tighten it, and with his other hand, he ran his thumb's fingernail over it. "Got it."

"Well done," she said. In that instant, she was looking up, and he was looking down. Her insides fluttered. They were the perfect distance from each other for a kiss if he but bent a little lower.

His blue eyes locked with her own, and she caught her breath. Then his gaze dropped to her mouth.

Alice moved quickly, releasing the horse and stepping away.

"And now I am left as a horse's chaperone," she quipped to lighten the moment.

"Indeed." His raspy tone weakened her knees.

When he said nothing more, merely taking her measure in a way that made her skin feel too tight, she asked, "Shall we head back to the Beasleys' home?"

"It is your home, too, is it not?"

A quick laugh escaped her. She had never considered it her home. It was her place of employment, not somewhere she could relax—except when playing her violin.

"You find that amusing?" he asked.

"I am grateful for the place I have in the Beasleys' household," she said, but when he edged closer, alarm fluttered in her stomach.

"May I assist you onto your mount?" he offered.

Of course! What a ninny!

"Thank you," she said.

In silence, he laced his gloved fingers, making a step for her use. Drawing up her skirt slightly, she placed the toe of her shoe in Lord Diamond's hands, feeling almost indecent. Then with experience, she popped up and onto the saddle.

For a moment, his fingers skimmed her ankle, raising her skirt higher, causing her to shiver, before he guided her foot into the iron-and-leather slipper stirrup. Then he released her dress.

"Thank you," she mumbled again, as if it was the only thing she could say.

When he looked up at her, he smiled slightly.

"How is it you are such a skilled horsewoman? Even the way you mount is done with assurance and elegance."

Her cheeks warmed under his compliment. *Should she lie to him?* Alice could see no reason. And she had enough lies in her life.

"In truth, I grew up riding, mostly in the country. I haven't ridden for a while, but one never forgets how to do it, no more than I would forget how to play music."

"I see," he said, finally turning away and reclaiming his horse, which was happily munching grass beside Susanne's Rowan.

ADAM DIDN'T KNOW WHAT had come over him. Obviously, he was not happy Lady Susanne had fallen, but the moment he and Mrs. Malcolm were alone again, the air crackled between them with undeniable attraction. He was acutely aware of her nearness, her floral scent, the exact gray-green color of her wide-set, intelligent eyes, the way a rosy blush feathered across her cheeks when he complimented her.

He wanted to spend more time with her. *Alone.* Now that he knew her to be widowed, his wish wasn't so outrageous, apart from the fact that she was in the employ of Lady Susanne's parents.

But to what end? Adam wished he could say his motives were pure. Instead, they were driven by sheer magnetic attraction.

With Mrs. Malcolm riding beside him while he led the third horse at a slow amble, he decided to ask her more about her life. Getting to know her better was a more honorable pursuit than wishing to kiss her again. Although his body adamantly urged him to do that, too.

Wincing slightly, he recalled his father's lesson from an early age. *One did not dally with the help.* He knew better than to lead on or do anything to display a lack of respect for the station of useful, loyal staff, who in turn respected their employers. It was all civilized and designed to protect the vulnerable from the powerful.

Without doubt, the Earl Diamond was correct.

And yet… Mrs. Malcolm didn't seem particularly vulnerable. Looking over at her, examining her profile, he thought her strong and brave and clear-headed.

"How long has it been since your husband passed away?"

She made a strangled gasp, which turned into a cough to cover it up.

"Do you think that an appropriate topic?" she asked without looking at him.

"Short of snooping around, how else will I discover the answer without asking? And I am not the type to pour a cup of gossip water. I would rather hear about you from your own lips."

"Why do you want to hear about me at all?" she asked. "You know what I am. What more is there to say?"

"I am the heir to an earldom, but that is not all I am. I like fishing and trying to beat my eldest sister at target practice with the bow. I enjoy riding, which you know already, and now I know that about you, too. I don't care for spiders," he added carefully.

Her head whipped around, her eyes suddenly dancing. "Are you afraid of creepy-crawlies, my lord?"

"Not *afraid*, exactly. I simply don't want them on me. Or near me. Or in my room when I am sleeping."

"I see." She smirked and looked away.

He enjoyed having amused her.

"Is there something you don't like?" Adam asked, hoping for a little tit for tat.

When she hesitated, he thought she might tell him something important or nothing at all.

"I do not care for watercress. I don't want it on me, near me, or in my room when I am sleeping."

Adam couldn't help himself—he started to laugh and couldn't stop for a few moments.

"If you kill any spiders that approach, then I will eat any watercress we encounter."

Her smile before she spoke made his heart stutter, then beat rapidly.

"Very well," Mrs. Malcolm agreed. "That seems a fair deal."

They had exited the park, and time was slipping away. Urgency made him bold because he might never have the chance again.

"Won't you share your story?" he asked, wanting more than ever for her not to be such a mystery. "Just as I am more than an heir, you are more than a governess."

Another long pause ensued until he was convinced she wouldn't answer. At last, Mrs. Malcolm spoke without looking at him.

"I have been widowed for two years, which is half a year longer than I was married."

He thought about her words. "How did your husband die? Was he a soldier?"

"Why would you think that?"

"Unless you married an older man," Adam began, "then I assume your husband was my age. And I don't intend to die anytime soon."

She shrugged. "He may have been a little older than you. I may be a little older than you, for that matter."

He hadn't considered that, but he knew better than to ask her exact age. It didn't bother him one way or the other. They were simply two people riding together.

They approached the Circus, the architectural masterpiece of John Wood, the Elder. Adam was glad to see it in her company, knowing she would be able to answer any questions he had. She was that sort of person.

As expected, when they entered the first of three semi-circular sections of the golden-stoned neighborhood, Mrs. Malcolm said, "Mr. Wood designed it after being inspired by a visit to Stonehenge. Sadly, he died shortly afterward, only three months into its building. It took his son the next fourteen years to complete."

"A lot more columns than Stonehenge," Adam said, looking along the crescent of homes in front of them and then around at the other two. Doric, Roman, and Corinthian columns stacked one above the other, moving up in complexity for each of every home's three stories. To be sure, it was clever and pleasing to the eye.

"Palladian architecture at its finest," he said.

When Mrs. Malcolm cocked her head in his direction, he confessed, "My mother grew up here, and she told me a bit about it."

Adam thought the facades were exceedingly interesting, with friezes high above and all around.

"What are the symbols?" he asked, just to hear Mrs. Malcolm talk.

"I have walked all three sections many times," she said. "There are emblems of the Mason and the Druids, and many items to do with science and art. Hundreds actually. I've seen a compass, flowers, boats, globes, birds. Even a paintbrush."

"A serpent," Adam pointed out over one door.

She sent him an arch look, and he wondered if she knew his given name. He shrugged.

"One point of interest," she said, "if you look at the parapet atop each home, you'll see the finials are all in the shape of an acorn."

Adam craned his head and looked. "Indeed. And why?"

This time, Mrs. Malcolm shrugged. "Some say they make reference to Bath's founder, King Bladud."

"I confess to being like Lady Susanne with Lord Sydney and his gardens," he said. "I have never heard of this king."

Mrs. Malcolm smiled softly. "I do enjoy reading about the details. Very well, if you want to know, he was a mere leper swineherd with many pigs at the time he came here. This could be anytime between 500 and 900 BC."

"That is a large span of 'anytime'," Adam pointed out.

"It is. As the story goes, he escaped being locked up for his leprosy, contracted in Greece of all places, came to Bath, and discovered the healing waters."

Adam frowned. "That doesn't sound correct. I've never heard these waters cured leprosy. Anyway, how did he become king, and of what?"

"You know good old Geoffrey of Monmouth's *Historia Regum Britanniae*?" Mrs. Malcolm asked her question the way most women discussed a novel of one of the Brontë sisters, only recently revealed not to be gentlemen writers with the last name of Bell. "He first mentions Bladud as a King of the Britons, son of King Rud Hud Hudibras," she continued, "but no one knows for certain if either were even real."

"What about his pigs?" Adam asked, entranced by her.

"Bladud noticed his pigs had good skin after wallowing in the warm mud of Bath."

"You are running rig on me now," he said, delighted.

"I am not, I promise you. Bladud tried the warm mud and cured his leprosy. His father restored him as heir to the throne, and Bladud founded Bath in order to bring restorative powers to others."

"What about the acorns?" He waved his hand at the many finials three stories above them.

"Oh, those." She arched a flawlessly shaped eyebrow. "All pigs love acorns. Didn't you know that?"

"Again, I am suddenly reduced to the position of pupil with you as my teacher." He appreciated her knowledge and told her so. "You are impressive, Mrs. Malcolm."

"Thank you."

Having traversed the Circus, they were now heading along Bennett Street and had lapsed into silence. Adam realized, in all the talk of pigs and kings, she hadn't answered his original question about how her husband died.

"Why don't you wish to speak of Mr. Malcolm?"

"Mr. Malcolm," she repeated. Then she said something more under her breath.

They turned onto The Paragon, which he thought a strange name for a street. It stretched for thirty-seven identical white front doors under thirty-seven triangular pediments, all three-story facades, also with matching wrought-iron railings out front.

On this street of sameness, Mrs. Malcolm's next words, so extraordinarily frank, shocked him.

"Because my husband was a bastard through and through. I don't mean that literally. He wasn't born on the wrong side of the blanket, as they say, but his nature was as base as they come. Therefore, you must excuse me if I don't wish to waste a moment of otherwise pleasant discourse on him."

Adam swallowed. *He hadn't expected that!* They circled around to the alley where a groom would take all three mounts, and Mrs. Malcolm would disappear indoors.

Wishing he could think of something to say that didn't sound trite or pointless, Adam finally blurted out what he felt. "Then I am truly sorry you married him."

"As am I," she said.

"And why did you come to Bath?" He had to ask. For of all the places in Britain or the world, he wondered how she had ended up there, where he had found her.

She cocked her head, then sighed. "Because of *Northanger Abbey.*"

He didn't know what to say since he hadn't read it.

"A favorite of mine," she added.

And that was all he was going to get out of her.

Soon, he had dismounted and raced the groom to help her down. She seemed to be in an ill humor, and Adam blamed himself. They could have simply continued discussing Bath or buildings, or even how long she'd been playing the violin, but he'd gone and pried into something painful.

How could he make amends?

Then he recalled what he'd seen on a notice at Sydney Gardens.

"May I escort you to the Hanoverian concert in Sydney Gardens tomorrow night? The musicians are performing at the Gothic Hall."

She froze motionless as a statue.

CHAPTER SIX

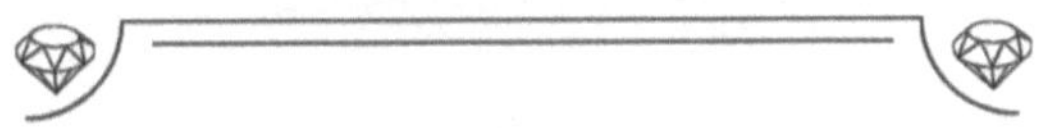

Adam heard the inappropriateness of his words and wished he could recall them to his mouth. He could not for an instant imagine his father or any of his own friends inviting a governess out, any more than a shopgirl or a maid.

Mrs. Malcolm turned to face him full on. Her expression was a mixture of doubt and regret, as well as something he thought looked like reproach. Again, he knew he ought not to have asked her.

"I cannot keep company with you *and* keep my post as a governess," she reminded him. "That is simply the way of it. And if you are courting Lady Susanne, then you shouldn't be asking me, anyway."

"I know," Adam agreed at once. "It was wrong of me to overstep the boundaries of what is possible." But blast it all, he wanted to go with her and witness again her pleasure while she listened to music.

"Lord Diamond," she said, her tone softer, "I sincerely thank you for the offer, no matter how ill-conceived. I assume by your good reputation with Lord and Lady Beasley that you asked me from a place of kindness. I will tell Lady Susanne you are interested in attending."

With that, she hurried inside, through the servant's door at the back entrance.

The devil take him! He had cocked that up. Although, he believed were circumstances different, she would wish to keep company with him. She hadn't rebuffed him as a predator, nor dismissed him out of hand.

As he strolled around to the front of the residence, Adam realized she had not satisfied his curiosity about the death of her husband. *The bastard!* Her fiery declaration of the man's nature had surprised him.

She seemed like a level-headed young woman. *How had she ankle-shackled herself to the wrong fellow, and what had become of him?*

At the front of the house, he knocked and was instantly admitted and met by Lady Beasley.

"Is Lady Susanne well after her ordeal?"

"My daughter is fine, a little shaken. Thank you for bringing back her horse. Is it injured?"

"No, my lady. Stung by a bee, but with Mrs. Malcolm's assistance, I removed the stinger."

"Truly?" Her ladyship frowned. "She is a woman of many talents. Surprisingly so at times."

"Where did she come from?" he blurted.

"Our governess? Why, London, I believe. Mrs. Malcolm was newly widowed and left the city, which was a trove of unpleasant memories from what I understand."

"And how did you find her?"

"She answered an advertisement. That is how one usually finds a governess. Why do you ask, my lord?"

"As you said, she is surprising for a governess."

When Lady Beasley narrowed her eyes, he added, "Both my older sisters have young children, boys and girls. She seems precisely the type of tutor they would appreciate, what with the musical talent and all."

Lady Beasley's face relaxed. "I see. You hope to steal my employee away from me." She chuckled. "You would be unsuccessful. Mrs. Malcolm has expressed an absolute disinclination for returning to London."

Since they were chatting openly now, he thought he would try one last prying question.

"How did her husband die?"

Again, Lady Beasley's forehead furrowed. "Do you know something? I don't believe she has ever told me." Then she shrugged. "I suppose it doesn't matter now. In any case, in a few years, my girls will have completed any course of instruction she can offer and will be too old for a governess. Then you may have her."

Adam swallowed the distaste of discussing the interesting, intelligent woman as if she were an object that could be easily transferred from one household to another.

"Thank you," he managed. "Although if she is disinclined to live in London, then perhaps not, for both my sisters have homes there."

Lady Beasley had finished discussing her employee.

"Shall I send my daughter into the drawing room to visit with you?"

"No," he said, perhaps too quickly. Yet he'd had enough of Lady Susanne's company for the day. He hoped to grow fonder of and be able to tolerate her rather vapid nature for longer than a morning's ride. For she was, in fact, a good contender to be a wife. Even the long-lasting attractiveness of her mother spoke well on her behalf.

He didn't doubt Mrs. Malcolm would age particularly well, too, what with her cheekbones, then realized he shouldn't be thinking of her at all.

"I think Lady Susanne should rest today," he added, "but my advice is she get back upon that horse as soon as possible to avoid a festering fear, one which might prevent her from riding in the future."

"Well said," Lady Beasley agreed.

He nearly departed before remembering the concert. While he could not possibly ask her ladyship for permission to take the governess on an outing, he could invite Lady Susanne *and* her chaperone.

"May I have the honor of escorting Lady Susanne to the Hanover musicians' concert in Sydney Gardens tomorrow night?"

"I am sure she would be most delighted."

"Perhaps you would allow Mrs. Malcolm to be the chaperone again, only because the experience at the last concert was greatly enhanced for both your daughter and for myself by the governess's knowledge of the music."

Although Lady Beasley raised an eyebrow, upon consideration, she seemed to think it a good idea.

"Yes, I do not see why not."

WHEN SUSANNE RUSHED into the sunny salon, she interrupted Alice instructing the two younger Beasleys as they translated a Latin passage of Homer's *Odyssey*. The eldest sister stopped in her tracks and listened a moment before bursting out in laughter.

"I am so thoroughly relieved that I missed out on all your lessons," she declared, then gave her sisters a pitying look.

"I think it's interesting," Pauline said.

"I like the story, but I would rather read it in English," Leila admitted.

"Do you need something?" Alice asked, not appreciating the interruption, especially if it was merely to breed dissatisfaction amongst her pupils.

"I came only to say we are going out again with Lord Diamond. To another concert. I know you will love it, and I enjoy being with him, so everyone will be happy."

Without waiting for a reply, merely assuming Alice would agree, Susanne departed.

"How splendid for you," Leila said.

Was it, though? Alice wondered. For she didn't think Lord Diamond was being sincere in his pursuit of Susanne. The girl might become overly attached and get her heart broken.

Alice was of half a mind to make him show his hand, so to speak. It would be easier on Susanne if she became a little hurt now when the relationship was new, rather than deeply wounded later.

This was not a ball, so Alice could wear one of her ordinary dresses without worry. Despite that, Susanne was trussed up as if she were going to meet the Queen herself. Recalling her own youthful days when she gladly took any excuse to wear her finery, Alice could only smile until she saw the dancing slippers.

"At least wear proper shoes," Alice advised while they were donning lightweight shawls for the summer evening.

"But these match my gown and gloves beautifully." Both were a turquoise color, the gown of satin, the gloves of silk, and each making Alice feel downright drab in her pale green cotton dress with plain white gloves.

"Mother," Susanne called out. Mrs. Beasley appeared at the top of the stairs.

"Please don't yell like that," her mother admonished. "What is it?"

"Must I wear proper walking shoes when my slippers match so well?" She lifted her hem to show her.

Lady Beasley sighed. "They shall probably be ruined, but the perfection of your ensemble makes them absolutely imperative."

Susanne clapped her hands. Alice turned away with a shrug. She probably would have done the same thing. But now, with her new circumstances, the wastefulness of butter-soft kid leather slippers being worn outside and the impracticality of hurt toes reigned supreme over fashion. Her charge was already peering out the front window.

"He's here," Susanne yelled to her mother who was still standing on the landing.

"I told you to stop yelling. Go on, then. His lordship needn't come inside. We can relax our decorum a little now that first, second, and even third impressions have been made."

With that, Alice found herself on the other side of the door, looking once more into the handsome face of Lord Diamond. An evening stretched before them in which she hoped to tamp down the stirrings she felt for him while trying to decide if he was playing false with Susanne.

The first inkling came when he managed to sit between them at the Gothic Hall, then proceeded to turn his head and ask her questions. Naturally, Susanne was also looking at her, but since she was on the far side of Lord Diamond, her charge took it upon herself to make moon eyes at the man's left ear.

Susanne also sniffed him surreptitiously, something Alice wished to do, too, for the man must be wearing the most expensive and manly cologne ever to come out of a London perfumery.

"It will be mostly Handel tonight, I assume. And I hope we shall be treated to his *Funeral Anthem for Queen Caroline.*"

"A *funeral* anthem," Susanne exclaimed. "How dreadful!"

"It's a complex and passionate piece," Alice told her. "It made many believe he and the queen were more than friends."

"An entirely forbidden romance," Lord Diamond remarked, his gaze flickering across her face.

"Yes," she agreed, trying to calm her rapidly beating heart. "The piece was first heard in Westminster Abbey. The acoustics must have made it seem as though Heaven itself was mourning."

"The acoustics?" Susanne asked, but neither did Lord Diamond's head turn toward her, nor did Alice respond. She couldn't take her eyes from his. "I doubt we shall hear the vocals tonight, but no matter, the music speaks for itself, written miraculously over the period of a single week."

Shivers danced down her spine, and she leaned closer to him. "A week, can you imagine?"

"I cannot," he whispered.

She could see her own twin images in his eyes and sat back. *What had gotten into her?*

"What are *acoustics?*" came Susanne's question interrupting—*thankfully*—the mesmerizing moment.

As expected, the anthem was the third piece played. Not all the ode, of course, although Alice would have gladly sat through the entire length of it. As it was, she closed her eyes and let the music wash over her and seep through her, startled when tears pricked her eyes.

As a few rolled down her cheeks, she felt his lordship pat her gloved hand. And then Susanne said, too loudly, "It is rather dour. I think I prefer a tidy, sentimental song like 'The Troubadour Was a Gallant Youth,' or 'Mary Anne.'"

Alice shook her head, but the young lady's words had certainly pulled her from the somber melancholy. She snickered at Handel being compared to tediously simple, drawing-room music, sung so softly by young ladies one couldn't hear it while seated a few yards away. And then she heard Lord Diamond chuckle.

Unable to help herself, Alice started to laugh. It erupted out of her before she could clamp her hand over her mouth, drawing the attention of those around her.

Embarrassed but unable to stop, she rose and ran down the makeshift aisle on either side of which chairs had been set up in the venue.

Bursting through the doors, Alice ran across the Sydney Gardens' main path toward the bowling green, where she leaned against an oak and tried to collect herself. However, after the uncontrollable laughter, she reverted to warm, salty tears and worse, to deep wracking sobs.

"Stop it!" she scolded herself, frightened by the wildly swinging depth of her emotions. "Alice, be still." It was something her mother used to say when she was an active child.

"Alice?" came Lord Diamond's voice. "Are you speaking to that tree by name?"

"No," she said, slightly affronted and realizing he was close. "What are you doing here?"

"Gathering myself. I couldn't stop laughing, so I followed you."

"And Lady Susanne?" she asked.

"I told her to stay put." He fell silent, and she was glad that in the dim light he couldn't see her face, which was probably blotchy.

She knew she should insist they return at once to the Gothic Hall, but she needed a moment. *Alone.*

"Will you leave me, please?"

"Is your given name Alice?"

She sighed loudly, so he could hear her vexation with him. "Yes."

"Mine is Adam."

Since she hadn't asked, she had no comment. But it was a good name—solid, masculine, friendly.

"My sister has a maid named Alice," he said.

She frowned at him. "That is of no import. A name doesn't signify one's station."

"I didn't say that it did," he pointed out.

They stared at one another. Then she recalled another Adam.

"My father had a groom named Adam." *Tit-for-tat,* she thought. Yet Lord Diamond didn't appear the least set down.

"When I think of you as Alice, you seem entirely different from who you are as Mrs. Malcolm, the governess." He took a step closer.

"Do I?" she asked. That night, standing in the darkness with a handsome man, she felt very different from Mrs. Malcolm, the governess. She was her old self, *Lady Alice.* A flighty, shallow ninny. She hoped not but feared it might be true.

"Yes," he said. "You are a different woman entirely."

She wanted to ask him what difference he saw in her when, to her amazement, he leaned in close and claimed her lips in a heated yet tender kiss.

Just as she hadn't been able to help the strong current of sorrow that swept through her from the music, now she couldn't beat back the wave of desire that pulsed in her veins, bringing her body back to vibrant life.

At once yearning for intimacy and craving his touch.

When his tongue touched her lips, he drew back. "Your cheek and lips are salty wet. Were you crying?"

He didn't move away. Instead, he wrapped his arms around the back of her, and she leaned her head on his chest.

"I confess I was. That piece by Handel got the better of me." No need to tell him it felt as though her whole disaster of a life had been represented by the funeral anthem.

"I thought it extraordinarily beautiful," Adam admitted.

"Soulful," she agreed.

"Sublime," he said.

Then they remained quiet a second until she looked up at him. When their gazes met again, he groaned. Their mouths fused hungrily together once more. Alice wanted to strip off her inexpensive gloves and dive her fingers into his dark hair. She wanted to strip off his clothing and do more than that. It had been a long time, and it had never felt like this.

Up until the moment Adam had kissed her in a strip of land behind the assembly rooms, her body had remained obediently dormant. Three and a half years earlier, after a painful deflowering and a disappointingly brief first time with Richard, she'd then experienced a series of her husband's hurried, selfish, oft-inebriated, and sometimes painful joinings in the marital bed.

Nothing had been remotely satisfying, but she had felt a feathering of need awaken. She hoped there was something more to experience. The few times she'd tried to make

Richard slow down or touch her a certain way, he'd brushed aside her request, caring nothing for her feelings.

Luckily for her, he'd moved on to mistresses and deep bottles of gin.

Now beside the oak, flames of raw desire engulfed her, dampening the place between her legs. At the same time, her senses were assaulted by Adam's sensuous kiss and his damnably delightful scent and the way he gently kneaded the flesh at her hip before his hands slid lower to cradle her rear end.

He tilted her hips against him, and her knees wobbled.

Shamelessly, she held on to him, both her hands clasping the front of his jacket. Reveling in the moments of pure pleasure, Alice moaned when he bit her lower lip, rasping it between his teeth before sucking it into his mouth.

She'd never been kissed like this before. It was a revelation, intoxicating, heady—she could barely recall her own name.

"Mrs. Malcolm!" It was yelled out loudly by Lady Susanne, who was a mere few yards away.

Struggling to free herself, it took far too long before Alice stood apart from Lord Diamond. And when she looked at the young lady, she simply didn't know what to say.

What could she possibly tell her to make it any better?

"How could you?" Susanne asked, sounding wounded and confused. "With *my* suitor? It's indecent."

"I am sorry," Alice said, her voice coming out barely louder than a whisper. Her mouth felt strange. But when she raised her hand to her lips, only to find it shaking, she lowered it again.

She hadn't changed at all, hadn't learned anything from her wreck of a life.

"Mrs. Malcolm has nothing to be sorry for," Lord Diamond said firmly. "I found her overcome with emotion from the music and sought to comfort her. I then took liberties with her person."

"You did!" Susanne agreed. "Grave liberties. I saw you. But . . ." She looked from one to the other. "But Mrs. Malcolm appeared to be *allowing* the liberties and taking some of her own."

"Nonsense," Lord Diamond said.

All Alice could do was stare at his profile as he tried to save her reputation, something no one had ever done for her before.

"I am taller and stronger," he insisted. "I wanted to kiss her, and I did. There was little she could do to stop me."

How chivalrous of him! Normally, she would gainsay him and take her share of the responsibility, but not for this. She couldn't. She was as low as she could go, and the thought of seeking employment again, perhaps landing somewhere far less acceptable left her frozen with fear.

Thus, she let him heap the blame upon himself and hoped he understood.

CHAPTER SEVEN

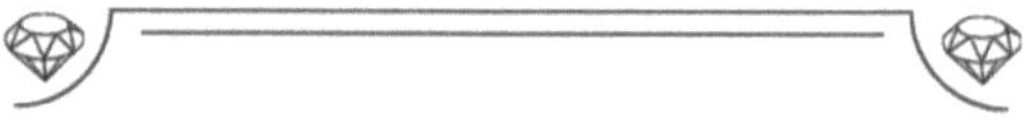

Adam hoped he had said enough to save Mrs. Malcolm from losing her position with the Beasley family, not to mention her good name. Lovers kissing in Sydney Gardens was probably nothing out of the ordinary. But a gentleman kissing a governess and being discovered by the lady he was supposed to be courting—that was beyond the pale, especially when the governess was supposed to be chaperoning.

Besides, it was indubitably his fault. Both times. This instance had been far better than the first. Instead of being punched in the stomach, he'd felt her body melt against his, inflaming his passions. He'd never experienced anything like it. Raw and hot and overwhelming until he had truly forgotten they were in a public place.

It must have been the darkness and the fact that they were practically alone with everyone in the Gothic Hall, listening to music. Or they should have been, except Lady Susanne had come out!

What now?

Lady Susanne allowed him to escort them home, although she would hardly look at him and wouldn't speak to either one of them, not even when he addressed her directly.

"Will you keep what you saw to yourself, my lady, to avoid embarrassment to Mrs. Malcolm, or any greater harm?"

The greatest harm would be if Alice, as he now thought of her, was sacked. He didn't know her circumstances but assumed her dead husband had not left her with much money, or she would not be working for the Beasleys.

For her part, Alice had shrunk into herself, turning away. If she behaved in such a guilty fashion, Adam feared Lady Beasley would know something had happened even if her eldest daughter said nothing about what she'd seen.

"Mrs. Malcolm, please do not accept any blame," he added, trying to warn her to stand tall, chin lifted, and maintain her innocence. "I hope you accept my apology. And to you, too, Lady Susanne. I should not have left you alone in the Gothic Hall. But if you speak of this, how will your sisters' governess be able to continue her lessons with a hint of ignominy hanging over her?"

Still, Lady Susanne said nothing. Nor did she bid him good night when he helped her out of the carriage.

Alice, on the other hand, looked him directly in the eyes. Instead of fury at his reckless behavior, she sent him a message of gratitude, which he did not deserve.

"Good night," she said softly, her voice still subdued. Then she disappeared inside.

He barely slept, wondering over her fate, although he also marveled at his obsession with this woman who had been a stranger to him not long ago. She made his pulse pound like horse's hooves and his heart soar, despite her being a widow and from a different class. He wanted to be near her, to find out everything about her, and mostly to kiss her again. Turning, he punched his pillow.

Was this how love started? Adam thought perhaps it was. Something inside her called to him in a way he had never experienced. And it certainly wasn't happening with Lady Susanne.

On the other hand, it was inconceivable to take this beyond a summer dalliance—love or not. He knew from Lady Beasley that Alice was finished with London, whereas the city was his beloved home. In any case, he could not be seen with her there. As soon as her station was discovered, the assumption would be she was loose, maybe even accepting money from him.

In Bath, though, if she were willing, he could bring her to his private residence and tup her soundly. Perhaps she was lonely and would enjoy such a respite, even if that was all he could offer her.

Unable to let matters rest, he stopped by the Beasleys' home as soon as the hour could be considered polite for visiting. Once inside, he wasn't sure what to do. *How could he speak to Mrs. Malcolm privately? And what of Lady Susanne?*

The latter appeared, summoned by the butler's announcement of Adam's arrival. Not surprisingly, Lady Susanne wore an expression of disappointment. Unlike the last few times, however, her mother did not enter with her, which was fortunate but disconcerting.

"I did not expect to see you today, my lord."

"I needed to speak with you, but I am surprised we are alone."

"My mother is out. I have sent for my maid, and she will join us presently. Meanwhile, we can speak candidly."

He swallowed. "Yes, that's true."

"Are you interested in courting me? More to the point, do you find me favorable above all other women?"

Adam ought to have expected the question, but he hadn't. He thought he would spend time apologizing and soothing and smoothing everything over. Instead, the normally easy-going, unopinionated Lady Susanne had gone directly to the crux of the matter.

And he had to consider her question. In all the agonizing over Mrs. Malcolm—Alice—during the prior night, he had not given any thought to whether he could continue to keep company with the young lady who had been kind to him.

Moreover, her mother was still his own mother's friend. He must tread carefully.

"The length of your hesitation doesn't bode well," Lady Susanne said. "Simply because I don't mind bending my likes to the gentleman with whom I keep company, and intend to do the same with the man I marry, it doesn't mean that I am in all respects a doormat."

"No, of course not," he said.

What an awful thought, to be under someone's foot in such a low manner.

"I am amiable, perhaps to a fault," she continued, "because few things bother me and because my own enjoyments are easy to do in my personal time, such as perusing fashion plates and strolling the shops to search for the latest dress designs. Thus, I don't push my own pursuits and pleasures upon others."

"No," he agreed, "you have not. You've been most accommodating."

She nodded. "However, I am unwilling to be with a man who doesn't favor me above all others."

Nor should she. His respect for her had grown immensely.

"I understand," Adam said.

"Even while courting," she added. "It should be apparent to both of us very swiftly if we wish for the other to be in our future. I was certainly content to have you as my suitor, then my fiancé, and finally my husband. I would forsake all others and not allow another to escort me around Bath. In return, I would expect you to want me exclusively and not to have eyes for my chaperone."

Her voice had raised in pitch, and he was glad the maid hadn't yet joined them.

"You have every right to that expectation," he said, knowing he could not meet it. "Unfortunately, my attachment has not grown beyond admiration for you as the daughter of my mother's friend."

"I understand." She considered a moment. "Then I am glad to have seen what I saw last night so as not to be misled into thinking otherwise, nor do we need to waste any more time with one another."

Adam was feeling as small as a garden slug. "I am sorry. I never meant to mislead you, nor do I feel any time we spent to have been wasted, for I truly enjoyed it."

She nodded. "Now that we have clarified what is and is not between us, perhaps we should talk about Mrs. Malcolm."

"What about Mrs. Malcolm?" came Lady Beasley's voice through the open doorway. She entered and looked around. "Why are you two alone together?"

Lady Susanne opened and closed her mouth, and Adam wanted to bellow in frustration. *Was he to take the blame for yet another indiscretion, this time not of his own making?*

"Not to worry, Mother," Lady Susanne said before he could begin to explain. "Mrs. Malcolm was here just a moment ago."

Adam was startled by her lie but grateful.

"Why would she leave the two of you in what could be considered a compromising position?" Lady Beasley asked, sounding annoyed.

Lady Susanne looked at him, her soft brown eyes widening. He racked his brain, then said the only thing he could think of.

"She went to fetch a book for me. Mrs. Malcolm has a copy of… of… *Northanger Abbey*, and kindly offered to lend it to me."

Lady Beasley appeared surprised. "I didn't realize gentlemen had an interest in Miss Austen's novels."

"And why not?" he asked. "They are well-written tales of… of…," *Damnation!* For the life of him, he couldn't think what an Austen novel was about since he normally read stories of adventure, usually older works, such as Defoe or Fielding.

"Lord Diamond is being polite, Mother," Lady Susanne said, saving him again. "Of course he hasn't read Miss Austen's novels of love and manners, but that one is different. Even I know it is set in Bath, and his lordship is immersing himself in our city."

"I see," Lady Beasley said slowly. "Nevertheless, this is impossibly improper. Susanne, come with me, and send a maid to find out what is taking our governess so long to bring the book to Lord Diamond." She turned to him. "I wish we could stay and visit, my lord, but we have a prior engagement. I returned home only to collect my daughter. We are late to a tea party."

"I apologize for my intrusion without an invitation," Adam said, thinking it couldn't have worked out any better. "Good day, ladies. I hope you enjoy your party."

Lady Susanne gave him a last look that gave him hope she didn't think too badly of him. And then he waited in the drawing room, hoping someone remembered to speak with Mrs. Malcolm. Otherwise, he might have a very long wait indeed.

As it was, in about two minutes she appeared, dressed in the dress she wore the first time he saw her playing the violin. His entire being sighed with relief at being in her presence once again.

"Lord Diamond," she greeted, sounding breathless as if she had hurried. "I confess I am confounded by a message delivered to me to bring you this book as quickly as possible."

She showed him the copy of *Northanger Abbey* she held in her hands.

"Moreover, I was interrupted during my French lesson with the younger Beasley daughters and told by the housemaid *not* to keep you waiting. I had to run like a mouse with a cat on her tail and dig this out of my trunk."

He bowed deeply because, despite having kissed her soundly, he felt nothing but the deepest respect. "It was a bit of a ruse, I admit."

"A ruse?" she asked. "To see how quickly I could make it from the third floor down to the drawing room?"

He smiled. She was enchanting. "No, definitely not that. Lady Susanne and I were caught in here alone."

"Oh." Alice's tone grew serious.

"By her mother," he added.

"Doing what?" she asked, narrowing her eyes.

Was she jealous? On his part, he would be green to the gills if he thought her kissing another man so quickly after their encounter.

"We were talking about the future and how there wasn't going to be one for the two of us," he said, hoping that made Alice the tiniest bit happy. "But we were alone. When discovered, I said you had left us to bring me your book."

"Clever," she said, although she did not sound overly pleased. "And where are they now?"

"Lady Beasley and Lady Susanne went to a tea party."

Alice nodded. "Lessons to broaden her thoughts would do that young lady better than a party."

"It's admirable how you care for them."

"The Beasleys have been good to me," she said, "and I would like to see the three girls happy and fulfilled."

"And what about yourself?" Adam wanted to know what she wished for her future.

"I am grateful our inappropriate behavior did not cost me my position, although it will be a little awkward around Lady Susanne for the time being. Even worse now I know you are ceasing to court her."

"I hope it will grow easier soon."

Silence fell, and they stared at one another. Adam wanted to step forward and sweep her into his arms. The desire was almost painful to resist, as if she were already pledged to him, his woman in truth, and he was being kept from her. Alice was like a princess locked in a tower, and irrationally, he wanted to liberate her as the prince in the Brothers Grimm fairy tale.

But even if he climbed that tower, he would find a widowed governess.

"You had best take the book," Alice said, holding it out to him. "Not that I expect Lady Beasley to follow up on such a petty matter."

As Adam reached out to take it from her, he realized she was gloveless. Quickly, he stripped off his own kidskin gloves, unable to pass up the opportunity to touch her bare hand. Sure enough, he was able to trace the underside of her fingers when he took the slim tome.

Staring at their hands, she visibly shivered, matching the trembling sensation inside him.

"Mrs. Malcolm," he began.

Her gaze flew to his, and she shook her head.

"Good day, my lord." With that, she all but ran from the room.

Blast! Cradling the book against him, he left. It was the ticket to seeing her again, even after Lady Susanne told her mother he would no longer court her.

A few days later, he received a letter from his own mother. Carolyn Diamond got quickly to her reason for writing by the second sentence.

We miss you, dear son. I hope you are well and behaving yourself.

He smirked. He was a grown man and could behave how he chose. Then he thought of his mother's green eyes and how she could give a dragon's stare when displeased, and his smirk vanished. Moreover, his father, a tall, personable man, could be firm—even a little frightening—when necessary.

Adam never wanted to disappoint either of his parents. He tugged at his cravat, which felt a little too tight, as he continued to read.

I heard from my friend, Lady Beasley, yesterday. It seems you have lost interest in her eldest daughter. That is a shame. I would not have minded linking our two families.

However, I know you have your reasons. You are a sensible man—mostly—and will find a woman who makes your heart sing. That is your father's and my fervent hope.

Although I wonder if Lady Beasley will still invite me for sherry next time I am in Bath.

Then she entertained him with news of his four sisters, which he appreciated, making him laugh and also miss them more than he'd anticipated.

When Adam finally put down the long letter, he couldn't forget his mother's words about a woman who made his heart sing. *Wasn't that precisely what Mrs. Malcolm did?*

He had felt unsettled since he first met her. Each time he was thrown in with both her and Lady Susanne, it was only Alice who interested him. And he could compare her to any number of women with whom he'd kept company, daughters of his parents' friends, ladies he'd met at balls and dinner parties. None gave him the warm and effusive feeling she did. Certainly, none made him want to bring her happiness even at the expense of his own.

But Alice caused that and more, leaving him staring out a window and wondering how he could steal her away for a picnic.

A picnic couldn't be against the rules for a governess. *Could it?*

He expelled a long breath, knowing perfectly well that it was. If she had a bachelor sniffing around her skirts, she would never be able to keep her employment. He must leave her alone since he did not intend anything more lasting for the future. Otherwise, it was unfair to her.

But oh, how he wished he could stretch out upon a picnic blanket with her, feed her morsels of tender chicken and grapes, drink wine, and then swive like rabbits.

If only he could speak with Clarity. His eldest sister would suss out the best course of action to make everyone happy. In lieu of her advice, he would have to figure it out as best he could.

CHAPTER EIGHT

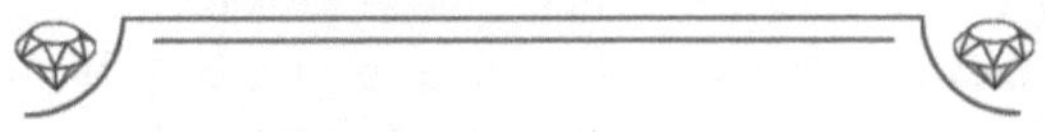

Alice had half-hoped she would be sacked after the incident at Sydney Gardens. At least she would be free to begin a torrid affair with the man who made her body sizzle like a rasher of bacon in a hot pan.

She sighed at the thought of how she'd tingled when he kissed her and of wanting him to do it again. *Had she learned nothing from her previous disregard for propriety and her foolish wildness?*

However, lessons continued as usual, and although Susanne gave her a nettled glare when they encountered one another in passing, nothing else changed.

While taking her break and strolling through Bath's bustling avenues, Alice's discontentment in her usual mundane practices made her realize everything had changed. For one, her thoughts were constantly on Lord Diamond, how he had held her when she'd cried and the way he'd taken the blame for their indiscretion, making sure her reputation hadn't suffered.

And secondly, when she went to bed at night, she contemplated the profoundly different life she might have had over the past few years if he'd been her husband and not Richard. When she awakened, she felt a sense of disappointment, knowing her chance at happiness had been wasted on such an undeserving man.

In truth, she didn't know Lord Diamond well, but he'd already shown more good character during their short acquaintance than Richard ever had. *Apart from the ill-advised, spontaneous kissing!*

As she left her favorite shop with not only fine instruments but also the best selection of sheet music, she startled. Lord Diamond was waiting outside. And she knew he was waiting for her, obviously not conducting any shopping of his own.

"How did you know where I was?" Alice asked, resigned to the fact that he was interested in her, only hoping she could navigate the situation without detriment.

"I followed you," he confessed, looking proud of himself. "It was easy. You mostly only go to two places, either here for musical accoutrements or to the Lilliput Alley bakery for Sally Lunn buns. Shall we go there next?"

"We cannot go anywhere together."

"I know that ought to be the case, but I cannot fathom why. You are not a debutante with an anxious mother, nor are you a titled lady with a lady's maid trailing behind. You are an independent woman, which is the most glorious creature imaginable."

Was he mocking her? She thought not. He was being arguably more honest than any man she'd ever known. However, because she had no family or chaperone, that was all the more reason she had to protect herself.

"Regardless of my station in life, I must preserve my reputation, perhaps with even more vehemence. Otherwise, the fall is too easy and swift."

"The fall?" he asked.

Lord Diamond was walking beside her despite her having intended to put him off.

"Yes, the fall into disgrace." Alice knew all too well the perilousness of letting down one's guard, especially for a handsome man.

Instead of taking her seriously, this particular handsome man smiled, then asked, "And would a delicious bun shared with me truly lead to disgrace?"

He had no idea, she thought. For indeed, it might. One thing often led to another, at least in her experience.

"I believe I deserve a reward from you."

"I beg your pardon," she said. *What was he on about?*

"You said it was unseemly to appear to have designs upon Lady Susanne while actually wishing to spend time with you, and thus I told her forthrightly that I shall not be courting her."

Again, Lord Diamond had shown his honest and good nature. But being seen with a nobleman was dangerous for many reasons she couldn't tell him.

"I am still a governess while you are a titled lord."

He sighed. "We cannot change who we are, Mrs. Malcolm."

She flinched slightly, but he continued without noticing, and they turned onto Lilliput Alley.

"And in all the annals of time, I am sure some other nobleman shared a Sally Lunn bun with a member of the middle class without the world breaking apart."

With that, he held open the door to the bakery. "And since we are already here, what is the harm?"

Alice peered inside, hoping not to recognize any of the patrons, just as she hoped every day. But it was worse if she seemed to be accompanied by Lord Diamond. People would see her differently. They might look twice. They might remember her from her old life.

Yet since she was causing more commotion by blocking the entrance, she went inside, breathing in the tempting aroma of warm bread. At the busy counter, they placed their order, which Lord Diamond paid for. With their purchase in hand, they strolled east toward a grassy spot by the River Avon and found an empty bench. Then silence fell while his lordship opened the bakery bag, offering her the sack to help herself.

After stripping off her right glove, she took one out but felt a little odd eating outside with him.

Undaunted, Lord Diamond, with both gloves off, drew out a still-warm Sally Lunn and bit into it. He sighed, as Alice had done the first time she'd tasted one.

"Chewy and light, a little sweet," he remarked. "It's rather perfect, just like being with you."

It would be perfect if Alice weren't terrified. Even if no one knew her as Lady Alice or Lady Fairclough, her employers might happen by. And being found in the company of a nobleman, even if only eating a bun, she knew it would not go well.

"I am nervous," she confessed. "I know we middle class can mix with you fine nobs, but you were incorrect in your opinion that I am independent. I am securely bound by the expectations of Lord and Lady Beasley. And what they expect is a moral instructor for their girls."

He nodded. "I promise not to kiss you here on the bench." His tone was teasing.

She sighed, closing her eyes momentarily. She wanted to laugh, but it wasn't funny. When Alice opened her eyelids, she fell into Lord Diamond's deep blue gaze. His interest was obvious. She'd seen the look before.

In response, frustration and resentment swirled through her. Being restrained from doing what she wanted was still uncomfortable and unfamiliar, although the lesson wasn't lost upon her. A little restraint ahead of time would have changed everything in her past.

On the other hand, she was already seated beside him and therefore decided to enjoy the moment. In any case, it was too late to go home and hide.

"These are best eaten sliced and buttered," she said. "I often take them home to have with a cup of tea during my free time." Then she finally took a bite.

"I won't accompany you to Lord and Lady Beasley's for butter or tea," he said, "knowing how that would alarm you.

I also promise not to ask any prying questions into your past." This time, he spoke seriously.

"Thank you."

"Then what shall we talk about?" he asked.

Alice blinked at him. How wonderful that he simply wished to converse with her. Most men wanted to dance, compliment, kiss, and then do more. Yet none she'd met had ever shown an interest in honest discourse.

"Tell me what brought you to Bath."

To her surprise, he went a little pink in the cheeks before answering.

"Believe it or not, I am escaping my life in London."

Her heart thudded painfully, having done precisely that herself, two years earlier.

"What do you mean?" In Lord Diamond's case, he might be engaged, secretly married, or running from debt. All those thoughts flitted through her head before she quickly dismissed them. Lady Beasley knew his family and would not have allowed Susanne within a furlong of him if he was involved in any such miscreance.

"The young ladies of Mayfair have known me or known *of* me for a few years, ever since I escorted my sisters to public events. Some families seem to have put me on a list of possible suitors."

Alice couldn't help pointing out the obvious. "Quite high on the list, I would imagine."

"Indeed, whether I wish it or not," he said. "And I do not."

"Why?" She knew she was being a nosy-poke, but didn't most men want the attention and obvious flummery of pretty ladies?

"They were all of a kind, like Lady Susanne." Immediately the words were out of his mouth, he gaped. "I cannot believe I just said anything so ungentlemanly, offensive, and…"

"Honest," Alice supplied when he trailed off, looking chagrinned. "I cannot speak for the other ladies you've met, but Lady Susanne seems younger than her years and has a stubbornness set against filling her mind through literature, history, or music."

He nodded sagely, clearly unwilling to say anything else that even hinted of a derogatory insult. She liked that about him.

"And yet, if I may point out, you are amongst the same sort of people here in Bath. You came calling at the Beasleys' home, and you went to a ball."

"I have also attended a few dinner parties," he told her.

"To what aim, my lord, if you wish to remove yourself from the marriage-minded females?"

"Not all of them," he said. "Only the pushy London ones. I would like a wife in the not-too-distant future, and where else can I look if not at balls and in the homes of the quality folk?"

Alice supposed he was correct, and yet there he was, on a bench with her, seemingly a lowly governess.

As if reading her thoughts, he added, "And in all the time I've been in Bath, I have enjoyed your company most of all. In fact, after I saw you on the street and returned your package to you, I began to search for the mysterious *lady*, which, in answer to your question, was why I was out in the small Season, attending dinner parties with strangers."

Alice had not expected such a confession. *He'd been searching for her!* Yet that was precisely the type of statement Richard would have made to press his case and make her think his devotion was genuine. Having been such a fool once, it was difficult to believe another man with an equally smooth tongue.

And thus, she quelled her blossoming enthusiasm for Lord Diamond. Or tried to.

ADAM COULDN'T BELIEVE how thrilled he was to eat Sally Lunn buns. And it wasn't because of their soft texture and lightly sweet goodness, reminding him of a French brioche. Rather, the simplest pleasure of sitting on a bench by a river had become extraordinary for doing it *with* Mrs. Malcolm. The only thing blighting his satisfaction was having promised not to pry.

Her romantic past did not matter greatly, but he wanted to know more of her previous life. If he was going to stretch the boundaries outside the usual sea of females in which he fished in order to pursue her, which he had all but decided to do, then he wanted some assurance. Even if they were merely going to have a secret affair, she needed to be of sound mind, free from any ties to nefarious individuals, and of acceptably virtuous character. The latter meant willing to cavort in his bed while not simultaneously doing the same in anyone else's.

He would wager his last farthing she was all three. Still, it would be reassuring to hear from her own lips. Thus, after his last bite, he deigned to ask a personal question.

"How did you meet your husband?"

She frowned over the rim of her cup. Then she set it down.

"I thought you weren't going to ask personal questions."

"I answered yours," he pointed out.

"You didn't have to," she said. "You chose to. I choose not to."

"But why? I am honestly curious as to where a governess goes to meet a man, even a dastardly bastard of a man, and get engaged."

"I see. Your question is to satisfy your idle curiosity."

He couldn't tell her it was nothing of the sort without alarming her, but it wasn't idle at all. Instead, it was searing, meaningful, determined curiosity. *Where had she been when she'd spied Mr. Malcolm? What had drawn her to him if he was such a wretch?*

Mostly, he wondered how he could feel jealous of a dead man, especially one whom she seemed to despise.

"You don't have to tell me," he finally conceded in the long hesitation. "It is only my wish to know you better, and what happened in the past has a bearing on who you are now, whether we will it or not."

She took in a deep breath. "Very well. We met at a dance, just like where those of you in the wealthiest classes meet. He saw me first, as I recall. He asked for the honor of a dance. He…." She hesitated, then lifted her chin slightly and looked Adam in the eyes.

"He distracted me with pretty words and flummery. I was naïve but didn't realize it. I thought I knew as much as any worldly woman. I was wrong."

The topic had made her morose, but he had successfully started her talking now, so he continued with another question.

"You were at a public dance, one for which you bought a ticket, I assume." He didn't think either the deceased Mr. Malcolm nor the female seated before him could have been at a private ball attended only by the wealthy or the powerful. He tried to imagine the throng of store clerks and shopgirls dressed in their Sunday best. Alice would stand out with her beauty, her learning, and the cultured manner she had.

"After dancing together, you decided to allow his courtship. Is that correct?" he asked.

She merely frowned, and he sensed there was more to the story she would not disclose. At least, not then and there.

"And did your parents approve? Where are they now? Why didn't you stay in London after you became widowed?"

"Those are many questions, my lord. How did you know I met my husband in London?"

"Lady Beasley told me where you came from before you arrived in Bath. I assumed if you'd come from there, then you might have lived there, too."

"You are correct. I did. My parents left for the Continent soon after my husband died. As to your last question, I needed to earn a living, so I came here to Bath for a fresh start."

"Because of *Northanger Abbey*?"

"Yes. It had captured my imagination early in my life, so why not here?"

"Many women would have thrown themselves upon the mercy of Her Majesty's government. We have programs for destitute widows."

She made a face at the words he'd chosen. "That sounds like giving up," she said, her voice soft. "The way ladies of your class often seem to do—stay home and do nothing, earn nothing, and be nothing."

The women he knew, at least in his family, lived full lives with a husband and children to look after, charities to run or assist, and personal interests of their own, be it art, music, gardening, or science. Thus, he thought she was being a little harsh on an entire class of people she actually knew nothing about, only surmising.

On the other hand, for her own life, she was pragmatic and industrious—both admirable traits. He supposed if he persisted and asked more about her courtship and marriage, it would in truth be mere curiosity, unworthy of him despite how much he wished to know.

Besides, the future was what was important, even if for them, it could only last until the autumn.

"You're smiling broadly, my lord. Is it the quality of the Sally Lunns?"

"Naturally," he said. "What else could make this the best bun of my entire life?"

Her cheeks became rosy again, and Adam's heart squeezed. She was not immune to him. And he was captivated by her. After the few times he'd been in her company, with their interesting discussions and capped by the most titillating kisses, he had decided he would pursue her and do so with bold keenness, as he had that day.

Pushing aside his previous inclination to leave her alone, *noblesse oblige* and all that nonsense, he gave in to his more ignoble instincts only because she seemed as affected by him as he was with her.

"Are you sometimes lonely, Mrs. Malcolm?"

"What an impertinent question!" But she hadn't raised her voice to cause a scene, so he continued.

"I only ask because we get along well and share a similar outlook upon many things, indicating our compatibility. Also, if I am not mistaken, in all frankness which I think you'll appreciate, we are attracted to one another in the physical sense."

This time, her cheeks went scarlet, but she did not stand up and walk away, so he hoped he was correct. Naturally, he would never have such a candid conversation with any lady of his acquaintance, but he didn't think Alice would be so delicate or easily offended. He couldn't imagine her needing smelling salts or having a fit of hysteria, either. She was made of stronger stuff.

"I understand what you are saying," she responded in a quiet voice. "You are making a proposition to me to keep company."

"Keep company," he repeated. *Was that her euphemism for swiving?* Because above all, he desired to roll her under him, bare her bountiful breasts, and take them both on a journey of sweat-inducing, tremor-causing pleasure. "Yes," he said, hoping she agreed as readily, "until such time as I must return to London."

"While I appreciate your offer," she said politely, and he knew she was going to turn him down, "I cannot risk my position."

It was that simple. He could offer payment that would equal her governess's salary, but he knew enough about her not to make such a crass mistake. Besides, that would leave her in the lurch, without employment, when he left for home.

Thus, the only way to get past her objection due to her station as a governess was to remove the impediment entirely. While he considered that, she chewed another bite.

"Our conversation ought to have remained firmly in the present," Alice said. "Do you know about Solange Luyon, a young Huguenot refugee and skilled baker? Somehow, she became Sally Lunn after coming to Bath in 1680. The story is that she was escaping persecution in France."

He shook his head. "Is that true?"

"Maybe, maybe not. Some say these buns are actually named for *sol et lune,* French for *sun and moon.*"

"Strangely, I prefer to think of a real person baking these," he mused, peering into the bag where two buns remained.

Alice chuckled. "Regardless of the name's origin, my lord, I assure you that a real person baked these." She rose to her feet. "I should be getting back now, but it has been an *interesting* diversion."

"I will escort you home," Adam offered, also rising.

"No, thank you. That would be unwise. I wouldn't want to run into… anyone."

He knew she was nervous about being seen with him, and thus, he would respect her wishes, at least for the time being. If only they could have had a moment truly alone.

Not that he was overly confident of his prowess, but she seemed to become more pliable, soften toward him, seem even to understand the depth of their connection whenever he touched her. It certainly reinforced the sense of rightness he felt in pursuing her.

Unfortunately, he had to let her go. After walking beside her for a few yards, he bid Alice good day. The lingering look they exchanged assured him she would welcome seeing him again.

CHAPTER NINE

Alice couldn't stop reflecting upon the unexpected yet delightful treat of taking tea with Lord Diamond. She had deflected his questions while answering some as best she could without lying. When they'd parted, she wondered when or how she would see him again, which was a scary spark of hope in her heart.

Try as she might, she couldn't eradicate it. Moreover, she ought to be insulted by his transparent proposal to begin an affair. She supposed he thought that wholly acceptable to a widowed woman of her class. Any other type of proposal was unthinkable from a man in his position.

And strangely, despite knowing the danger, she had considered it.

Thus, a day later, when Lord Diamond came to the house, her pulse raced, even as she doubted he could have come regarding her. Even more unlikely when Alice learned he had asked to speak with Lord Beasley. The news that he'd requested a meeting with the master of the house spread from the butler to the housemaid. Swiftly, by way of a tea tray and another maid, the tidbit made it all the way up to the salon in which the girls were identifying continents on an atlas while Alice gave them a geography lesson.

"I thought Lord Diamond and Susanne were no longer keeping company," Pauline said after Leila gave a squeal of excitement.

"But why? They seemed a good a couple as any," said Pauline pragmatically, pouring the tea for all of them after the maid departed. "Anyway, why else would a man want to speak to Father unless it were to ask for our sister's hand?"

Alice's stomach clenched. *Was he going to offer for Susanne?* If he did, she ought to speak with Lord Beasley to mention her own doubts about his future fidelity. A man who could spend time freely with her while still having an intent toward another woman could not possibly remain faithful. She knew this from experience.

And what of Susanne? Alice couldn't imagine she would want a husband whom she had witnessed kissing another woman.

"Let us stop speculating, girls," Alice said, although her own brain continued to do precisely that. "Pauline, please locate Madagascar. That is where our bountiful empire gets most of its vanilla."

A few minutes later, the same maid who had dashed up with the tea service and the pot of gossip water returned with a request from Lord Beasley that Alice go to his private study.

"Me?" she exclaimed.

"Father wants to speak with our governess?" Leila exclaimed. "Oh dear! I hope you are not sacked."

With her heart pounding under the speculative looks from Pauline and Leila, Alice touched a hand to her hair and went downstairs.

She was going to be let go. Adam had asked Susanne for her hand, and the young lady had accepted as long as Alice was sent packing.

It made perfect sense, and no sense at all!

She knocked on the door to the room which she hadn't been into once in nearly two years of employment.

"Enter," came Lord Beasley's sonorous tone.

Feeling light-headed, she pushed it open, watching as both Lord Beasley and Adam rose to their feet. Susanne was nowhere to be seen.

Alice nodded by way of greeting to Lord Diamond, who was looking at her intently as if studying a butterfly pinned to a board, and then she greeted his lordship, a man with whom she'd had few encounters.

"You wished to see me, my lord?"

"Yes, Mrs. Malcolm. Come in. Take a seat so we may resume ours."

She did so, finding herself next to Adam while Lord Beasley was seated opposite.

"I shall get directly to the point. This young man wishes to court you. Are you amenable?"

Her mouth opened, but she snapped it closed when she realized she had no words.

Was it a trap? If she said yes, she might be sent away within the hour.

"You may speak freely," Lord Beasley said. "That is why I am here and not my wife, who might be displeased to know Lord Diamond favors you over our daughter."

Alice felt the heat rise in her cheeks.

"It is our own fault," his lordship continued. "This young man obviously prefers brains to beauty. Susanne is too old now to stuff sense and facts into her head. Nevertheless, as pretty and amiable as she is, I have no doubt my daughter will find a suitable husband. But we are here to speak of you. Although you are a widow, you are a single female. Under my roof, Mrs. Malcolm, and thus, you are under my protection."

"Thank you, my lord. My mind is spinning, I admit. I would hate to displease Lady Beasley, who has been a good and kind employer, and I would be equally loath to give insult to Lady Susanne."

Lord Beasley nodded. "Well said. However, my wife chose to employ a widow, not a confirmed spinster. Thus, she knew the risks that hiring a marriageable woman entailed. Moreover, Lady Beasley considers you the best governess we've ever had. Thus, as far as I am concerned, your position is not in any danger up until the moment you marry. And then, of course, we will be sorry to see you leave."

She spared a glance to Lord Diamond, who was staring at her and nodding at everything Lord Beasley said. Apparently, they were in complete concurrence despite Alice thinking it was the strangest thing she'd ever heard.

"My lord, are you saying you are granting permission for me to be courted in public by Lord Diamond?"

"If you wish, yes."

She blinked and turned to Adam. There was no question she would like to spend time with him, even while accepting that a courtship leading to marriage was unthinkable. Her past precluded it. Moreover, he had been rather direct in saying they would keep company only until he left. Thus, letting him spend time with her seemed pointless, destined to lead to heartbreak, at least for her.

Yet while her mind flitted from side to side, she couldn't deny how much she liked being with him. Perhaps, after two years of solitude, not to mention a year and a half of misery before that, she deserved some happy moments with an attentive, intelligent man.

Without Lord Beasley being able to see, Adam winked, and her decision was made. If she told him plainly at the start what distance they must keep—for she was unwilling to risk becoming pregnant—then perhaps he would be agreeable to a casual friendly arrangement until he had to leave Bath.

At the very least, she would greatly enjoy a companion to take her to concerts, despite how others might think they were truly courting with an eye toward engagement and marriage. As long as he knew her limitations, then she would maintain her self-respect.

"I would like to spend time with Lord Diamond," Alice said, carefully choosing her words.

"That's settled then." Lord Beasley looked at Adam. "As far as I know, Mrs. Malcolm needs no chaperone. If she wishes to employ one, that is her prerogative. All I can say is that I want no scandal, no impropriety, nothing that will shine an unfavorable light upon my household or my daughters' governess. Is that clear?"

"Yes," she answered.

"Good, but I was speaking to Lord Diamond. I know your parents, do not forget."

Adam nodded. "Even without the threat of incurring their wrath, I assure you, my lord, I will do nothing to disparage either Mrs. Malcolm or your household."

"Very well," Lord Beasley said. "We all agree it is an odd circumstance, but this is not the Middle Ages. If you wish to court my governess, so be it. Meanwhile, I have work to do."

He stood once again, and Alice and Adam did the same.

"May I have a word with her alone in the drawing room?" Adam asked.

"Briefly, for I am paying her to instruct, not to flirt."

Alice's cheeks warmed. And then she thought of the other two concerned females.

"My lord, will you explain your decision to Lady Beasley and Lady Susanne?"

He sighed. "Indeed, I shall. And heaven help me when I do it."

Alice led the way to the drawing room, amazed at the turn of events. But Adam didn't wait until they were in the relative privacy of a room, even one with servants' ears at every door.

"That went well. I hope you are pleased."

"I am bewildered," she confessed, "both by your wish to court me and his lordship's acquiescence."

"But are you pleased?" Lord Diamond persisted.

That was the primary emotion, so she told him, "Yes. I look forward to an outing."

They entered the drawing room, and Adam even closed the door behind them.

She stared, then smiled. "I confess I feel like a naughty child."

He grinned back at her. "As do I. But I thought hard about this and could see no reason why we shouldn't enjoy ourselves while we are able, as long as Lord Beasley agreed not to terminate your employment. I didn't want to incur your anger from the start."

"I am amazed at your courage in speaking to his lordship on such a matter. You were like a dog in a doublet." She chuckled. "And Lord Beasley shall have to be equally brave to tell her ladyship of his decision."

Suddenly, he reached for her hand. "Will you accompany me to a concert and after, let me finally be alone with you. Recall I reside in a townhouse on the Royal Crescent."

She recalled only too well, but she was not going to see it.

"I am only agreeing to attend a concert or go riding with you. Anything we can do in public. Nothing more. I must emphasize that I am pleased to have your companionship while you remain in Bath, but I intend to stay here and keep my employment."

He grinned. "I trust one thing will lead to another."

She shook her head at his cocky manner. "You cannot mean what you are intimating."

"I know we've only known one another a brief while—"

"Very brief, indeed," Alice said.

"But you feel it, this thing between us, like magnetism, if I had to name it."

She wouldn't lie and say she didn't, but she didn't have to bare her soul or her desires.

"I would be very happy to go to a concert."

Lord Diamond stroked the back of her hand with his thumb, making her shiver. Then he released her.

"Tomorrow night. I shall collect you at eight."

Going to evening events would expose her to those from whom she wished to hide.

"Since I do not have an appropriate wardrobe," she protested, "I would prefer to go to daytime concerts, meaning we must wait until the week's end."

"You may wear a bed sheet for all I care," he shot back. "I predict you'll end up doing so by evening's end, anyway."

Her insides fluttered at the way he was looking at her. It was going to take every ounce of self-respect—not to mention the fear of any ramifications should they go too far—to keep her from giving in to her attraction for him.

"An afternoon concert," she insisted. There was less chance that the high society types visiting from London would be awake and out any earlier than dinnertime.

"I would prefer the evening one," Lord Diamond said.

Alice sighed. "I think we must delineate precisely what can be between us."

"Between you?" came Lady Beasley's voice. "What on earth is going on here?"

"Not again," Lord Diamond muttered.

ADAM LEFT THE BEASLEYS' home satisfied everything was going along better than he could have hoped. By being frank with Lord Beasley and later, more awkwardly, with Lady Beasley, he'd been given permission to court Mrs. Malcolm.

In his heart, he didn't believe he even needed their consent. However, better to have a smooth path at the outset. Besides, he doubted Alice would have agreed to anything if she hadn't received both of her employer's blessings, albeit rather ungraciously provided by the lady of the house *after* she'd heard what her husband had to say.

"If you prefer a governess to my daughter," Lady Beasley had quipped, "then I wonder at your judgment. Regardless, while there is no accounting for taste, young man, I understand there is also no way to fathom the mercurial and oft-spontaneous yearning of the human heart."

With that statement, she had left him to invite Alice to go riding again. It was the best way he could spend time with her until he could get tickets to the daytime concert.

And she had agreed. He had never been happier than when Alice was at his side. While she only had Saturday afternoons and Sundays free during the day, she had nearly every night to her own devices, too. He found it the strangest thing, having to wait a week to be able to tour the Roman Baths with her, climb the Gothic abbey's clock tower and bell tower and see the city from the top of the cathedral, or ride again through Victoria Park.

However, after some persuading and him being on his best behavior for two weeks, she agreed to let him take advantage of her evenings, too. He filled them with any event in which she showed an interest, never a dance or place where she had to mingle with the *ton*.

Adam restrained himself from taking advantage of anything else until she was ready, although time was not in his favor. Determined to win her over like a gentleman should, he treated her as if she were a lady of his class. Doing anything else, such as pressuring her into being alone or plying her with jewelry, would be reprehensible, no matter how tempting her soft lips. Thus, while his ultimate aim was a torrid affair before his imminent departure, he took his suit slowly, as if truly courting her.

Strangely, even after a few weeks in which she comported herself as well as any lady, she was reluctant to return to the assembly rooms for a ball or accompany him to a private dinner party.

"Absolutely not," she declared when Adam said they had been invited to the home of a friend of his from London.

"They will love you," he assured her, but she was adamant.

He assumed she felt herself a fraud amongst the titled and wealthy people. She would have to get over that were he to convince her to attend. Any female accompanying him anywhere, as long as she wasn't crude or behaved in a low manner, would be accepted by his acquaintances. Members of his class would understand that he was enjoying a *special* friendship. It was done, and often. Nearly every king, in fact, had a lover chosen from the middle class or lower, even actresses!

But with Alice, convincing her to enjoy a dinner party had to be undertaken slowly. Everything to do with her had to be done at a leisurely pace.

Except the workings of his heart. That spontaneous organ Lady Beasley had once mentioned had charged ahead as fast as a fully stoked steam engine zipping along the track from interest to admiration to love.

Adam knew it for what it was because when Alice wasn't with him, he was thinking of her. When she smiled, he was happy. When she was nearby, he felt contented—and, naturally, he was also growing exceedingly frustrated. An entirely different kind of yearning than Lady Beasley had meant tortured him, both daily and every night.

Each time their gloved hands brushed against one another, he wanted to pull Alice into his arms. When their arms touched and her warmth seeped into him, he could imagine her naked beneath him. He did, in fact, imagine that, and all too often.

Was it any wonder, he finally asked her consent to kiss her again?

He could have got down on his knees and thanked the good lord when she said *yes* in her breathy way, which indicated she was as affected by their close proximity as he was. Instead of dropping to the damp grass like a supplicant, he drew her close in the safety of the Beasleys' back garden, hoping none of the family were watching. But truly, he didn't give a tinker's damn if they were.

When he claimed her mouth under his after weeks of behaving like a monk, Adam had never felt more like a parched man being given a sip of delicious water. He drank her in, every soft nibble he took of her lips, every taste of her tongue, every sweet brush of her skin against his.

"Marry me," Adam breathed against the skin of her neck, feeling her freeze instantly.

CHAPTER TEN

The devil! How on earth had that outrageous question popped out of his mouth? It must have been the worrisome knowledge that they were running out of one precious commodity he could not replace. Andrew Marvell's "winged chariot" of time was soaring without slowing.

And just like the narrator in that famed poem, Adam hoped Mrs. Malcolm would set aside her inhibitions and let him tup her.

Certainly, the more he thought about never seeing Alice again, the more he wanted to hold on to her with both hands. But binding her to him in matrimony was out of the question. She was meant for a Mr. Malcolm type of man, except loyal and kind and not a cheating bastard. A man who wore a beige coat made of cheap kersey, who went to work at a mercantile or, if very fortunate, at a bank. She would give him children, which she would raise to be smart like herself, and stay at home to keep house, maybe hiring a woman to do the laundry.

If Alice could cook, which he didn't know, perhaps she would have a nice dinner on the table when her husband came home, needing his feet rubbed.

Ugh! The whole thing, while he knew it went on in hundreds of thousands of households across Great Britain, seemed a mean life for a dazzling woman who had the quality and fineness to take her place in any salon in Mayfair or Paris.

Yet Adam could hardly imagine the uproar in London if he returned with Alice on his arm, dressed her up like a lady, and then people found out her true identity.

Luckily, she seemed to have realized the ridiculousness of his proposal even before he did, and he wasn't forced to retract it.

"Kiss me again," Alice demanded, which was better than her storming off in a fit of pique because an eager nobleman had asked her to marry him and then instantly changed his mind, regretting it.

In any case, he had no problem complying with her request. His arms went around her, and she plastered herself against him. He let her feel his desire, and she didn't recoil. She crushed her breasts to his chest and held on while he ravaged her mouth.

It was not the perfect end to an evening. The *perfect ending* would have been if she'd allowed him to take her back to his grandparents' townhouse on the west end of the Royal Crescent.

Adam rattled around with the most minimal of staff inside the five floors, not that he ever went into the large cellar or the spacious attic rooms. He would have dearly loved to slip Alice inside and up to his bed.

Still, it was as close to bliss as he was going to get that night.

Having weathered the ill-advised proposal, he decided to think with his head before he spoke. He tried. He focused on the path in front of their horses or the view from a bridge in the park, the divine music of an orchestra or the tragedy of a well-performed play.

Yet oddly, nearly every time they were together, Adam could imagine asking her again if she would become his wife. There was always a single moment in which he had to struggle not to let his heart speak.

He was certain she knew he was falling in love with her. For every time he wanted to tell her of the dreadful battle raging inside him, between what was proper and what he wished could happen if the situation permitted, she asked him to kiss her once more, thereby thoroughly distracting him.

"Please," he asked one Sunday after they'd been to the Theatre Royal, the luxuriously red-and-gold appointed venue in the middle of Bath. "It's one of the most sought-after tickets."

Adam had arranged entrance to a ball at the deceased William Beckford's former residence, the Lansdown Estate. Reputedly one of the wealthiest commoners in Britain, the novelist and art collector had donated his land and residence to the Methodist Kingswood School. With the grand opening of the exclusive preparatory school, a festive evening was expected in the large common rooms of the main building. Everyone in the upper echelon of Bath society wanted to attend.

Being an earl's son had some benefits, and tickets became instantly available at his asking. However, when Adam surprised Mrs. Malcolm with them, it was he who was surprised when she flatly denied him.

"I do not wish to go to a ball," she said. "Not any. Never."

"I know you can dance and even enjoy doing so," he argued. "Don't tell me you're still smarting over the incident with that silly shawl."

"I have told you before that I have no interest in fancy dinner parties or dances." She crossed her arms over her beautiful breasts, which he could easily imagine worshiping with hands, lips, tongue, and teeth.

"Fine!" he said, feeling tweaguey. "Either agree to run away with me to deepest, darkest Peru or dance with me at this ball. One or the other. Those are your only two choices."

"You are absurd," she said, but there was laughter in her voice.

"I tell you, Mrs. Malcolm, I am not going to take no. Wear that burgundy gown and come to a single dance with me."

When she hesitated, he gave her a look his mother used to say would melt butter and make one think they'd swallowed sugar at the same time. With his blue eyes held open wide and his lower lip pulled up into a pout, he hadn't used the expression since he was a youth trying to get an extra helping of vanilla sponge cake.

It had worked then. It worked now, too.

Alice put a hand to her chest. "Oh! Very well. I shall come to the dance if you make me a promise."

"You have made me extremely happy," he told her, wondering if he should use the look again to get her to go to bed with him or if that would be pressing his luck too far.

"Will you promise not to try to maneuver me back to the Royal Crescent again?"

She was on to him. His heart sank for he could not make such a promise.

"Ever?" he asked, starting to make his meltingly sweet face again.

"At least for the duration of the ball," she said.

"I can promise that," he agreed, thrilled to think of having her in his arms again even for a waltz.

And she did wear the dress, but nearly spoiled it with a lace fichu across the décolletage, hiding her splendid cleavage. *What a marplot!*

The Kingswood School was decorated with everything that school boys would never need nor even be allowed to see, solely for the sake of Bath's elite and for those down from London for the event. Lanterns covered the grounds around the massive residence, summer flowers filled vases, and the aroma of fine food filled the air. The tickets had been absurdly expensive to raise money and to make certain only one class of people would be in attendance. And these party-goers expected the best of everything.

"I see friends from London and as far away as Edinburgh."

As if overwhelmed, Mrs. Malcolm said nothing, head down, her gaze upon the floor. She seemed smaller and shrunken as if she might vanish entirely.

"You are the loveliest woman here," Adam vowed, hoping to quell her nervousness.

Her head shot up, and she looked at him, nodded, and regained some of her usual spirit.

Keeping her arm safely tucked under his so as not to lose her in the throng, they made their way through people who were eager to see whether the Queen and Prince Albert had come as they were rumored to do. He didn't care as much about royalty as dancing with Alice. The crowds made it difficult to get through the entrance chamber and into the school's common room turned into a ballroom.

As soon as the next piece began, however, they were on the dance floor.

ALICE WISHED SHE HAD never agreed to attend. She was nearly certain she recognized people from her old life, although no one whose name she knew. It had been many weeks since the dance she had chaperoned, weeks since she'd had the pleasure of being in Adam's arms, except for a few precious kisses that left her breathless and light-headed.

She'd given in to him, donning her only ballgown, because of her intense desire to dance with him again. However, with the crowd of Londoners attending, she knew this was a mistake. As they crossed the polished floor, she wished she could disappear beneath it.

After ten minutes without incident—no one had called her name—she relaxed slightly. Because of the rarity of this treat, determined never to put herself in this perilous situation again, Alice decided to make the most of the music and dance every dance.

"I shall take no other partner all night," Adam vowed during their first waltz. "After all, who is to stop us from enjoying only one another?"

"No one, I suppose," she agreed. Although she wondered if they would draw unnecessary attention by doing so. But in such a crowd, perhaps no one would notice. Thus, they didn't vacate the dance floor after the piece ended, but continued on to the next one.

"Your eyes are sparkling like gems," he said.

Alice smiled. This was the best night of her life, without doubt. In the warmth of the room, his cologne tickled her senses, making her long to give in and go with him to his home. She could learn if his promises of bliss were true or some wild fantasy he'd made up.

After an hour, they needed a respite.

"At this ball," Adam predicted, "there will be faultlessly chilled champagne, even if ice had to be carted from the North Pole itself."

In what would become the students' dining hall, they found every manner of refreshment. Not only the aforementioned beverage but little pastries, trays of fruits and cheeses, and thinly sliced bread, morsels intended to satisfy the partygoers until the late-night supper.

"There's a good view of the gardens from the far end," their server informed them, nodding toward the double doors opposite.

With glass in hand, they carved a path through the other guests seeking claret, lemonade, or the champagne Alice and Adam now sipped while traversing the long room toward the back. Double doors of clear panes showed an estate lit with a hundred lanterns.

"A romantic place, don't you think?" he asked.

"It is," she agreed, not remembering the last time she had felt this happy. "Rather at odds for a preparatory school."

"Maybe we should go outside and enjoy more than just a view," Adam suggested.

Side by side, they peered out. She knew it would result in another astonishing kiss. Thus, she nodded.

Out upon the terrace, Alice considered how far into the garden she would go with Adam, both figuratively and literally as they surveyed the expansive lawn, hedges, and playing fields.

"We won't go too far," he said, and she wondered at his meaning. In any case, they strolled down one path away from the main building, and eventually stopped beside an ancient stone wall.

He raised his glass of champagne. "To your health, Mrs. Malcolm."

She raised it, too, seeing his expression had grown quite serious.

"What are you thinking?" she asked, looking at him over her glass as she sipped.

"That we are meant to be together."

She rolled her eyes. "You said you wouldn't try to entice me back to the Royal Crescent tonight."

"I am not," he vowed. Then his face broke out into his usual wickedly handsome grin. "I wouldn't stop you if you agreed, of course. But I meant something else entirely. I meant I am of the firm opinion that we ought to be together *permanently.*"

A small gasp escaped her, but he rushed on.

"Let us make this courtship a real one. We have Lord Beasley's blessing, but I know you fear for your position as his family's governess. Thus, I am telling you that in the long run, it will not be an issue."

Alice knew Adam meant she would not need employment in the future because his ultimate goal was marriage. It was a headstrong young man's fancy.

She shook her head. "We have kept company barely two months," she stalled. And then Alice lied to him. "You cannot have formed that strong of an attachment."

For her part, she was entirely taken with him. Her heart was filled with thoughts of Adam during the day and dreams of him at night. Always, there was the anticipation of heartbreaking sadness when he finally left. But she had to convince him he was dealing with unrealistic fantasy. "The courtship would be longer than your time in Bath."

"I was rather hoping you had formed an equal attachment," he said. "After all, we have spent many more hours than I did with Lady Susanne. Yet with those fleeting encounters I had with her, a concert, a few minutes in the drawing room, and a single ball, no one would have raised an eyebrow had I said I'd fallen desperately in love and wished to become engaged to her. That is how these things are done amongst my class."

She breathed deeply, staring at him. She had to make him understand. For her, there was no going back to London, not while Gerald Fairclough still threatened her freedom and her finances. Debtor's prison was almost preferable to the alarming way he'd accused her of murdering his brother, with no way for Alice to prove she hadn't. After all, she had been there when Richard died, so close she'd seen her husband's nasty final moments.

"You truly do not know me, nor I you," she warned him.

Adam tapped her glass with his, then drank the last of it down. "Everything I do know, I love. And I shall endeavor to make you feel the same."

Alice squeezed her eyes closed a moment. Her earlier actions and decisions had shadowed her right up to that instant, making the future she wanted a hopeless whim. When she opened them, she had to tell him once more how impossible was his pursuit of her.

"You are heir to an earldom. That much I already know. The only son of a powerful family. I am not suitable for you in any manner, neither my widowed status, my age, nor my current position as a governess. Your parents will put a stop to our mutual admiration as soon as they learn of it."

"Is that what worries you?" Adam's face brightened. "I can assure you Lord and Lady Diamond are kind people. Open-minded and open-hearted. They would never interfere with my private matters of the heart. Besides, I have my own townhouse in London and have lived separately from them for the past three years."

If he thought that would smooth things over, he was wrong. A powerful earl such as his father could make many things happen to his liking.

"That will make no difference. I know your world," she said carefully.

"Do you?" He smiled indulgently, thinking she did not.

After all, how could a governess understand the *ton*?

"*I* barely understand them," he said, "and I have grown up with their strict rules and somewhat peculiar manners."

"I know of what I speak," she insisted. *Yet what could she say about her experience without giving away her past?* "When I was in London, I was in the household of more than one family. Bitter, strident, judgmental people, each and every one."

"Gracious!" he said. "You were a governess for the wrong families, I warrant."

"I was involved with the wrong people, to be sure, but I believe in this case, when an earldom is at stake, I will not be welcomed as your blushing bride."

"How can I convince you otherwise?" he asked.

Her laugh was mirthless. Having to convince him of her unsuitability was painful. She turned away from his dear face and started to walk back the way they had come, despite knowing it would prevent her receiving another of his kisses.

As he fell into step beside her, she asked, "How many heirs marry women who are not virginal young ladies, recently presented at court? How many marry widows? Can you name even one?"

Adam hesitated, probably casting his thoughts to the people he knew.

"Strangely, I cannot come up with a single marriage as you describe. But that matters not in the least."

She wanted to stamp her foot with frustration. "It does, my lord. More so if the female has a history. And mine is all wrong and unacceptable."

"I have thought much about this," Adam insisted. "Indeed, I have fought my own innate prejudice about taking a governess as my wife. Selfishly, I wanted to make you my mistress and nothing more, but that's no longer enough for me. Besides, no one in the *ton* would know or care about your prior marriage to Mr. Malcolm."

"If they did know, they would care. You are fully aware of that. It is why you fought against your saner, more reasonable self."

Eventually, she might have to tell him more—how she'd been thoughtless and reckless, bringing the curse of a marriage to Richard upon her own head and the ramifications upon her family. If he pressed her, she would make him understand that her being a governess was the least of her worries.

"I appreciate what you have told me of your parents. But I maintain that apart from attending a few events in Bath, there can be nothing more between us. Please, Adam, let go your romantic notion," she begged, taking the steps to the terrace.

"Lady Fairclough?" said a female voice at the top of the steps.

With her blood instantly thick from fear and her skin clammy, Alice forced herself not to turn, flinch, or make any sign of recognition.

Adam, however, looked in the speaker's direction.

"I believe this lady is addressing you," he said.

Alice glanced sideways at him, hoping the stranger would go away when she ignored her.

"Lady Fairclough, is it you?" the voice persisted.

Adam hesitated. Alice turned at last, keeping her face placid. Staring at the woman, Alice frowned as if she had no idea who she was or why she was speaking to her. In truth, she recognized her as a ballroom acquaintance from years earlier who might have been an old friend of her late husband, too.

"I am sorry, you are mistaken," Alice said firmly and continued past.

As they re-entered the Kingswood School's main hall, she held her breath for a moment or two, stiff with worry the woman would call out after her. Heads would turn, others might know her name and know her, as well.

When nothing happened, Alice released a sigh of relief. If Adam wasn't holding her arm, she might fall to the polished wood floor from the rush of terror that had surged through her, leaving her shattered and exhausted as it dissipated. Just like that, the best night had become the worst.

"What was that about?" Adam asked.

"I know not," Alice said, her voice weedy, but then she tried to make a joke. "Someone in need of spectacles, apparently."

"Indeed." He set his glass down and hers, too. Ignoring their unfinished conversation, he asked, "Shall we dance?"

She knew him well enough—he was postponing the discussion of marriage until he had her alone in his carriage. Strange to be back in a life of champagne, festive ballrooms, and persuasive, titled men.

How had she let this happen?

Of late, Alice had detected an unwelcome restlessness during the long hours she spent playing her part with her Beasley pupils. Where before she had accepted the tedium of a dull, chaste life, Adam had awakened in her the desire for a richer existence.

Having grown up with parties and concerts, a library at her disposal, scintillating conversation across many a dinner table, and dashing, sparkle-eyed suitors after being presented at court in the Queen's Drawing Room, Alice had given it all up. A governess enjoyed none of that. And in exchange, she had stopped worrying, stopped looking over her shoulder.

Now, thinking she should tell him her head ached and leave immediately, she was desperately clinging to that boring, lonely, *secure* life.

The alternative was too frightening, represented by a stranger outside who'd called her name.

But Alice didn't claim a megrim, and they didn't leave. When she allowed him to take her again upon the dance floor, she soon spotted another familiar face from London—an acquaintance who would probably also yell out *"Lady Fairclough, where have you been?"* if she were noticed. It signified the end of her time in Bath.

"I am ready to go home," she said.

Alice would have to do something drastic. Even before that evening, he had mentioned her moving to London after he left. For he had been clear in his determination to make her his lover, while she was equally determined not to give in.

Tonight, Adam had asked her in earnestness to become his wife. Tears pricked her eyes again as they exited the grand hall. If she told him the truth, he would feel duped and possibly hate her. If she didn't tell him, he would not allow her to slip back into her secluded world, despite her professing her absolute delight at being a governess for the rest of her days—*an outright lie.*

Worst of all, Alice couldn't resume her easy-going enjoyment until the Autumn. For if she continued this dangerous game of going into society, dressed as though she were still a member of Mayfair's upper echelon, her ruse would be revealed. Eventually, another person would say her real name in Adam's presence.

The horrible past and everything she had lost would be on display for anyone to pick over, like a falcon with a rabbit in its claws. She could not face such humiliation once more.

Worse, if her brother-in-law found her, she would be dragged back to London, possibly in chains.

"Is anything amiss?" Adam asked when the music ended.

Possibly everything, Alice thought, unable to shake the feeling of dread.

"No, not at all." Only that she was already planning her escape, something she had known might be necessary when she agreed to let him escort her around town. Having loved every minute of his company, she would pack the memories in her trunk along with her belongings when she fled Bath.

He squeezed her arm.

"You are awfully quiet."

"A little tired is all." In fact, each time they went out, she felt the wearying strain of living a lie. And tonight, her worst fears had materialized, draining her of any joy.

Within minutes, they were in a horse-drawn fly heading back to the Beasleys' residence. Finally, in the seclusion of the small two-seater cab with the driver in front of them, he turned her face toward his with a finger upon her chin and seared her mouth with his own.

When his lips touched hers and she slid her arms up and around his neck, holding on to him, sorrow slithered through her. When he tilted his head and his strong hands roamed her, his palm coming to rest on her breast, she wanted to weep for missing out on this man for the rest of her life.

"You smell divine," he murmured against her mouth.

"As do you," she returned. He always did, and she would remember his scent for the rest of her days.

He nibbled down her neck, and her body responded, thrumming and throbbing with need. In the morning, she would wish, as she always did after denying them both, that they were actually a couple.

If only Adam Diamond could truly be hers to love.

All she had wished for was to enjoy the small Season with him before he returned home. It was becoming clear her wish could not come true.

She had allowed her heart's desire to risk the new life she'd made for herself.

It had been worth it!

CHAPTER ELEVEN

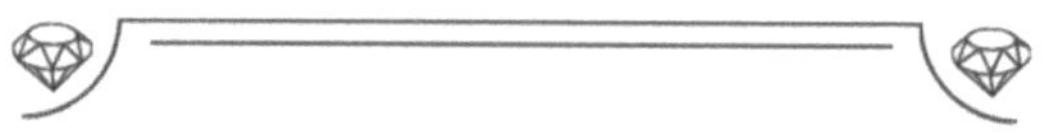

"Lady Beasley, I have been waiting nearly fifteen minutes," Adam fumed. Something was very wrong. Alice had not answered his recent missive, nor appeared at the bakery they frequented. "I asked your butler to tell Mrs. Malcolm I was here. Do you know where she is?"

Adam had paced the downstairs, going along the passageway to peer out into the back garden. He had returned to the drawing room, then made his way through the set of connected rooms to the salon in which he'd first heard her play the violin. And then he'd gone full circle.

Finally, Lady Beasley appeared as if she had no idea he was even there. Her ladyship pursed her lips a moment, then she tilted her chin and sniffed. Her expression was one of deep disapproval.

"You have formed a deep attachment with my girls' governess, have you not?"

Adam did not intend to speak of his personal life with Lady Beasley, but when asked outright, he hated to lie. He could speak the truth, he hoped, without getting Alice in trouble.

"We share a love of reading and have been comparing our interests and swapping books." *And swapping kisses,* he added silently. But as an excuse to show up uninvited, he'd brought with him the book Alice had once lent him, which he'd set aside and all but forgotten. "I know no one else in Bath who has the same grasp of both historical and contemporary literature."

That ought to please her ladyship since Alice could impart her wisdom on the younger daughters. In fact, he knew no one else who had the same manner of thinking and expressing herself as Alice. He was entirely enchanted.

Apparently, his expression disclosed his profound admiration. Lady Beasley crossed her arms and sighed deeply.

"Your mother would be most displeased to learn of your behavior. An earl's son, playing with the emotions of a middle-class female."

Adam clenched his jaw and counted to five, so he didn't say anything impertinent. But he was not playing with Alice's emotions. It was his own which had been sent spinning. After the Kingswood ball, in which he had set aside the bias he had against her class and declared his intentions for an engagement, she hadn't jumped at the chance to elevate herself. Instead, she had set herself against him. In the carriage ride on the way back to the Paragon, Alice had kissed him passionately in return but refused to speak about marriage.

As soon as he found her, he was going to overrule her objections regarding being a widowed member of the middle class and plead his case. Or simply kiss her into submission.

"While I appreciate that you have a long friendship with my mother, this has nothing to do with her, nor even with you, although I mean no disrespect. Simply because Mrs. Malcolm lives under your roof, it ought not to mean you can control other aspects of her life outside of the work she does for this family. Thus, I wish to speak with her."

"As do I," Lady Beasley said. "I welcomed her as an employee, even with the short list of references she provided because there was something capable about her. And without doubt, she was knowledgeable in many areas, just what my girls needed for a well-rounded education. And now, look what has happened." She sighed. "She was the perfect governess."

Adam's chest tightened. "Was?"

"She departed without notice yesterday morning. Packed up her things and left."

Blood was rushing to his head. She had left her beloved position. *How would he find her? Should he even try?* Alice's abrupt departure could only mean she had no wish to continue with their blossoming friendship.

"I do not understand." And he didn't. Their last kiss had been magical. After the ball, as soon as they entered the carriage, they had been a flurry of mouths and hands. He was certain her feelings for him were growing at the same breakneck speed as his for her. They had made tentative plans to meet, and then she had simply not shown up.

At least now he knew why.

"Are you saying she has left your employ or departed from Bath?"

Lady Beasley spread her hands and shrugged.

"As I understand it, she has done both. Mrs. Malcolm slid a note of resignation along with a message for each of my girls under my bedroom door early yesterday. With no explanation and only muted contrition, she stated she could not continue in her post."

Lady Beasley had begun to pace the room, working herself up into high dander.

"A month or at least a fortnight could be expected from anyone in her position to allow me the opportunity to find a replacement. But I received not even an hour's notice. It is a shame." She stopped and sighed again. "I liked her. I held her in high esteem for the education she could give my girls. Moreover, I trusted her with their future development into knowledgeable young ladies. To say I am disappointed would be to state my feelings mildly."

Adam knew how she felt. Disappointment warred with anger, although he knew when he stepped outside and could examine his emotions, both would give way to sadness.

"All I can say, my lady, is that I am sorry you have lost an excellent governess."

"As am I," she agreed. "And I hope you had nothing to do with it." Her cheeks turned puce. "My goodness, I truly hope you had nothing to do with it," she repeated. "Your mother definitely wouldn't be pleased, and then your father would have to get involved, too."

It took Adam a moment to understand of what she was accusing him. One thing he was certain, Alice was not with child. At least, not with his.

"On the matter of which you intimate, I can assure you there is no merit to your insinuation. And I would hope you do not start spreading any such hearsay about your former employee."

"I shall not give her references," Lady Beasley declared, "so I cannot imagine how she will find her next position."

Adam thought the clever Alice would land on her feet and find another post if she chose. *But why leave this one and start over?*

"She said nothing of why she had to go away?"

"She did not," her ladyship confirmed. "You know, I thought it a pity you didn't find my Susanne to your liking, and now, I imagine you feel the same. But it is too late for you to find a respectable wife in Bath after being tangled up with Mrs. Malcolm. Everyone is talking about it. I can only surmise that is why she left. I bid you good day, my lord."

Without waiting for his response, she departed, leaving him still holding Alice's book which he'd intended to return.

That night, seated in the drawing room of his too-large home, looking at the view of Victoria Park with a glass of brandy in one hand, Adam finally opened Austen's novel. He had meant to read it previously but had been content keeping hold of the book, so he would always have a pretext to go see her.

He had never even cracked the spine before. To his amazement, when he did, the bookplate on the front cover held the answer to the mystery that was his Alice, as he'd come to think of her.

Alice Malcolm Jeffrey, Stonely Grange, Caversham

She was *not* Mrs. Malcolm at all! *Maybe she wasn't even a widow.*

He turned the page and the next one before flipping to the back where she'd written a note about how much she'd enjoyed *Northanger Abbey*. It wasn't a note to him, merely something scrawled on the back of the last page.

She had dated the note 1838, which would explain her youthful and effusive words about the satirical Gothic tale of terror and manners.

Reading it again, he smiled. At least he had a place to start.

STONELY GRANGE WAS, IN a word, crumbling. If Alice had to pick another word, it would be *dilapidated, decrepit,* even *creepy.* Someone might kindly say it was a diamond in the rough. However, it was more like a diamond being reclaimed by the earth from which it sprung. It had once been polished but was now a murky shadow of its former glory.

Was there even a single window without a broken pane?

Yes, those that were completely boarded up.

That made her laugh. It was good to be home, even if she now had a hole where her heart had been.

The only staff still there were those glad of a free place to live. They no longer received wages, so she supposed they weren't really staff, nor could she ask them to do so much as boil water for her tea.

Thus, Alice had moved another rung down the ladder of life. She'd given up her steady role as a governess with her meals prepared for her and a clean bedroom for the frightening insecurity of being an impoverished lady.

A new existence but with her old identity.

She couldn't maintain either long, or she would starve. With her savings, if she wished to keep some of it in reserve, she could probably manage for a month, time enough to decide where she would go next. The mistake had been going to Bath instead of a country village. The old temptations of a sparkling, lively city had lured her to the only other place in England with its own full Season.

She couldn't make that mistake again.

No more balls or dinners or concerts. No more gentlemen like Lord Diamond.

"Adam," she murmured his name aloud, allowing the heartache to remind her he had been real. She'd made sure to accept a long and luxurious kiss from his firm lips before she'd bid him goodnight the final time. His hands had lingered at her waist, holding her close, and she'd slid her own up his chest to grasp his broad shoulders.

In the span of the kiss, she'd memorized the feel of him under her fingers, the taste of his lips, and the fragrance that made her want to howl with desire. With him not knowing it to be a kiss goodbye, he'd been tender and happy. Then he'd allowed her to run inside, where she'd quietly packed up all her things and written her notes of goodbye to Lady Beasley and her daughters.

She hadn't allowed herself the indulgence of a private message to Adam. That would have been too hard, not to mention too tempting to tell him where to find her.

"As I live and breathe, it's Lady Alice," said the head gardener while she made her way across the lawn. What a difference from when she'd left after becoming engaged, traveling in a fine coach and six. A lifetime ago, it seemed.

"Good day, Henry. How are you?"

He tugged on his cap in his familiar way. "I cannot complain, m'lady. We'll have a good harvest this year."

"You've become a farmer, then, instead of a gardener."

"Had to," he said, maintaining a cheerful smile. "What with the chickens, pigs, and cows, those of us here live well."

"I am glad to hear it. Do you think I shall be welcomed after… everything?"

Surprise crossed his weathered features.

"Indeed, m'lady. It's your home, after all." He smiled and looked at the manor. "Almost nothing is the same inside, mind you. Most everything was sold off by the men who came. There are still rooms a plenty, mind you, empty ones at that." But he chuckled at his little jest, not sounding the least bitter.

"I shall be happy for any place to lay my head." Alice had endured a long journey first by train, then by mail coach, packed with other travelers. And then she'd walked from the depot at the last tavern for two miles.

"Who remains here?" The last letter before her parents fled to Spain where they could live cheaply and well, her mother had made it sound as if hordes of raiding marauders had taken over. In truth, it was merely the staff moving in as they could no longer afford their cottages. Of course, her mother had also blamed her. *Again!*

"Ol' cook calls it home and still makes a fine meal for all of us. Her daughter and a housemaid, who'd nowhere to go, stayed to help. My daughter's middle boy, Bert, remained as well." Then he shrugged. "Mr. Neble left and Mrs. Smythe, too. A butler and a housekeeper need a family to care for and a staff to manage."

That might have been the longest speech Alice had ever heard from the man. But maybe in the past, they had simply never had the need to chat.

Then he nodded and tugged his hat again.

"Thank you, Henry. I shall see you later, then."

"Yes, m'lady."

She cringed slightly at the term. It had been two years since she'd been addressed thusly. At first, it was strange to style herself as a *missus*, but now, hearing Henry's respectful greeting, she felt herself a fraud. A lady didn't marry a wretch who spent all his own money and then went after hers. A lady didn't bring calamity upon her home and all those who depended upon it.

But what did that make her parents, who had folded like a bad hand of whist?

Alice continued closer. Knowing her mother and father weren't inside made it easier and more welcoming. She'd always loved her family's country home. The location, on the fertile banks of the Thames, made it the prettiest place on earth when she was a child.

She sighed as the door squeaked loudly when she opened it. More of a groan actually, as if the house were announcing its displeasure at the return of the wayward daughter.

No Mr. Neble any longer in the front hall with his straight posture and tidy appearance. No Mrs. Smythe who smelled of lemon oil.

"Hello," she called out into the echoing front hall.

Strangely, it wasn't as bad as she'd feared. The furnishings were whittled away to the bare minimum, with no paintings or vases or even the mirror that used to hang over a small rectangular table, which was also gone. Yet the floor was clean, and the place smelled fresh.

Alice set down her bag, having left her trunk at the tavern depot, hoping she could borrow a wagon to collect it later. A yawn split her mouth, reminding her how tired she was, nearly desperate for a bed.

To that end, she went to the back of the house and into the long, stone-walled kitchen.

There was the same cook, Mrs. Georgie, as everyone called her. Seeing her, seated, drinking tea, ever the mistress of her same familiar domain, Alice felt tears fill her eyes.

Spying her, Mrs. Georgie's eyes opened wide before she silently set down her mug.

"Good afternoon," Alice said.

Their cook rose to her feet, still staring as if she was seeing a ghost or goblin.

Alice wished she would say something, even if it was to scream at her for ruining the life they had all shared at Stonely Grange *before* Richard, Lord Fairclough came along.

"My word. Is it you, Lady Alice?" she said at last.

"It is. I hope you will allow me to stay," she said.

"Allow you?" Mrs. Georgie repeated, furrowing her brow. Then she came around the table and without warning wrapped Alice in a fierce hug.

With that gesture, her tears began to fall. She sobbed until she was entirely wrung out. And the entire time, the cook, smelling faintly of cinnamon, continued to hold her.

"There, there," Mrs. Georgie soothed.

"I'm terribly sorry," Alice said at last. Her apology was too small for everything she wanted it to encompass, but at that moment, she was simply apologizing for being a burden on the struggling household.

"Don't you dare apologize to the likes of me, m'lady." Mrs. Georgie held her away from her soft round body so she could look into Alice's face. "You look dead on your feet. Are you hungry, thirsty, or just tired?"

"Yes," Alice said and managed a wobbly smile. "All three, but if you give me a drink of water, then I shall skip eating until I have slept, assuming there's a spare bed."

"Sit down here." Mrs. Georgie pressed Alice down onto the wooden bench by the well-used maple table. Then she snagged a second cup and filled it from the brown Betty earthenware teapot. It was so customary a sight on their cook's workspace, Alice nearly started to cry again.

Before pushing the chipped mug toward Alice, Mrs. Georgie added sugar and milk.

"Just the way you like it," she said.

When a plate of biscuits appeared, Alice shook her head.

"You are being too kind, and you do not have to wait on me."

"Nonsense. I'm just looking after family, same as I would my Jenny. Stay there and drink the tea. I'll go find my girl, and we'll make sure there's a bed with clean sheets."

She was halfway out the door when she turned.

"Where are your things?"

"I have a bag in the front hall, but I left my trunk at Mr. Ashley's."

"A single trunk?" Mrs. Georgie asked, then shook her head. "Things have certainly changed. I'll get Henry to hop in his wagon and fetch your trunk from the tavern."

"Thank you." Alice could have put her head down on the table and fallen asleep, but she stayed upright, drank the tea, and ate nearly the entire plate of biscuits before the cook returned.

"Come along, m'lady, we've made up a bed for you. Not your own, for your pretty four-poster is long gone. I wouldn't want you to see the state of your old room, anyway."

Alice didn't want to see it either, not yet. "I am grateful for any bed I can sleep in at this moment."

She followed Mrs. Georgie to one of the small guest rooms where every effort had been made to make it comfortable with a simple bed frame and mattress. As promised, there were bleached sheets that looked so inviting, Alice wondered if she would ever rise from them again. A small, painted dresser, probably brought down from the attic, was the only other article of furniture. Without a chair or washstand, it wasn't even as nice as what she had as a governess at the Beasleys' home.

"It's perfect," she declared, receiving another hug from the cook. Henry appeared at the door with her trunk.

"Thank you. How kind of you to fetch it."

"Yes, m'lady." He tugged his hat and disappeared, not used to household duties.

"Can you manage?" Mrs. Georgie asked.

"I don't understand," Alice said. The cook's meaning escaped her, and it must be due to her tiredness.

"Undressing and all," Mrs. Georgie said, looking chagrinned.

Alice nearly laughed, but she realized the woman was serious. She had never seen Alice make do for herself.

"Oh, Mrs. Georgie. I haven't had a lady's maid for going on two years."

"Truly?" the woman exclaimed, eyes widening. "Imagine that!"

Alice did chuckle that time. "It's true. Just like you and Jenny and most every other woman in the world except the very few, I can undress and put myself to bed."

Mrs. Georgie laughed, too. "I guess you can, m'lady, and good for you."

With that, she departed.

Alice hoped she hadn't destroyed some long-held belief of the cook that the titled class were helpless creatures because from what she'd seen, for the most part, that was true. But when forced to fend for herself, she, at least, had done so and quite well.

And that was the last coherent thought her weary brain put together. She took off her shoes, hat, and gloves, and stretched out on the lumpy mattress. It felt like the height of luxury. And then, she knew no more.

CHAPTER TWELVE

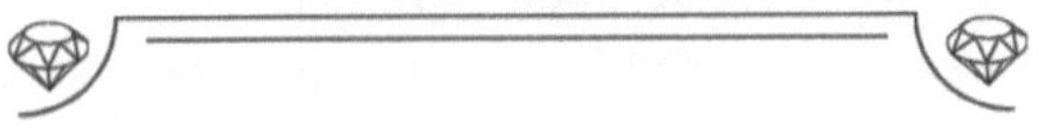

Alice was enjoying her fourth day of being home. Settled into a routine with the help and permission of Mrs. Georgie, Jenny, Henry, and a few others who made up the household, she had been accepted into their midst. She ate what they ate and where they ate it, which turned out to be in the formal dining room because they still thought it to be an exciting lark.

The gorgeous mahogany table that had been there all Alice's life had been sold, along with the crystal chandelier. But Henry and one of his grandsons, who helped provide food for the household, had crafted a new table from barn boards. With a lace tablecloth over it, it served the purpose well. With the mismatched chairs, enough for all of them, Alice thought it a merry group.

While her parents' former staff wouldn't let her clean, do laundry, or even beat the few remaining carpets, they let her exercise the two old horses, help in the gardens, and even assist in the kitchen.

By Mrs. Georgie's side, Alice snapped the ends off the runner beans and peeled potatoes, grateful they had food. She hadn't yet needed to delve into her meager savings. No one had asked her for back wages, for which she was exceedingly grateful.

Henry's grandson, Bert, a tall youth of eighteen, burst in through the kitchen's back door, leading to the herb garden.

"You made me jump," Mrs. Georgie said. "If you do it again, I'll take my ladle to your backside. See if I don't."

"Sorry," Bert mumbled. Today, he didn't do what he usually did, which was scan the room for Jenny. Instead, he said excitedly, "We have a visitor!"

Mrs. Georgie looked at Alice, probably thinking the last thing they needed was another mouth to feed.

"Shall I see who it is?" Alice offered.

"It's *your* home, m'lady." She said it without animosity, as if Alice had become the hostess the moment she'd arrived back at Stonely Grange.

"Very well." After wiping her hands upon her apron, Alice turned to Bert. "Where is our guest?"

"A carriage drove into the stable yard, and Granddad told me to fetch someone. Looks to belong to a right nob, m'lady, if you'll excuse my saying the word."

Alice nodded and went to go out the same door the lad had come through.

"No, m'lady, Granddad said he'd send the snout-nose to the main entrance, if you'll excuse my saying the word."

"Why don't you stop saying such things, then?" Mrs. Georgie berated, and Bert dipped his head.

"It's no matter," Alice said, "but I'll go out back and intercept our guest. Seems a bit silly to stand on ceremony when there are no chairs in which to be seated afterward."

Mrs. Georgie chuckled. "You have the right of it, m'lady."

Alice had her fingers on the door handle when the cook stopped her.

"Your apron," Mrs. George reminded her. "You aren't the hired help."

Sending the cook a wry smile, since no one was paid anymore, Alice shrugged. "The honest garment of an honest worker," she quipped before heading outside.

She hadn't gone but five or six steps when she saw *him*. Adam had descended from a fine carriage and was standing in the yard. Her heart squeezed, the breath left her lungs in a *whoosh*, then returned in a gasp, and her mind denied the possibility of his being there.

How had he found her?

"YOU ARE THE GARDENER *and* the groom?" Adam asked, trying to work out why the older man who had been tending a plot of vegetables had dropped his hoe, hurried over, and said he would bring the horses some water.

"No, m'lord. Rather, yes, m'lord. Actually, we don't have a groom no more."

The driver Adam had hired at the Reading train station jumped down.

"They're spirited beasts, Henry. They might lift you off your feet," he warned good naturedly, obviously knowing the older man.

Adam could easily imagine the short and slight Henry sent flying with a flick of the lead rope.

"I'll be fine," the gardener said with a chuckle. "Got a couple buckets roundabout here somewhere."

But instead of hurrying off to find them, he looked at Adam.

"Nothing to worry about, m'lord, but Mr. Shaw, here," he hooked a thumb at the driver, "has brought you round back."

"Naturally, I did," the man said, crossing his arms. "No point in going to the front, now, is there?"

Adam had no idea what they were jabbering about.

"Nonsense," Henry said. "If his lordship wants to enter through the front, he may." The gardener addressed Adam again. "I say, if you want to go around to the front, my grandson has gone inside to send someone to greet you."

When the man gestured toward the back of the house, Adam let his gaze follow where he pointed. While the gardens were kept well enough, the house needed care. There were roofing tiles missing, trim hanging askew, and a distinct air of shabbiness.

He knew from his parents' country estate that a manor house such as this ought to have an army of staff constantly maintaining its upkeep. Instead, he'd seen a single wizened old man and a youth who'd disappeared inside.

The white-painted door through which the purported grandson had gone suddenly opened.

"Never you mind, m'lord. Here comes her ladyship now," the gardener added.

A lovely, honey-haired female exited the house, wiping her hands on her apron. She stopped after a few feet and gawked at him.

Adam stared back at Alice. Despite her changed appearance, he would have recognized her anywhere. Today, she wore a functional kerchief on her head with her hair coming over one shoulder in a long braid. Her dress was a plain, faun-colored cotton and over it, she wore an apron. He would swear it was a maid's apron.

Yet the old man had called Alice "her ladyship." The mystery thickened, but at least he'd found her. By the expression upon her face, she was none too happy that he had.

"I shall send word when I need to be collected," he told Mr. Shaw, and then he left the two men behind. Although trying to maintain a dignified gait as he approached her, Adam wanted to run, irrationally thinking she might vanish before his eyes.

"My lady," he greeted, unable to keep the teasing tone from his voice. "No longer Mrs. Malcolm, the knowledgeable governess?"

"I doubt the quantity or caliber of my knowledge has changed any. How did you find me?" she asked bluntly. No smile, no kind and gentle greeting as he'd hoped. But as she shielded her eyes from the late sun turning her hair to a thick, golden rope, her gaze flickered over him from head to toe.

When the youth who'd accompanied her had taken Adam's trunk from the driver and the others had departed, he answered her.

"You left me a clue, *Lady* Alice."

She visibly startled before she regained her composure.

"My book," she said after a moment. "I wondered whether it was one with my bookplate in it. I gave it to you in such a rush that day."

"Yes, the bookplate."

She shook her head, perhaps at her own carelessness.

"Why did you come?" she asked.

That question was not one he could easily answer, especially not standing in the stable yard. And thus, he said the most obvious one.

"To return it."

She offered an exasperated huff. "You could have sent it by messenger."

Deflated by her reception, Adam took her words like a kick in the gut. She really wasn't happy to see him and would rather the book had shown up in brown paper, delivered by a stranger.

"Are you not pleased to see me?" He hated to ask, feeling vulnerable in an unfamiliar way. Not that he'd expected her to run into his arms and let him sweep her off her feet, but the underlying hostility he detected was new and unwelcome.

"It's not that," she said, glancing around her. But she said nothing more, with unfathomable emotions swimming in the depths of her lovely eyes. Maybe the hostility was shame at her circumstances, but it looked more like fear.

What had he stumbled into?

If the gardener hadn't called her a lady, Adam might have assumed she'd taken a lesser position than a governess as a scullery maid.

"You have a piece of potato peeling on your apron."

Absently, she brushed it off. "You didn't come all this way, a hundred miles, to return my book, nor tidy my clothing. What do you want?"

"It wasn't a hundred miles, only about seventy-five. At this moment, I want to go indoors. I would like a glass of cool ale if you have it. I wish to speak frankly with you, and then I hope to have a bed to sleep in. If after all that, our business is concluded, then I shall leave tomorrow."

"Our business?" she repeated.

Was she going to deny him entrance and the barest of explanations? He waited while she chewed her lower lip.

"Fine, then. Come inside, but I warn you, Lord Diamond, my family's home is a shell of its former state. And there are no servants, only friends who live together because they have nowhere else to go."

He couldn't deny that statement shocked him. *No servants?*

And her last statement, did that include herself?

"What about you, Lady Alice? Do you have nowhere else?"

"Especially me," she said quietly and led him inside.

Adam hadn't known what to expect indoors—maybe pigs being kept in the drawing room and pigeons in the pantry. Instead, it was room after room of emptiness. It appeared as if the Jeffrey family had moved out, taken their belongings, and left a handful of people behind.

Friends, Alice had called them. Yet they were behaving as staff. He'd been immediately offered tea by a woman who must be the cook. A younger one introducing herself as Jenny said she would make up a room for him, then looked bewildered and asked Alice where his lordship should be placed. They had gone off together to find something suitable, giving him time to walk around the ground floor.

There was nothing in the drawing room except an ugly candlestick on the floor by the hearth and a single torn ottoman, making an already large space seem cavernous.

The same for each room he wandered into except the dining room, which had a crude semblance of a place to eat. On the second floor, he pushed open a door expecting more of the same, and his breath caught.

It was a library with shelf upon shelf of books.

That's where Alice found him sometime later.

"Astonishing, isn't it?" she remarked.

He turned from the shelf he was scanning, this one full of history books. With her apron and kerchief off, she looked more like the woman he knew and with whom he had fallen in love if he was entirely honest with himself. Yet still, she did not appear like the lady of this house or any. Far too plainly dressed and with too much worry upon her face.

"This room does seem to be a miracle when every other room has been decimated of what one might consider normal furnishings. How was it spared the Viking raid?"

She laughed, looking years younger, like a teenager.

"A few days ago, I walked in here, my favorite room in the house, prepared for the worst. I swear I shrieked so loudly Mrs. Georgie—that's our cook, before and still—she came running. I asked her exactly what you asked me. How could it still be a library?"

He moved closer to her, hoping to catch her familiar scent.

"What was her answer?"

"The idiots who took everything thought a bunch of musty books had no value." Her smile when she finished that statement was breathtaking.

"And who were these illiterate blunderheads?"

Her smiled died. "They are no longer important."

By the set of her lips, she wasn't going to tell him. At least not then.

"Where is the rest of your family? Your parents? You said they left the country?"

Nodding, she strolled over to the closest shelf and ran a hand across the lined-up spines, straightening one that was less than half an inch out of order.

"I am an only child. Two others died before the age of five." Then a book caught her fancy. She drew out the thin volume, opened it, and smiled. "My parents are in Spain. Two years ago, they fled this disaster for which they blame me."

With that, she snapped the book closed and replaced it.

"Two years ago, you said you were widowed. Is that true?"

"It is." She immediately changed the topic. "We have that ale you requested, as well as some cold chicken and bread. Are you hungry?"

"Thank you, I am."

The dining room, which he'd already noticed, was . . . rustic but functional. After taking him in, she went to fetch the food herself.

"I shall return shortly."

Adam watched her leave and speculated upon the state of Stonely Grange and the "idiots" who had taken everything. When she returned with a tray, he rushed forward to take it from her.

"You are in an extraordinary circumstance, are you not?"

Alice sat at the table, despite not having brought herself any food, and gestured for him to eat.

"I suppose this life is nothing I could have imagined," she agreed. "But I am fortunate to have a roof over my head, nonetheless."

"Will you tell me your story?"

When she briefly closed her eyes as if shutting him out, he persisted, "Aren't we close enough friends for you to confide in me? I promise you I am not the least judgmental, and I hold you in the highest esteem."

He waited. Her eyelids fluttered open, and she examined her fingernails, tapped them on the table, looked around the room, and even sighed.

"And I am persistent," he added, for he was not going to ride away and leave the mystery of Lady Alice Malcolm Jeffrey in his wake.

"You are," she agreed, looking at him again. "I am still astonished to see you."

He had hoped by expressing his admiration, her gaze might appear more joyful, but that was not the case.

"I never expected you to be sitting here," she admitted softly. Then she shook her head. "A few years ago, I married Lord Richard Fairclough. I thought he was a decent, kind man. He was neither. I left my home here and traveled to London with him, from a dream to a nightmare, as it were. He was a drunkard, always very *arf'arf'an'arf* no matter the time of day. He was also a hopeless gambler who was either easily bilked or extraordinarily unlucky. And a profligate spend-all."

"But did he have any bad traits?" Adam asked, hoping the jest would make her smile. After all, the man was dead. However, Alice barely lifted one side of her luscious mouth in a mostly wry expression.

"Luckily, we never had children, and even more fortunately, he died. And that is my story. Not a particularly interesting one."

"I beg to differ." Adam had hung on her every word, looking into the depths of her gray-green eyes. He wanted to remove the sadness he saw there but didn't know how to go about it.

Moreover, he knew the story had more to it, with facets she hadn't yet revealed.

"Who ravaged your family home?"

"People to whom Fairclough owed money, I believe, sent here by his brother. The house was gifted to me by my parents. In turn, it had been gifted to my father with the same restrictions regarding selling it. While my husband could not sell the estate outright by the terms of its legal trust—*thank God!*—naturally, he owned everything in it.

There was nothing I nor my parents could do but let everything be taken and sold to pay Fairclough's debts."

"How awful." Adam had lost his appetite, but she spoke so matter-of-factly, he knew she'd long ago accepted the circumstances. She certainly wasn't grieving over the reprobate, nor devastated and heartbroken.

"Thoughtlessly, or perhaps maliciously, Fairclough did not leave our London home to me. It, too, was sold quickly by his brother, Gerald, the new Lord Fairclough. Thus, with no money and no roof over my head in London, I left and decided it better to be a governess than a tragically impoverished widow. No one recognized me until I started dressing up and going out to places a governess should not be."

"With me," he finished.

"Yes, but I did enjoy our outings," she confessed, offering him the first real smile since he'd arrived.

Suddenly, he recalled the name, and Alice's speedy departure made a little more sense.

"You left Bath because of that woman who addressed you as Lady Fairclough?"

"I did."

"But why?" Adam hoped she would continue talking. Inside, he was a little shaken to think of all the times they were together with her pretending to be the middle-class Mrs. Malcolm, and he'd believed her.

"If it happened once, it would happen again," she explained. "I allowed myself the indulgence of going to a ball, being in a setting which would bring my true identity to people's minds. And I didn't want Lord and Lady Beasley to know whom they had actually hired. They would have sacked me for the ruse, and I would have had to leave, but then, everyone in Bath would have known who had been in their midst. You know how the servants' grapevine works, do you not?"

"I believe I understand the concept," Adam said wryly. "Yet you left, anyway."

"On my own terms. And without all the snooty nobs in Bath—"

"Your fellow nobs, if I am grasping the situation correctly."

"Yes," she agreed. "My father is an earl and my mother is a viscount's daughter. They hoped I would marry in my first Season. With my mother's unusual chaperoning skills, too lax when I needed her and rather forceful when she saw an opportunity to push me in the wrong direction—into the wrong arms, as it were—my parents got their wish."

"Are you saying your parents approved of Fairclough?" Now that Adam knew the name, memories of a thundering reprobate floated through his brain. He'd never met him, but the man had once lost so badly at cards, it was the stuff of legend at White's. And he was equally unfortunate at common wagering, losing so much he was right up the list with Beau Brummel.

"Approved is too strong a word," Alice said. "They didn't really care who it was, as long as he was from our class, of course, and he didn't mind that my dowry was not a large one. He thought he would have this estate to sell. I didn't find out until later that my father had never told Richard of the restrictions on the deed. In any case, unable to stop our belongings from being sold, my parents packed up and left for the less expensive and far sunnier Spain."

Adam could not imagine such negligent parents leaving their offspring, and a female, at that, to fend for herself. *How could his Alice have come from such weak and cowardly people?*

"And now you are back, is your plan to remain here indefinitely?"

Again, she sighed. "I honestly did not know what I would find here. Stonely Grange might have been burned to the ground for all I knew. Believe it or not, even seeing it like this, in its ravished state, I am vastly relieved. And then, of course, there is the library."

"Therefore, the intrepid Lady Fairclough—"

"Don't call me that," she interrupted with a scowl.

"And so, Lady Alice intends to live in her hulking, empty house with her handful of *friends*, reading her beloved books until . . . ?"

"Why must there be an until?" she asked, blinking at him.

"I don't know that there must. But is that the life you want? Peaceful, I suppose, but devoid of that fun and companionship you enjoyed with me in Bath."

With a shrug, she looked away. "I think I will stay as long as I can. And when I cannot, then I shall go be a governess somewhere remote, thereby removing the possibility of a nosy-poke yelling my name."

He wondered if she would prefer that life to being with him.

"Do you intend never to reclaim your place as a member of the *ton*, nor return to London?"

She shook her head. "I cannot return to London." Rising to her feet, she added, "I promised Mrs. Georgie that I would help make preserves, or was it pickles? Anyway, something to do with jars."

Adam had stood, too, and now he moved around the table, wanting to put them back on the same footing they had been before she had vanished. Hoping she would allow him, he reached for her hand.

When she didn't flinch or pull away, he took the other one, too. Feeling as if he were coming home, he pulled her close.

"I missed you."

She nodded but was staring in the vicinity of his pale gray necktie.

"It was unkind of you to leave without saying goodbye or telling me where you were going."

"I know," her voice was husky. "If I spoke with you, you would have asked all sorts of questions. Or tried to stop me."

"Alice, I don't care if you are a lady or a governess. You know that, don't you?"

"I suppose so."

He released one of her hands so he could tilt her chin up and look into her eyes. *How he adored her clear, interesting eyes!* They reminded him of the solid strength of all nature—rocks and trees and ancient beings.

Except at that moment, he could see the glittering of unshed tears.

"Tell me," he said.

After a moment, she swallowed. "I missed you, too. I thought I would never see you again."

He didn't wait. Adam leaned down and kissed her, reveling in the familiar jolt of warmth and desire. She felt it, too, by the way her hands came up and her fingers clasped his jacket, holding him in place.

When he slanted his mouth across hers and demanded access with a sweep of his tongue along her soft lips, she leaned against him. Opening her mouth to his gentle assault, at the same time, she laced her fingers behind his neck, holding on to him as if her life depended upon it.

No one was going to interrupt—no Lady Susanne nor Lady Beasley, no butler nor assembly room manager. And she no longer had a governess's morality to protect.

Nothing and no one outside of the two of them mattered. Adam lost track of how long he explored her mouth, caressed her tongue with his, and felt her ardent reciprocation.

"Alice," he said against her mouth. "*My* Alice."

Was she? In his heart, he felt she was. But she was an enigma, and he had no idea if she—

"Take me," she whispered. Then added, "Upstairs."

He drew back, thinking to sweep her into his arms, but she grabbed his hand, gave him a shy smile that set his blood to boiling, and led the way.

CHAPTER THIRTEEN

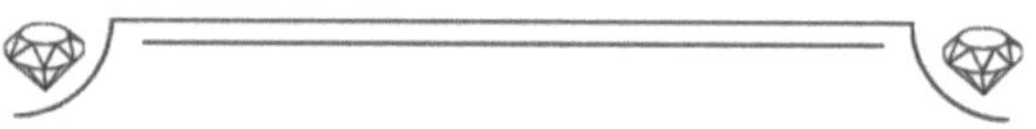

As soon as Alice drew him into her spartan room and shut the door, she looked at it through the eyes of a future earl and gave in to nervous babbling.

"It's not fancy, nothing like the room I grew up in. Actually, the room I grew up in is along the hall, but Mrs. Georgie didn't want me to stay in it as it is entirely changed. She thought it would make me sad, but I don't mind any of this. Not even this plain bed."

Alice circled the room, pacing from door to window to bed and back again. While she spoke, Adam stood in the center, his gaze following her movements, although his eyes had darted to the bed at its mention.

"I am glad not to be playing the part of a governess anymore. The family was kind, and the Beasley girls were attentive enough most of the time. But I lacked the temperament and patience. And at times, I—"

"Alice," he said, his voice soft and sensual. "Come here."

She swallowed and joined him, toe-to-toe on the floor that had no carpet, and she knew for herself how cold it was under foot at night.

"We don't have to do anything at all. I am simply happy to be with you again." But one of his hands was stroking her arm and the other her back, sending waves of desire pulsing through her.

"I want you," she said, glad she could be completely honest at least in that regard. "I am no longer a governess with a reputation to uphold, and being a widow has some benefits. I am . . . autonomous."

He cracked a smile. "That's a good word for a city, but I have never heard a woman describe herself as such."

"Independent, then. Free to make my own decisions. And at this moment, I choose to be with you. As long as you recall I am not a virgin, nor a simpering innocent."

"I don't give a damn about deflowering virgins. I care only whether there is any other man in your heart."

"There is not."

"Am *I*? In your heart, I mean?" Adam looked both sensually sure of himself and achingly vulnerable.

She leaned closer and kissed him. "You are."

It didn't take long for them to be naked and under the covers. Alice's body knew what was coming and had never wanted to join with a man more. So why was he slowly driving her mad instead of sweeping her under him and plunging inside her? Richard had never taken his time.

First, Adam rose above her and settled between her legs. Leaning on his forearms, he dipped his head and took her lips under his again. The weight of his tall, firm body was a teasing torment in itself, and she couldn't help lifting her hips trying to get him to engage.

"Patience," he said. "You certainly don't have that governess temperament." He feathered kisses down her neck, making her arch into the pillow to offer him more.

Biting her lip, eyes closed, she decided to endure whatever manner of swiving Adam wanted. To her delight, it entailed him kissing and nibbling his way across her bare skin, side to side and always downward. Each of her breasts was treated with deft attention, the likes of which she'd never experienced. Even her nipples were tasted and flicked with his tongue until she could barely breathe.

When Adam went lower, she held her breath, staring down at him, fascinated, terrified. At the last moment before he touched her core with his mouth, she started to scramble for his shoulders to stop him.

"Easy," he said, as if calming a wild horse. *"Shh,"* he added, and then blew across her curls.

She froze. *What new magic was this?* Everything in her world was now focused on the smallest part of her body.

Delicately, he parted her petals and blew again.

Dear God! She moaned, which became a groan when that skilled tongue of his touched her sensitive nubbin. She brushed her hands across his head but gave up trying to move him or to stop him.

Letting her arms fall to either side of her, she settled back and allowed his ministrations. At first, he was satisfying her needs, but then, when his tongue strokes became slower, she realized he was teasing her.

"Beast," she muttered.

He chuckled and kissed her inner thigh.

"Are you ready for me, Lady Alice?"

That made her laugh in return, a relaxing release because the rest of her body was tense and tight.

"I am, and you know it, Lord Diamond." She knew what came next or thought she did.

"Let me make sure." His mouth was back upon her, but this time, he wasn't teasing. Every lick and suck were deliberate, intended to drive her mad, she feared. When he inserted a finger into her passage, she gasped.

In seconds, he had tongued her to a frantic frenzy. Alice couldn't hold still, nor could she stay silent. Her body, which seemed coiled like a spring, suddenly unfurled, starting low between her hips where his finger now stroked inside her and surging in a spiral of release while a keening sound of pleasure escaped her lips.

"Now, you're ready," he murmured.

Before she could understand what had happened—what *had* just happened?—Adam settled his arousal at her slick core, looked her straight in the eyes, and entered her.

They sighed at the same time.

Alice couldn't help a lopsided smile. But when he started to move, her smile slipped. From her brief experience with Richard, the swiving was nearly finished. For the first time in her adult life, she was enjoying it and didn't want it to end.

Putting her arms around him, she held on as Adam set the pace. When he slid a hand along her leg and raised her thigh, she hummed at the new sensation of his shaft going deeper.

Opening her eyes, Alice couldn't help watching his handsome face changing as he passed through the stages she had just experienced, until it was obvious he was going to spend. Before he did, eyes closed, gritting his teeth, he released her thigh and slid his hand between their heated bodies.

When he caressed her sensitive bud again, she moaned.

"I cannot possibly," she said in answer to his touch. She had done something so incredible once, Adam could not possibly expect her to do it again.

"You can," he said. "You will. Close your eyes and let go."

Doing what he said, Alice stopped fighting it. As before, she was sent to a dizzying height by her own muscles releasing the tension that had grown within. A moment later, Adam drew out of her and spent upon the bedding before collapsing in a heap on his stomach, his head turned away, groaning.

For some reason, his utter exhaustion, as if she'd worked him a like a plow horse, tickled her, and she started to laugh.

After a moment, he spoke into the sheet.

"What are you laughing at, woman?"

That sent her into another fit of giggles. It felt like bliss to be in bed with him, after he'd played her body as well as she played the violin. *Even better!*

"I am . . . happy," she said. "That is all."

"That's everything," he said, finally turning to look at her. "You deserve to be happy."

"Do I?"

Alice wasn't so sure about that. Her mistakes had cost everyone.

"I should get dressed and make an appearance. I wouldn't want anyone to think we were doing . . . anything."

He shook his head. "I can't believe you went from answering to Lady Beasley to now answering to your former staff."

"I am not," she defended herself. "But they have been good to me, and I have responsibilities here. You can stay and rest but do come down fully dressed."

He grinned at her.

"And try not to look like *that*," she pleaded.

"Like what?"

If anything, his expression became even more smug. Turning her back on him, she rose and dressed under his watchful eyes, but soon, his eyelids grew heavier. Adam was asleep before she left.

IN A SINGLE BED THAT MIGHT have once belonged to the missing groom but had been placed in a guest bedroom on the second floor, Adam lay down after a plain but tasty supper. Before that, he'd eaten for the first time with a gardener and a cook, discussing the land and the strong community of people in the neighboring town where both had been born. They'd even played a few hands of whist.

In a room without another stick of furniture except the bed, not even any curtains, he thought about Alice. She'd been a little edgy all evening and too quiet, perhaps embarrassed by what they had done.

Moreover, she had refused to come to bed with him or to let him return to her room for the night. They'd had a brief discussion in the hallway in loud whispers.

"I don't want the staff thinking I have become as common as a barber's chair."

"I thought you said they were friends, not staff," he had pointed out.

"Don't mince words," she'd said. "I have tried hard to redeem myself—"

She broke off.

"Redeem yourself? From what exactly?" he prompted, wishing he could see her face better. But she was in the shadows, as was he. Everyone was given a single stubby candle, and no oil lamps burned in the passageways. It was as if they had literally returned to the Dark Ages.

"From nothing really," Alice said quickly. "I suppose from marrying the wrong man," she added, but he knew it was something else. "I don't want anyone thinking I am loose with my person, that's all."

"Of course not." He thought of the reputations of his sisters and didn't press the matter, despite knowing a widow had more freedom than any other female, at least in his class.

Thus, he had gone to bed alone, surprisingly able to fall asleep quickly since he'd traveled many miles and then had the best swiving of his life.

Naturally there was no way to know short of asking, which he wouldn't, and perhaps he was being a vain arse, but he thought Alice had been surprised by her climax. It was rather satisfying to think he'd brought her to a heady finish such as she'd never had before.

As he'd told her, he had no interest in deflowering a virgin, yet seeing the look of shock on her face when she spent not once but twice made him believe her the most innocent woman he'd ever tupped. Certainly, she was the least experienced widow he could imagine.

In the morning, practically bouncing out of bed, Adam felt happier than he had since the awful instant he learned she'd left Bath—perhaps happier than he had ever been. More than that, he felt a peaceful joy because she hadn't sent him away. Quite the opposite, they had finally consummated the intense attraction between them.

Not only was he eager to do it again, he wanted to do it with her for the rest of their lives. He'd awakened to the absolute knowledge that Alice should be his and his alone. After all, everything was different now. They were on an even footing socially, and thus, he no longer need worry about what people would think if he came home with a governess in tow.

He found her in the kitchen, seated on a stool, drinking tea. The cook was nearby, stirring porridge over a massive cast iron, wood-burning cookstove. Next to it was the ubiquitous Rumford roaster set in its brick housing in the wall, and on the other side, a bread oven.

"Good morning, Mrs. Georgie," he greeted the older woman first, hoping for a goodly portion of breakfast. She looked over her shoulder with a friendly nod. "And good morning to you, my lady." Adam wanted to restore Alice to her rightful place, even if only by showing her the respect of her title.

"Good morning." She still had that slightly wary look upon her face, which she'd worn ever since they'd swived. "Did you sleep well?" she asked him.

"I did. Thank you." Adam took the other stool. "I would say I slept like a baby, but I can recall my youngest sister as a baby awakening every few hours. Bri fussed and cried and woke up the entire household."

"Bri?" she repeated. "An unusual name."

"It is short for Brilliance," he told her.

The cook glanced over her shoulder again, and her expression mirrored Alice's.

"Do you not know any of my sisters?" Adam asked.

"I don't," Alice said. "Lady Beasley mentioned you have two older ones and two who are younger. The older ones were probably out in society before me for I do not remember meeting them."

"Probably so. They are Clarity and Purity, both with husbands and children."

He saw her exchange a look with Mrs. Georgie.

"And your other two sisters?" she asked. "Are they out in society yet?"

"To tell you the truth, I have lost track of whether Bri and Ray, short for Radiance, have been presented at court already."

Another wide-eyed exchange.

"In any case," Alice said, "I am sure I have not met any of them. While I doubt whether any of them would remember my name, I am certain I would remember any or all of theirs."

Then she changed the subject. "Are you ready for some tea and porridge?"

While porridge wasn't his favorite way to start the day, he agreed to a bowl of it.

"The weather is fine. May I take my mug and bowl outside? And will you join me?"

With an encouraging nod from Mrs. Georgie, Alice rose to her feet, her mug in hand, and accompanied him out the door and onto the back terrace. Unfortunately, there was no furniture. They sat together on the granite steps leading to the gardens.

"You have a lovely home."

That made her laugh. "A spartan home at present, but I agree."

After another moment, he asked, "What do you intend to do?"

Alice cradled her cup in her hands. "About what?"

Was she being obtuse? "About everything?"

"Thank you for the clarification. I am enjoying a little peace and quiet, or I was until you came along, all curious and handsome."

It was his turn to laugh.

"Truly," she added, "those are unsettling traits. In answer, I can honestly say I do not know. I cannot sell if I wanted to, as it must go to my heirs. And yet, it is doubtful I shall have any children. Moreover, if the roof starts to leak or any other calamity, there won't be anything left for them to inherit."

Adam thought she was too young to make such an assumption about her fertility. But on the other point, he wondered if he could offer assistance.

"One of my brothers-in-law is a solicitor. I wonder if there is some clause in the will that allows you to sell due to hardship. I cannot believe you are forced to let an estate like this crumble away. It would be better to sell while it still has a good roof. You could pay these people any wages owed to them with the profits."

Alice shrugged, not looking inclined. "I would hate for them to lose this home with no way to earn a living."

"And you, too, I imagine. You would hate not to have it to come back to."

"I have always liked Stonely Grange. I cannot imagine not having it. I was thinking of asking in the town if there are any wealthy families nearby who have been looking for tutors and—"

"You wouldn't?" Adam couldn't hide his surprise. "Anyone hereabouts will know you as Lady Alice. And I do not care if this is the year of Our Lord 1851, titled ladies cannot be governesses or tutors. It is simply not done."

"How else can I make money?" she asked. "How shall I survive?"

"You can marry me, and then you won't need to worry about it."

CHAPTER FOURTEEN

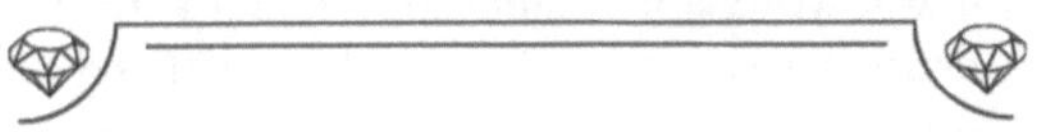

Alice's mouth dropped open slightly, and Adam wanted to kiss it at once. This was his third time asking rather spontaneously, but in this instance, he had no regret, nor wish to reclaim the words.

His proposal was a reasonable solution, and he liked the idea tremendously.

Yet when she spoke, she surprised him.

"If I weren't a lady by birth, would we be having this conversation?"

He failed to see what that had to do with anything.

"That's not fair. I asked you twice before."

Her mouth twisted. "You did it with great reluctance."

Adam shrugged and dragged his spoon around in the smoothly cooked oats. "I was attracted to you from the moment I saw you on the street and retrieved your fallen package."

"Because you thought I was a lady."

He laughed. "You *are* a lady who was playing the part of a governess. Regardless, at the time, you simply carried yourself in a way that was appealing, so yes, I thought you were a lady."

"If you'd known I was a governess, you wouldn't have spoken with me," she insisted.

"You weren't really a governess."

"I was! I did the work and was paid for it. And may I point out that you didn't speak to the housemaid with whom I was walking."

"The blasted maid didn't have honey-colored hair that caught my attention, nor a wiggle to her arse that made my blood boil."

His statement was met with silence.

"If you want to say I am superficial," Adam continued, unable to believe he had to defend his intentions, "then I say, yes, it was your appearance that caught me first. And then your violin playing, and after that, dancing with you and talking with you. Then, of course, kissing you and making you so angry I thought your head would shoot off your body like a cannonball from a cannon. And at every step, I expected there to be something that turned me away, something that dissuaded me from wanting you apart from the impossibility of my marrying a governess. Instead, everything about you drew me further in."

She took a deep breath, and then she faced him.

"How about rashly giving away my innocence and marrying a man who was a scoundrel? Are those reasons for your admiration? I am a destitute earl's daughter and disgraced, too. If recognized, I would bring only shame and embarrassment to any man associated with me, including you."

He reached for her, but she bolted from the step, spilling her tea while scrambling out of his reach.

"As Mrs. Malcolm, wherever I go, I can live peacefully and respectably."

"You're living a lie," he snapped, rising to his feet, "*if* you call it living."

She drew herself up, shoulders back. "Now you are the one who is not being fair. I had no choice, and I made the best of it."

He had pricked her pride, which was stupid of him.

"I apologize. You have done remarkably well in dire circumstances, fending for yourself, finding a place to live and a way to make money. All of those are things most pampered ladies would not be able to do, nor even conceive of, and if they did think of such a plan, they wouldn't do it, believing such employment beneath them."

Alice lifted her chin. "I doubt I shall ever look at anyone making a wage in the same manner as I did before."

They had strayed far from the original topic.

"Please, my lady, resume your seat."

After a moment, she did, and so did he. Adam, as his sisters would tell her, was a persistent chap. Thus, after another silent moment, he tried again.

"Lady Alice, will you marry me?"

She said nothing, only staring at him as if he'd grown a second nose. While she considered his proposal, he ate the porridge and set the bowl beside him so he could drink the now-cold tea.

Finally, knowing she was still looking at his profile, he said, "I doubt a man has ever waited so patiently."

"I doubt a woman was more caught off guard than I," she said.

"Then you haven't been paying close attention," he told her. *What were the correct words to make her understand?*

"When I still thought you were a governess, I confessed my ardent admiration and asked for your hand. You gave me platitudes about your station and mine, all the while knowing our stations in life were the same. And after yesterday, we know we fit perfectly."

He stopped looking at the tree line in the distance and turned to see her blushing. A widow who blushed when a man referred to tupping. He liked that about her. He liked everything about her.

The question was, *Did she feel the same?*

After another long silence, she muttered, "We hardly know one another."

Relief trickled through him. It wasn't a definite answer, neither accepting his offer, nor closing the door entirely upon a union. Instead, it was a sensible statement, albeit inaccurate.

"That is not true," he disagreed. "We have spent many hours together in Bath. But if you want to know more, then ask me a question, and I shall ask you one in return."

For a moment, he thought she might not play the game, but she nodded.

"How is it your sisters all have such strange names, and you escaped that fate?"

Unexpected, but a fair question.

"I did not escape. My full name is Adamas, which in Latin means—"

"Diamond," she filled in. "Thus, you are Lord Diamond Diamond. Your parents are an amusing pair."

"Aren't they, though? At least I escaped my mother's second choice, Adamare. Do you also know what that means?"

By the way her cheeks reddened again, he would guess she did. Leaning closer, he kissed her, loving the way she turned to him and kissed him back. They were already a couple as far as he was concerned.

"It's my turn," he said when he finally drew back.

"For what?" she asked breathlessly, starting to lean against him.

"To ask you a question."

Straightening immediately, she had the look of a skittish doe. "If you must."

"How did you really meet your husband?"

"Completely irrelevant," she snapped.

"I am merely trying to learn more about you. It wasn't a public, middle-class dance in London."

Alice twisted her lips, making him want to kiss her again. But then she relented.

"Very well," she said, while threading her fingers in the fabric of her skirts. "I met Fairclough the way most people of our class meet, at a private ball."

"And then?" he asked.

"You asked how we met," she protested. "That is all. He came up with the master of ceremonies, gained an introduction, and asked for a dance."

"Your turn," he said.

"Why aren't you married already?" she asked. "You are dash-fire handsome and extremely kind and obviously well-off."

"I am so flawless I should marry myself," he quipped. His words had the desired effect. Alice started to laugh, and he joined in.

Eventually, he took her chin between his fingers and captured her gaze.

"The answer is obvious, I believe. I simply had not met the right woman."

She shrugged and tried to look away, but he stopped her.

"Adam," she warned.

The way she said it sent a sizzle of desire to his loins.

"Yes, Lady Alice?"

She sighed. "You need a nice, innocent young lady. I have told you that before."

"I don't want a nice, innocent young lady. I want you."

Her eyes narrowed at the perceived insult, which made him laugh again.

"You are far more interesting than any other lady I have ever met. I tried not to love you, but I fell hard, anyway. And now I can embrace my feelings for you."

She stiffened. "Why now? I am no different now than I was in Bath. Lady or governess, what difference?"

"None," he agreed. "I was willing to go to my family and tell them of my choice for a wife, the fabulous Mrs. Malcolm. It will be easier now."

"Will it? Are they all of similar opinion that you must marry within your class?"

He stayed silent, thinking. "Honestly, I am not sure. I've simply always been surrounded by my peers."

"You are a snout-nose!"

"What? Don't be ridiculous." Then he paused. "Well, aren't you, too? Aren't we all to some degree? Did you befriend your housemaids and play cards with your butler when you were Lady Alice or Lady Fairclough?"

"No." She paused. "I remained with my own class for socializing as people do, no matter what class they belong to. I suppose that is why, as a governess, I made no friends. I was used to being with ladies and had no idea how to make new middle-class acquaintances."

She bit her lower lip.

"What of your parents? What if they are horrified at my having been a wage-earner?"

"They will think you utter perfection."

She sighed. "You intended to make me your mistress."

Ah, that was stuck in her craw, was it?

Any way that he arranged the words, she wouldn't like his explanation. Most men of his situation knew one thing—widows were for having fun. One escorted them around town with the idea there was a possibility for a sexual encounter at the evening's end. Moreover, widows from a different class were *not* for marriage, not when one was the heir to an earldom. Why, he didn't precisely know.

What he did know was that his friends would have teased him mercilessly had he shown up back home with a widowed governess as his wife. His parents, he hoped, would have accepted whomsoever made him happy, but there might have been the slightest shadow of concern.

Yet he had dismissed all of that and had asked her anyway, both when he thought her a governess and now. As far as he was concerned, he had redeemed his more dishonorable notions.

"At least say you won't dismiss my suit out of hand. Let me stay here a while, and we can learn more about one another."

Suddenly, her gorgeous smile appeared, and his heart beat faster.

"It is one of the benefits of being not only a widow but, for all intents, an orphan as well. I can do as I like."

"And you *like* me." Adam put his arm around her slender shoulders and pulled her against him. "Do you not, my lady?"

"Indeed, I do."

CHAPTER FIFTEEN

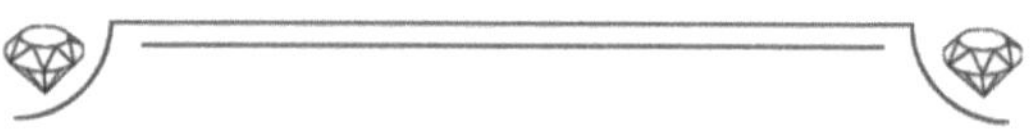

Alice could not have imagined any such situation as the one she now found herself in. A single lady living with a bachelor in a grand yet dilapidated house.

Not to mention in extremely immoral circumstances.

If anyone ever found out the unusual arrangement, even a letter of recommendation from the Archbishop of Westminster himself could not save her reputation.

At first, she was determined to keep Adam from returning to her bed. However, he was such a rum duke of a man and, as she'd discovered, so charming, he was irresistible. It was much more than that, however she hated to examine the way he had taken up residence in her heart. That was too terrifying.

They spent their days working on small projects no one else wanted to tackle, silly things like pruning the rose bushes and fixing the garden trellis. When they took a break, it was so she could show him more of her beloved library. They ate with the others, played card games and riddles in the dining room since it was the only one with enough chairs, and then retired to their separate rooms.

After the first night, though, Adam crept to her door when the house was quiet, having learned the way in the dark.

With no maid to disturb them in the morning by opening curtains and bringing tea, Alice didn't worry they would be discovered. Thus, when he fell asleep in her bed after swiving, she allowed him to stay. Eventually, when they did awaken with the sun, she sent him back to his own room.

Nearly a fortnight went by with the same behavior. Her heart was full of joy because of him, and she wished they could remain hidden in Caversham. However, due to his serious expression one sunny day when he was observing her shelling peas for Mrs. Georgie on the veranda, she knew.

"Something is wrong," she said.

As if they were married, he leaned in and dropped a kiss upon her lips before picking a fresh raw pea from the bowl and popping it into his mouth.

"Not exactly. But I shall have to return to London soon."

Her heart fell. Her stomach seemed to drop with it. Before him, for two years, she had been used to a life of solitude, teaching the Beasley girls and expecting nothing else but her books and the occasional free concert in the park.

Now, however, she had let herself grow used to Adam's company. His tender lovemaking, his wicked humor, his beloved eyes.

She swallowed the lump of sadness, recalling how his life and the promise of a sweet future was ahead of him. And hers was lost in the mire of the past when she'd made more than one mistake.

"Come with me, Alice. Marry me. You know how I feel. We are perfect together."

Her hands started to shake as she lowered the bowl to her lap. Tears blurred her vision.

For a second, she let herself think about being his wife. But only for a second. As soon as she was recognized as the former Lady Fairclough, too many questions would be asked. Richard's brother would once again take up his former hostile threats and his unreasonable demands for money.

How could she drag Adam into any of that? She couldn't, not when she loved him beyond measure.

Moreover, if she tried to explain her reluctance, tell him of her feelings, he would demand to know everything. He would want to know why the woman who had given away her heart wouldn't give him her hand as well. And when she disclosed the entire ugly truth, then she would see the respect and admiration leach from his gaze.

Alice couldn't bear to have him look at her with disdain.

Better to send him on his way, back to his upstanding family and his untarnished life in London. *So why was she selfishly taking the hand he held out to her?*

Adam drew her to her feet, and the bowl fell to the floor, scattering the peas.

Mrs. Georgie would be annoyed.

He made her face him, and a few tears spilled over.

"Lady Alice Malcolm Jeffrey, will you do me the honor of becoming my Lady Diamond? I can keep you in the manner to which you are familiar," he gestured around them.

Despite crying, his words made her laugh, too. Then she hiccupped, making him smile.

"Adamare," she whispered.

"Am I?" he asked, running a thumb across her cheek to catch a tear.

"Most definitely that name fits, *a passionate lover.* I cannot imagine how anyone could be more giving than you."

"Are you accepting my proposal now that we know one another better?"

Putting her hands upon his cheeks, she drew his head down so she could kiss him. Slowly, she tilted her head as he had taught her, fitting her lips against his, breathing him in as she opened her mouth to taste him.

His hands came around her back, dragging her close against him.

Time stood still as they kissed. She needed nothing more than that to be happy.

Finally, Alice pulled away, wishing she could take her heart back from him because it already ached with loss.

"I hope that was a kiss telling me yes," he said.

His deep blue eyes were joyful, reminding her of a beautiful September sky.

"I am sorry," she said, slipping from his hold and running into the house.

Luckily, no one was around as she ran up the back stairs and to her room. She half-expected Adam to follow, so she wasn't surprised when she heard a knock.

"I cannot," was all she said.

"It's me, m'lady," came Mrs. Georgie's voice.

"I am . . . not feeling well at present," Alice called out softly.

"I know all about that," the cook said. "May I come in, anyway?"

Mrs. Georgie had never asked to enter her room before. Despite feeling wretched, Alice was curious.

Wiping her face on her sleeves, she opened the door. In an instant, she was enfolded in the cook's arms.

Unfortunately, that caused her tears to fall faster. But Mrs. Georgie only gave her a minute to wallow in self-pity. And then she set her away.

"Don't be a ninny," she told Alice firmly.

"What do you mean?" She sniffed and dug in her pocket for a handkerchief.

"That young man wants to marry you."

"How did you know?" Alice asked. The servants' grapevine must work on a steam engine!

Mrs. Georgie shook her head. "It doesn't matter how I know. Why won't you accept him? It's as plain as the nose on your face that you love him."

Alice touched her nose unthinkingly. "I wish I could, but it's impossible."

"And why is that? You're a widow, but still a young woman. I know you're not grieving that arse you married."

"For one thing, Lord Diamond is going to be an earl someday. He needs a fresh, new lady who has never been married."

"Not true at all. I don't know much, but even kings and queens marry widows and widowers. Besides, that's for his lordship to decide."

"No," Alice said, starting to pace the room, glad for once it was empty because it gave her space to walk. "I must decide for both of us because . . . because . . ."

"Do you want to tell me what happened? Mayhap I can help you see clearly how to leave the past where it belongs. I know you would rather have your mother—"

"God, no!" Alice exclaimed. Not that she held anyone to blame except herself, but her distant, indifferent parents had turned out not to stand behind her, nor even beside her, when problems arose. She'd fended for herself when she had most needed support.

"I should have confided in *you* the first time Fairclough came to this house," Alice said. "He followed me from London after . . . well, after we were discovered alone, only kissing, mind you," she added, not wanting the cook to think badly of her. "He had done the honorable thing, or so I thought, and asked for my hand. Then my parents had whisked me back here, most likely so I wouldn't reconsider marrying a stranger, nor discover more about his less-than ideal nature."

Mrs. Georgie shook her head. "We didn't have as close a friendship as we have now," she reminded her. "But I wish I had told you I thought the man had tiny, beady, untrustworthy eyes even then."

"He did, but I didn't notice until too late. And my mother thought him extremely handsome."

"*Pish!*" Mrs. Georgie said. "Your former husband was like an ogre compared to Lord Diamond."

That wasn't exactly true, but it made Alice smile for the first time. Her mother was a terrible judge of character and had passed that trait down to her only daughter—until it was too late.

"I wish I had come to the kitchen, asked to peel some potatoes, and had a chat with you. My life would be so different."

"You probably wouldn't have listened to me then, but I hope you listen now. Your life can still be different. Take the chance that nice gentleman is offering you."

"I wish that I could."

"Then tell me why you cannot." Mrs. Georgie sounded heated. "I am no fool, and neither is Lord Diamond. If it's because you were previously wed, that's no matter. He doesn't care about that, so why should you?"

"In London, I was threatened by my husband's brother." Alice hated hearing the words out loud.

Mrs. Georgie frowned. "What kind of threats?"

"Frightening ones about how Richard died. I swear I had nothing to do with it, except . . ."

"Except for what, m'lady?"

"Wishing it would happen. Praying, in fact, nightly for some way to be free of him." Her voice broke, remembering her desperation.

Mrs. Georgie shook her head. "You cannot credit your hopes and prayers with a man's death."

"If I return to London and Fairclough's brother discovers me, I don't know what he will do."

"The Fairclough brothers already stripped this home of everything of value—"

"Not our books," Alice reminded her.

"Except for the books, because the men they sent were too stupid to realize their worth, and because we stood at the door of the library with guns and knives drawn."

"Did you?" Alice's eyes widened with wonder.

"Yes!" Mrs. Georgie said proudly.

Alice hugged her again. "I had no idea."

"I knew you would be back, even after your parents moved away." This time Mrs. Georgie's voice cracked with emotion. "I was shocked at how they left."

Alice couldn't say the same. Her parents held no great sentiment for the country home that had passed down to Alice from her grandfather and his father before him. Even though she'd been in London, she knew her parents felt a sense of relief when everything had been taken, forcing them to move. The burden of Stonely Grange had been lifted.

"Then how can I possibly go away again? How can I leave you all who stood by to protect our home?"

Mrs. Georgie shook her head. "Marry that young man. Don't let the Faircloughs spoil anything more for you. Maybe someday, you'll decide to refurbish this place. Then come back and we'll be here."

Alice started to think she ought to take the wise cook's advice. After all, Adam was nothing like Richard. He had already spent many more hours telling her and showing her how he felt. There was still another concern.

"What if his family doesn't like me?"

Mrs. Georgie tucked a stray wisp of hair behind Alice's ear.

"No worries about that, m'lady. Everyone has always liked you, some too much, and that was your problem. You didn't gather the wheat into the garner and burn up the useless chaff." She stroked her cheek. "Lord Diamond is the wheat."

"I know." Alice wanted to give in beyond anything. *Could she really take a chance that Gerald would leave her alone?* After all, it had been two years since she'd fled.

"Besides," Mrs. Georgie added, "now that you've fallen in love, and I've seen how happy you are, I cannot let you be a dried-up governess again. Go be Lady Diamond, as you were born to be."

The next tap upon the door, which was still open, proved to be Adam, his beloved face coming around the opening.

"I didn't mean to intrude."

"You didn't, m'lord. You are in the right place," Mrs. Georgie told him, "and just in time."

ADAM KNEW HE LIKED the cook. Whatever she had said to Alice, she'd changed *something*. How Mrs. Georgie could shift his lady-love from being dead set against marrying him to melting into his arms and agreeing to *consider* being his wife, he didn't know. Yet the woman had done it.

"We must have another discussion," Alice said when they were seated together on her bed, a place Adam preferred to every other place in the house, perhaps in the entire world.

"I am not certain you have thought about this all the way through," she said, sounding more like a governess than a lover. "I ought *not* to marry you, you understand."

"Why not?" he asked, leaning over to nuzzle her neck.

"You will be an earl," she reminded him, pushing ineffectually at his shoulder. "Don't you want an heir? If so, then you should look to someone like the dewy Lady Susanne."

"Are you saying you are too old to bear children?" He laughed. "I would have to gainsay you, Alice, for my mother was older than you when she bore the last two of my sisters."

She shook her head. "But what if I cannot?"

"What if pigs can talk and horses can fly?" he asked.

She sighed at his nonsense. Adam grasped her hand and fell backward onto the mattress taking her with him.

"I am an uncle to two boys already. The Diamond earldom shall not die out, and if Clarity's son became the next earl, then finally, we would have a family name different from our titled name. Viscount Hollidge, the Earl Diamond. It has a pleasant enough sound to it."

She turned to look him in the eyes.

"Are you saying you don't mind if the earldom slips from you to your sister's family?"

"My sister's family *is* my family. We are all one. You will learn that when you become a Diamond. It wouldn't matter if it were Clarity's son or Purity's son. They are all my blood, and I'm sure either would make fine earls. I honestly don't see the difference, although right now, they are both naughty, mischievous boys. And so was I, once."

Her eyes widened to saucers. Adam knew she'd never heard of a titled nobleman being so cavalier about his primogeniture rights. But he was surprised by her look of utter disbelief.

"My late husband made certain of my virginity," she said.

Adam wished he didn't have to think of her with Fairclough, but he simply nodded. It was a common practice when there was a title or a fortune involved.

"He told me he had to be certain any issue came from his seed," she added.

Adam winced. It would do no good to be jealous of a dead man, something he had to keep reminding himself.

"Fortunately, there were none," Alice said. "And that begs the question, was he unable to have children, or is my body barren?"

"If he drank a lot as you said—" Adam began, thinking the man probably had a lobcock at best.

Suddenly she smiled. "It wasn't only that. He and I were hardly ever intimate. I vow you and I have already swived more than occurred over the course of my entire marriage. He was exhausted from drink and too spent from his mistress."

Fairclough was a fool. Adam had been with mistresses, and none compared to the satisfaction he found with Alice.

"If you have your regular monthly courses, then the problem was probably with him." He shrugged at her querying look. "Four sisters," he reminded her. "But as I said, it doesn't matter."

She closed her eyes, and he held his breath, awaiting her answer. Finally, she squeezed his hand.

"If you truly mean what you say, then I am deeply relieved. You have caused most of my misgivings to vanish."

Adam squeezed her hand in return. "Then you agree, we shall wed?"

"Lord Diamond, you are an incredible man. I can only hope I am worthy of your confidence."

He decided to strike while the branding iron was scalding hot.

"In order to travel back to London together, and to raise no questions about how we've . . . *um* . . . kept company these past weeks," he said, "would you be averse to marrying here, now?"

"I am not bothered where or when," Alice said. "However, your family may feel cheated."

"My parents have already enjoyed my older sisters' two extravagant weddings and expect two more. They won't mind missing one. Besides, they themselves eloped to Gretna Green."

"Did they?" Another look of astonishment.

He nodded, liking that wild and wicked fact about the Earl and Countess Diamond when he'd learned of it a few years before.

"What about a marriage contract and a dowry, which I don't have, not to mention a house I cannot give you since this one legally must remain with me or my children?"

"Children," he repeated. "Think of the fun we shall have *trying* for them."

Despite still trying to lead him to Fiddlestick's end and throw up opposition, she laughed.

"If you are in agreement, my lady, then I shall send word to the Bishop of Oxford and procure us a license."

"You say that as if you know him personally," Alice mused.

"When he was merely the Dean of Westminster, just before he was appointed bishop by Sir Peel, Wilberforce dined at my parents' home, and I was in attendance. We got on very well despite my barely being twenty. We are lucky your home is in his diocese. He will allow us license to marry in your local parish church, and I shall pay for a feast for all of your *friends*. After that, I will take you home."

"Home," she repeated.

He detected the uncertainty in her voice. "I have a modest townhouse on Arlington Street."

Her eyes widened. "There is nothing modest about the homes on that street."

"Compared to my parents' home on Piccadilly, I think of it as such. We shall settle in for a day, and then I will introduce you. They shall want to throw a party, of course. And you'll meet all my sisters and my two brothers-in-law. Nice fellows. Did you know we have a country estate in Derby? Not quite as spiffy as yours, for it's a little more crowded, both with people and chairs."

"Don't tease," she said, pinching him through his shirt and coat.

"I won't. After all, devoid as your house is of furnishings, I've spent the happiest time of my life right here with you."

"And I, you," she said. "The small bed helped bring us together."

He laughed. "We should never have a bigger one."

CHAPTER SIXTEEN

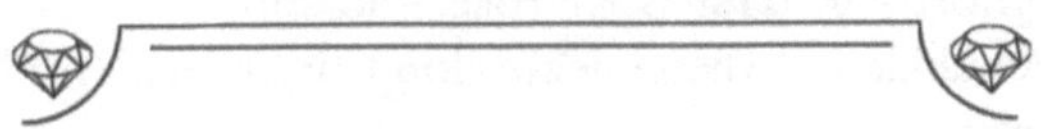

Adam had heard every jest and barb about getting leg-shackled, stuck in the parson's mousetrap, priest-linked, yoked, and *noozed*. He felt only delight that he had finally convinced Alice to become his wife.

If he had been among his randy friends in London, they would have said he would soon become like a butcher's dog, lying beside something without touching it. An old saying that most certainly wouldn't apply. Nor did he sleep like a cow with his back to his new bride. Another foolish saying.

He and Alice grinned whenever they glanced at one another, and they swived nearly as often as they grinned. Even he was getting sore.

Therefore, he hated to draw a thundercloud over his sunny lady, but he had to tell her.

"We have to go home." It had been a week since the wedding day in St. Peter's Church, Caversham. Each day after, she'd come up with something they had to do for the house before they left, a task which couldn't wait.

But his life in London could no longer wait. For while he was not yet in charge of the Diamond estate, he had his own home to run, a sizable portfolio of investments to keep an eye upon, and certain chores his father had designated regarding all their holdings from the time he gained the age of eighteen. And he had been away longer than he'd planned.

Naturally, his parents would be delighted when he returned with a clever, beautiful wife, and therefore, neglecting some of the family responsibilities would undoubtedly be forgiven.

"We leave tomorrow," he said, hating to sound as if he were in charge of her and hoping she didn't serve him a dish of nails in response.

"Tomorrow?" Her voice rose. "So soon."

He chuckled. "Alice, please don't fight me. You know I had to return."

"Perhaps I should stay here and join you later, after . . ."

"After?" he asked when she didn't finish. Not that he cared about her answer, for he had no intention of leaving without her. Skittish woman that she was, he knew he could be old and gray and still waiting.

"I understand your nervousness about meeting my family, but they will love you."

"You probably should write to them first," she suggested. "We'll post a letter in another week or so, and when we're assured of its receipt, we shall go to London."

"You are a minx." He drew her close and kissed her soundly. That always got her to bend to his wishes or at least let him take her to bed. "I have already sent word. But you can write a letter introducing yourself if you wish while we're on the train, and I'll send it to their house by courier when we get home."

"That's hardly the same," she said, putting her arms around him and returning the kiss.

"Alice, we must leave tomorrow." He still wanted to have a private word with Mrs. Georgie and with Henry, but then his task there was finished for the time being. "Do you hear me, *Wife?*"

Her cheeks pinkened whenever he said the word.

"Very well, *Husband.*"

And his shaft hardened whenever he heard that one. This married life was better than he could have imagined.

ALICE WAS ON TENTERHOOKS from the moment they got on the London-bound train at Reading Station, across from The Great Western Hotel. An hour later, pulling into Paddington Station, her insides had turned to quivering jelly.

"You have come over all pale," Adam said. "I promise, we'll just go to my... *our* home and get you established as its mistress. When you're comfortable—"

"In a few years," she joked.

"Yes," he agreed with hesitation, "in a few years, we'll venture out of our den and visit my parents. Speaking of which, will you write to yours and tell them you have a new husband?"

"I suppose I ought to, although they didn't particularly like my old one, not once they got to know him."

Instead of making him jealous, he laughed. She relaxed. Adam Diamond was a diamond of the first water as much as any female. It must come from being the middle child, the only boy, the heir, having good looks, and being entirely self-assured.

And he loved her!

Because of that, Alice tried her best to shed her worries and leave them in the plush interior of their first-class carriage at Paddington Station. After a hansom cab ride of twenty minutes, Adam led her into her new home.

The three-story brick façade that greeted her was in the most desirable situation facing Green Park. The entry gave way to a marble foyer with a staircase to the right and a door beside it, as well as double doors on the other side of the hall.

"Wife, this is our extremely capable butler, Mr. Lewis. Mr. Lewis, this is Lady Diamond, my wife. I am going to give her a brief tour and get out of our dusty traveling clothes."

They went upstairs, leaving the butler with his lifted eyebrows after such a brief introduction.

"Mr. Lewis will get the footman to handle our trunks," Adam promised and tossed open a door to an impeccable drawing room of manly burgundy and gray decor.

"Anything you don't like about any part of the house, you may change. I want you to make it yours."

"You are a generous *husband.*" At the word, his blue eyes darkened to midnight, and his arousal became apparent.

She had discovered the power of that single utterance the first day after their wedding, especially if she dropped her voice to a sultry whisper.

"Let me show you our bedroom," Adam said. "We'll meet the rest of the staff later. By then, Mr. Lewis will have told them all of your arrival, your name, and your beauty."

Adam's master bedroom was as attractive and nicely furnished as the rest of his home. He must have felt as though he were living in abject squalor at Stonely Grange. Moreover, his room smelled like his cologne, which he'd run out of while living away from London.

She stood in the middle of the spacious chamber, with the four-poster bed at one end with its dark blue and silver brocade canopy, and hugged herself. The blue curtains were silk, the patterned wool carpet was thick and soft under her shoes, and the mahogany high boy wardrobe and low chest of drawers were polished to a clear shine.

"How did I get here?" she wondered.

His low chuckle made her skin rise in goosebumps. A sizzle of fiery wanting darted through her when his arms came around her from behind.

"Now?" she asked, pretending not to be as filled with desire as he was. "We are dusty from the road, not to mention tired."

"All the more reason to strip off these clothes and lay down in my big comfortable bed."

"I thought we would have a small bed the rest of our lives."

"I did say that, didn't I?" He began undressing her while nuzzling her neck the way she loved. "We'll try this one out. If you don't find it entirely to your liking, we'll drag it out in the back and burn it. Then we'll send for your little doll's bed."

She laughed at the thought of such antics. But as soon as the cool air brushed her bare skin, she grew serious, helping him out of his traveling clothes with equal swiftness.

And then they slowed down. They had all the time they wanted with no one to interrupt. Adam took an eternity to touch and kiss every part of her body until Alice thought he was trying to drive her mad.

When he finally slid inside her, she grasped hold of his back and was soaring within a few strokes of his thick arousal. He answered with a quick and powerful release.

Relaxing together afterward, her pale hair on the pillow beside his dark mop, he brushed lazy fingers across her bare shoulder.

"I cannot wait to show off the prize I have brought back from Bath."

Alice gasped. It was the last thing she wanted to hear.

"You have gone positively rigid, sweet lady," he said. "Tell me why."

"Recall you said I could stay in my den for a year if I wished." She did not want to go into society, not in Mayfair. She would be recognized. People would talk, and Adam would know what kind of woman he had married.

"I don't care in the least that you are a widow or previously married. And if anyone comes from Fairclough's estate seeking debt money, I shall take care of it."

"You won't pay a single penny," she vowed.

"I shall not. The law is the law, and I don't believe *you* owe a penny, either. But let us enjoy life and face whatever comes together."

She took in a long breath. He was correct. She couldn't hide now that she was the newest Lady Diamond.

THUS, A WEEK LATER, ALICE was at a dinner party at his parents' home on Piccadilly, being feted as the new Diamond bride. His parents were as welcoming as he'd said they would be. And his sisters spoke to her as if she were one of them. No one gave her a sideways glance nor chastised Adam for having a quiet, private wedding.

"Not Gretna Green, at least," his father said, and his mother laughed.

"There was nothing wrong with our anvil wedding, was there, my love?"

"Nothing at all," the earl agreed.

And whether they were disappointed in their son's choice of a bride, she couldn't tell. They seemed to be genuinely happy for them both.

Nearly as soon as she'd met his mother, the lovely red-headed countess had declared, "We must have a large celebration to let everyone know our son has taken an ideal bride."

When it was brought up again by his eldest sister, Clarity—"Everyone loves a party, especially with newlyweds"—Alice reminded Adam on the way home that she was no longer equipped with a suitable wardrobe for her new life. She had even worn the same dress to meet the Diamonds that Lady Beasley had given her, as it was her finest.

"I have nothing suitable for balls and dinner parties." Alice thought it as good an excuse as any to remain at home. What's more, she would rather keep her simple governess clothing. He couldn't take her around Town in those plain cotton gowns.

However, to her husband, this was no deterrent.

"That's easy to remedy, and I think you'll find it enjoyable, too," he said.

The earl's coach came to collect Alice the following day, and Adam was correct. She enjoyed an outing with all the Diamond females, except Brilliance who was visiting a friend in Richmond. They took her to their favorite dressmaker on Oxford Street. Luckily, the establishment was not one which Alice had patronized in the past and to which she still owed money.

Soon, she had gowns befitting her new station. Regardless, she accepted none of the invitations that came to their home.

"You have a dress for every occasion," he said over dinner two weeks later, "and some for events I cannot even imagine."

She gasped. "Did I spend too much? When your mother or one of your sisters said I should buy something they thought looked good on me, I did as they suggested. I admit I was rather like a sheep under their tutelage, but I wouldn't gainsay them for all the world. However, I didn't intend to put a strain on our finances."

He only laughed. "You did nothing of the sort. But I noticed they helped you to choose some dresses in which I would very much like to see you. Before I remove them, of course."

She chuckled. They swived with enthusiasm nearly every night, and she couldn't imagine having missed out on her passionate, talented husband and having gone the rest of her life without knowing such pleasure.

She shivered even thinking of his touch, his tongue, his firm buttocks...

"Your cheeks are becoming all rosy."

"Because I love you, and I am happiest staying home alone with you."

"Every evening?" he asked.

"Yes, *every* evening," she insisted.

"Didn't you enjoy the dinner with my family?"

She sighed. "Of course I did. They were kind and fun, and they love you so much that some of it spilled over to how they treated me."

"Then I cannot understand your reticence. No one will care that you are the former Lady Fairclough. Two years have gone by, so you are well out of mourning."

She would be recognized, and Adam would learn the truth about her. Alice had known it would happen, yet she had married him, anyway. *Selfishly, thoughtlessly, but how could she go against her heart's fondest desire to be with him?*

She could only try to postpone the inevitable a little longer.

"We have barely exhausted the card games we know. Then we can fill our evenings with chess and charades and cribbage and—"

"I haven't grown tired of doing any of those things with you," Adam said. "But I want to show you off. I want everyone to know how proud I am that you accepted my proposal. Mostly, I want to dance with you. I love the happiness in your eyes when we waltz."

"We can waltz right here," she said, knowing she was running out of time. Adam wasn't like Richard. He wanted to take her out because he loved being with her and truly wished to share their happiness with his friends and acquaintances.

Thus, she finally accepted an invitation. Dressed in her favorite new gown of sapphire-blue silk, she made her first public appearance as the new Lady Diamond.

Adam had chosen the event, a large party at his parents' oldest friends' home on Belgrave Square. Alice had never met Lord and Lady Fenwick, but most people in London knew of the elderly couple and had at least one kind word to say about the enchanting and enchanted pair.

"Good evening, young Diamond," Lord Fenwick said, shaking Adam's hand. "I hear you have been captured quite completely and no wonder." His bushy white eyebrows rose. "Look at this lovely lady who did the catching. I suppose you walked into her net with a large smile."

Lady Fenwick let her husband have his fun, and then she addressed Alice.

"Welcome to our home, Lady Diamond. We are so happy for both of you. I know your life hasn't always been easy," she added.

Alice stiffened, but their hostess continued, "But now you are in a good place with an excellent family and the finest of men. We've known your husband all his life, haven't we dear?" She turned to Lord Fenwick.

His eyes were merry. "Indeed, we have. Seen young Diamond swaddled and diapered and in leading strings, bawling like a brat. Helped him learn to fish and shoot, didn't I?"

Adam happily agreed that he had. "Lord Fenwick has been a constant presence of advice and instruction."

"As well as teasing and terrible jokes," his wife said.

Lord Fenwick laughed. "All true."

"In any case, my husband and I hope you have a long and happy marriage, just like ours."

Alice had tears in her eyes when she thanked them and moved away so they could receive other guests.

"They are wonderful people," she said to Adam, who was searching for guests he knew.

"I've always thought so," he agreed. "I don't know anyone who doesn't."

"They had knowledge of my previous marriage, it seems."

"I believe Lady Fenwick was alluding to it, yes, but nothing more. They were genuinely glad for us, as everyone shall be."

Unfortunately, Adam was incorrect. The party was large and spilled over into every public room in the Fenwick's large home. Adam took her to the dance floor as soon as the musicians signaled the first dance. She relaxed as they moved together easily. Yet she could see heads turning when people realized who she was, back from obscurity.

When they walked toward Adam's friends to whom he wished to make introductions, fans raised and heads leaned together as they passed. Alice was certain guests were whispering about her.

The whispers would reach her husband's ears, eventually.

While Adam remained by her side nearly every moment, and all the people she met were kind, there was a few minutes when he was diverted by his father and a member of parliament. Alice remained talking with his sister, Purity, and her husband, Lord Foxford.

"We're leaving early," Purity said. "We've stayed the perfect amount of time so as not to insult Lord and Lady Fenwick, but our youngest is having nightmares. We like to be there if he awakens."

"Some people think we're a little over-indulgent with our children," Lord Foxford said. "But we don't give a rat's arse for their opinion."

Alice laughed at his words, although Purity frowned slightly.

"Come along, Foxy," she said before addressing Alice once more. "I will see you at Mother's luncheon at the end of the week, won't I?"

"Yes," Alice said, thrilled to be included, truly as if she were one of the Diamond sisters. "I am looking forward to Gunter's. It's been a long time since I was there."

"I don't like to leave you standing here," Purity fussed. "Where is that brother of mine?"

Alice shrugged. "He'll return any moment. Please, go, look after your children."

Conveniently, Lord and Lady Foxford also lived on Belgrave Square, which was how Lord Foxford was able to gain an introduction to Purity at another of the Fenwicks' parties.

The dutiful parents disappeared into the throng, and Alice took a moment to look around her. There wasn't anything to be afraid of. She was an upstanding woman, married to a good man. No one had cause to drag up the past or say anything untoward.

"Lady Fairclough," came the voice of the last man she wanted to see, his low tone close in her ear like a lover.

She whirled around to see Richard's younger brother, the current Lord Fairclough. With her heart beating hard in her chest, so she was sure he could hear it, Alice tried to gather her wits.

"I am no longer that," she reminded him. *Thank God,* she added to herself.

"I must admit, I am surprised to see you back in London, out in public as if you hadn't a care in the world."

She wished that were the case, that she was nothing more than a carefree newlywed, enjoying a party amongst her husband's friends.

"What do you want?"

His eyes flickered coldly over her face. "I want what I have always wanted. For you to pay your and your husband's debts."

"*You* are the new Lord Fairclough."

"I did not inherit his wife," he said with a sneer, "for which I am eternally grateful, but somehow, I inherited Richard's debts. And he had vowels a plenty."

"Vowels?" she echoed. *What was he saying?*

"IOUs, of course."

She didn't want to know the language of her dead husband's seedy world.

"After you sold our London home and everything from my country estate, I consider the debt paid." Alice thought that was a brave statement, said boldly, but his nostrils flared and his dark eyes narrowed.

Slowly reaching out, Gerald grasped her upper arm tightly, wrapping his fingers and squeezing tightly in a grip she knew too well. The brothers looked very much alike, and he even clutched her arm in a similar fashion to her late husband when he was displeased. It was disconcerting at best to be standing beside him, but she refused to yank her arm away and make a scene.

Still, familiar fear infused her, and Alice glanced around to see if anyone noticed with whom she spoke.

"You couldn't wait for my brother to die," Gerald spat out bitingly, getting to the crux of the matter. Two years ago, he had accused her instantly of becoming a merry widow.

"He didn't *merely* die. Richard killed himself with drink, don't forget."

"Unlikely. My brother's death is on *your* hands. And if he drank too much, it was because you drove him to it."

That accusation would not stand. Alice kept her voice firm despite trembling inside.

"I had nothing to do with it for the little I saw my husband. I was of no use to him once he'd spent every cent we had, including everything I brought to the marriage."

"So now my brother was an alcoholic and a spendthrift? I suppose next you'll accuse him of being a wife beater."

She looked down at his fingers still wrapped tightly around her arm.

"Take your hand off my wife," Adam's voice was soft yet steely harsh.

CHAPTER SEVENTEEN

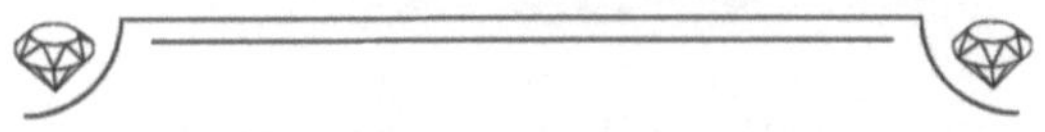

Alice stepped back at the same time as Gerald released her.

"What's going on here?" Adam demanded.

"Just a little family reunion," Gerald said. "I must admit, she has gall showing up here as if nothing ever happened. Did you even know she is considered a pariah for her youthful behavior?"

Alice flinched and glanced at her husband. His expression was inscrutable.

"Your opinion of Lady Diamond is inconsequential to me. I suggest you stay away from her in the future. Your family connection has entirely vanished, and I would like you to do the same."

Gerald's face reddened, but he turned and walked away.

Alice wanted to collapse against Adam's chest and have him soothe her, but she didn't want him to think Gerald—or memories of Richard—could make any difference to her. Instead, she took a deep breath.

"He always was a toady, worshipping his degenerate brother as if everything the man did was either well thought out or plain good sport."

Adam nodded, then offered her his arm. "Let's return to the ballroom and enjoy the rest of the evening."

She hesitated. "What if he is correct and people are talking about me . . . about us?"

Her dear husband shrugged. "If they are talking about you, it is only to wonder what makes you so special you can capture two titled gentlemen within four years. And if they speak about us, it is only to say how lucky we are to have made a love match. For I do love you, my lady."

"And I, you."

ADAM HATED TO DO IT. But Fairclough had been so nasty and Alice was so reticent, he decided he had best dig a little into her background. He didn't want to ask anyone too close to his family, for if they knew something awful, then it would be awkward in the future. Thus, he didn't go to the Fenwicks who knew everyone, nor ask either of his brothers-in-law.

Instead, he did something that he loathed. He consulted back issues of *The Times* society pages. In the McClary reading room on St. James's Street, right around the corner from his own home, Adam read the gossip from four years earlier up until Alice's first marriage announcement.

His wife had been a bit of a wild young woman, as it turned out. The newspaper's journalists who covered London's upper-class members noticed her dancing at least three times in a single evening with the same man! They made note of her comings and goings from backyard gardens and in Vauxhall, on more than one occasion looking breathless at the side of some swell. The papers also chronicled as with whom she sat at dinner parties and concerts, and how closely she was chaperoned.

Moreover, to Adam's dismay, Richard Fairclough had been engaged to another lady at the time he and Alice were discovered. *The Times* was almost gleeful to disclose the sordid details of one young woman's heartbreak and the other's near ruin but for Fairclough offering for her hand in marriage. Still, the papers labeled him a dishonorable rogue and Alice, a sorry jezebel. She had disappeared from London's social scene at once, going back to Caversham until her wedding day.

At that time, Adam learned, they moved into the less desirable neighborhood of Gloucester Street. It was a place of respectable citizens, some with noblemen in their family tree, but who lived by more meager means than what he would have expected of Lord Fairclough.

Adam decided the best way to deal with anything he learned was simply to ask her. He refused to live a life of doubt.

Therefore, at dinner, over the first course of pottage, he broached the subject. He hadn't rehearsed, so perhaps the question came out badly.

"Did you know your previous husband was already engaged when you let him spend time with you?"

He hadn't meant to blindside her, but Alice dropped her spoon, letting it clatter upon the bowl's rim and splash the tablecloth. He waved away the footman who left his station next to the sideboard to assist.

"You may leave until the next course is ready. Thank you." He sent the man on his way. He ought to have done that before he began a private conversation.

Alice dabbed at her lips. "I was aware. But how did you know?"

Adam didn't want to tell her the extent of his investigation or how many newspapers he'd read, knowing it would not go over well. After all, she was the one who had told him he shouldn't marry her. It wasn't fair now to look for reasons she might be deemed unsuitable.

"It doesn't matter how I know. And now that I think of it, I don't care about your answer. I apologize. It's petty to rehash the past."

"This is because of Gerald Fairclough's rudeness the other night, isn't it?"

"I suppose he made me curious."

"He will say worse about me before he stops. Thus, if you have any misgivings, you may as well tell me now or pass over them and let them go."

That was the forthright, practical governess he'd fallen in love with.

"I agree. I have no misgivings about us. But you seem so entirely different from the person who would get involved with an engaged man and…" He trailed off.

"And hurt someone like Miss Dumfrey. That was the lady's name. I am not the same person I was. At the time, it was all a lark, and I had no intention of sticking with Richard more than I did with any of the men I knew at the time. I was waiting for my heart to beat fast, the way it did the first time you talked to me on the street and gave me back my rosin."

Adam loved the memory of first seeing her on Great Pulteney Street. "I thought the package contained fancy lace gloves for an assembly."

She nearly smiled, but it didn't reach her eyes. "I needed wax for my bow. I had no need for lace gloves in Bath until I met you, but I must have gone through hundreds of pairs when I was younger."

Alice picked up her spoon. "Believe me, I wish Richard had remained faithful to Miss Dumfrey and left me alone."

"He would have been someone else's problem," Adam agreed.

"But I probably would have got myself into trouble, in any case," she confessed. "Of similar ilk, too, knowing my thoughts and actions at the time."

Adam pondered that. She was all but stating she would have been caught kissing another man.

"On the one hand, I wish you hadn't been involved with a rake. On the other, I am glad you married a man who died young because regardless of what or who came before me, I think we are right for one another. I would have hated missing out on you."

Her smile lit up the room.

"I didn't know a man could be like you."

Adam had an inkling what she meant. While he'd had his own wild moments, his father had instilled in him a deep respect for the fairer sex. He could hardly escape their intelligence, virtue, and kindness when living with his mother and four sisters.

And if it had taken him a little extra time to realize he could just as easily love a woman from the middle class as the upper one, then he, like Alice, was no longer the same person he had once been. In his case, he'd traded in a distinctly prejudiced view, which he hadn't realized he had, for a broader way of thinking.

"I won't ask you any more questions," he vowed.

"Thank you, but to satisfy your curiosity, Richard's heartbroken fiancée was anything but. She was angry, as I recall, more than she was devastated. I believe Miss Dumfrey already knew he was a blackguard, and she had made a mistake in agreeing to a marriage. Shortly afterward, she married a Scottish baron and moved away."

Adam coughed. "It seems she got the best bit of beef, leaving you the gristle."

"Indeed, she did."

They fell into silence until the next course arrived.

"One last thing on this subject," Adam said. "Tell me if Fairclough bothers you any time you are without me. You are my wife now and thus, fully under my protection."

"I will."

He hoped Alice understood the value of having married into a close and powerful family.

ALICE HAD BEEN SURPRISED by her husband's question. And the more she thought about it, the more she realized he must have asked someone about her. Hopefully, her new family didn't know anything of her shameful past behavior.

She was sure her new sisters-in-law had never acted with an ounce of impropriety.

All she could do was comport herself from then on in a way that would make Adam proud to be her husband. Before going out, she always told him where she was going, or at least made sure their affable butler knew.

And when she did venture onto the streets of London, she took her new lady's maid, the sometimes sweet, sometimes salty Jillian. It had been years since she'd had a maid dedicated to her service. Having a person at her beck and call seemed odd, especially after being a governess when her household status had been nearly on the same level as the Beasleys' house maids.

Regardless, Alice found herself chatting with Jillian from Ireland as if there was no difference between them, enjoying her company. If her old self, the debutante who had no female friends due to her own devilish behavior, could see her now, she would be shocked.

"I would like to purchase some cologne for Lord Diamond," she told Jillian, and they headed along Jermyn Street to Floris. Despite the perfumier making her sniff every other fragrance in the shop until her head was light, Alice made her purchase of Adam's familiar citrusy, woody, and amber scent.

As a clerk held the door open, Alice nearly walked directly into Gerald Fairclough, who was entering at the same time. Swallowing her alarm, she waited for him to step aside. When he didn't, she tried to go around him. He blocked her to the left and then again, to the right, all the while scowling at her with such loathing, it made her skin crawl.

"Move aside," she demanded, using her best supercilious tone despite a trickle of fear.

Cocking his head, he looked at the pretty bag she held in her hands, then at Jillian, and back again.

"It doesn't matter what sweet scent you put on your body, Lady Fairclough, you will still smell like a whore."

Jillian gasped. "Here now, you aren't to speak to my mistress like that."

Alice appreciated her maid's quick defense, but she needed to stand up for herself.

Gerald sneered. "Is that too harsh a description for a woman who traded her virtue more than once until finding a man who fell for her pretty face? My besotted brother gave up a fine woman with an even finer fortune for you. And what did he get for it?"

Alice wasn't going to trade barbs with Gerald, not when the clerks in the store behind her were undoubtedly listening, and Jillian was hanging on every word.

Her former brother-in-law was trying to strip her of her dignity as Lady Diamond, but she wouldn't let him drag her into a battle of insults in the street.

Instead, she looked him in the eyes and again calmly said, "Move aside, or I shall call for a constable."

His response was a bark of laughter. "I doubt you want to be anywhere near the Metropolitan police."

His threat of persecution over how Richard died still unnerved her.

"Is that my new sister-in-law?" came a familiar voice.

Alice cringed, not wanting any of the Diamond females anywhere near Gerald Fairclough.

Adam's flame-haired, green-eyed sister, the very image of her mother, managed to squeeze in past Gerald and stand directly beside him. He looked down at her with obvious curiosity.

"Greetings, Lady Radiance," Alice said, wishing she had stayed home and sent her maid by herself to buy the wretched cologne. This outing was taking on all the traits of a music-hall farce.

"Radiance," echoed Jillian, taking in the only red-haired Diamond sister. "And she is, too."

Radiance sent her a friendly look, then focused on Alice. "I am so glad to have run into you. I know your problem.

The streets here are filling with dung, and I find you trapped in a doorway by this pile of manure."

Gerald's expression turned thunderous. Naturally, Radiance took no notice.

"There is so much manure on our city streets, some say we'll be buried in it five feet deep one day. I just read a letter to the editor of *The Daily News* from one Charles Cochrane, President of the National Philanthropic Association. He suggests a city-wide plan of using men and boys as street-orderlies like they use in Cheapside and Bishopsgate. Honest work for honest pay and entirely clean roads."

She looked up at Gerald as if he might be interested in the project. "They use shovels, brooms, and wheelbarrows to remove the dung all day and all night." She even leaned closer to him. "Thus, no horse-shit on the street!"

He couldn't pretend not to understand the fiery lady. Thus, turning his back, he walked away.

Alice was astounded, a gloved hand to her mouth. When she looked at Jillian, she wore a similarly impressed and horrified expression.

Too late, the shop clerk who had assisted her approached the three women. "I hope you weren't inconvenienced, my lady. Please tell Lord Diamond that Floris Perfumers sends its utmost gratitude for his continued gracious patronage."

"Yes, of course. Thank you." Alice and Jillian stepped outside with Radiance. Alice couldn't help glancing around to make sure Gerald wasn't lying in wait, but she saw him striding down toward Pall Mall. He had ruined her day and perhaps soured her maid's view of her.

"He's a right arse, isn't he?" Jillian asked, breaking the tension.

Radiance laughed immediately, and Alice took a deep breath, then released it. "He certainly is."

Just like his dead brother! And with her own mother's help, Alice had stepped willingly into their world. If only she could figure out how to leave it behind now that she was back in London.

"I hope you don't mind that I stepped in and insulted him," Radiance said. "It seemed like good sport. But I must finish my shopping and get home before anyone notices I dashed out unaccompanied. Don't tell my brother."

Then the young lady leaned forward and embraced Alice briefly, dropping a kiss on her cheek before disappearing back inside Floris.

"She's a force of nature, that one," Jillian said. "If you don't mind my saying, m'lady."

"She is, to be sure," Alice agreed.

Insulting Gerald was the least of her problems. But short of hiding in her new house, she had no idea how to avoid him in the future. In any case, Adam wasn't about to let her do that. He was the opposite to Richard, and when her husband wasn't in his study, at the exchange, the bank, his club, or with his father discussing Parliament, he was with her.

One morning over coddled eggs, he said, "Recall when we discussed the Great Exhibition with Lady Susanne?"

"Indeed, I do." Alice caught his intent at once and dropped her napkin so she could clap her hands with the excitement of a child going to the fair. "Are we going today?" she asked.

"I have the entire day free to spend with my wife walking through the wonders of the world."

With the throng of people—twenty-five thousand on opening day—Alice hoped no one would notice her and doubted she would run into anyone she knew. The Crystal Palace, which housed exhibits not only from Britain but from around the world, was a place so large and novel the newspapers repeatedly stated the structure's enormous measurements.

Built in only nine months from glass and cast iron fabricated in Birmingham, it contained 293,000 panes, including the largest sheets of glass ever made, and 3,330 columns of iron.

However, when they arrived, it was not as crowded as she'd expected. At her query as to its waning popularity, Adam chuckled.

"It's Friday," he pointed out as they passed through the turnstile at the main entrance.

She shook her head, not comprehending.

"The entry price most days is only a shilling," he explained, "but they charge a pound today and on Saturdays."

"To keep out the masses," Alice surmised, embarrassed by the two-tier system as a few months prior, she was part of that class that would only pay twelve pence.

Once inside, she could think of nothing but the awesome ingenuity of people. Half of the nineteen-acre building contained inventions and goods from the British Isles, and the other half from fifty countries in the rest of the world, as well as another thirty-nine colonies.

Everywhere, colorful red, white, and blue banners hung with the names of the countries and the type of item they were exhibiting—be it *Manufactures, Machinery, Raw Materials,* or *Fine Arts.* The noise and the aromas were overwhelming, both the rattling of machinery in the distance and the nearby fragrance of produce from colonial Trinidad and spices from the India exhibit.

"Magnificent," Alice exclaimed, her head on a swivel, trying to take it all in at once. Directly ahead was a tall elm tree growing indoors under a barrel-vaulted roof, and near it, a massive fountain made of four tons of pink glass if the sign could be believed. They lingered a long time in the section from India with the vibrant textiles and the life-size stuffed elephant carrying a—

"Is that elephant wearing a four-poster bed?" Alice asked, going closer.

Adam read the sign. "It's a *howdah.* Their version of a horse and carriage."

And then, they stood before the famous Koh-i-Noor diamond, given to Queen Victoria upon being made Empress of India.

Adam whistled loudly at the large stone and read the translation of its Persian name, "Mountain of Light."

She squeezed his arm. "You are a larger Diamond by far, my love, and I much prefer your warmth and wit to that cold stone. Plus, it's rather dull, don't you think? Not a hint of sparkle compared to you."

"But I recently bought it for you." He sighed as, momentarily, she believed him. "I guess I shall have to return it to the Queen."

They both laughed, passing it to walk through the representation of a medieval court. But Adam's eyes widened when they approached a tall nude statue. He stared up at the alabaster sculpture on a rotating pedestal with an orange-red canopy and matching curtain as a backdrop.

"Does it say, 'Here stands the likeness of Lady Diamond'?" he asked, leaning over to look at the description.

"Adam!" she exclaimed, her cheeks feeling warm as she examined the unclothed female form. "*Ssh!* What will people think?"

"That I have seen you entirely bare, which I have, and I've admired the artistic beauty of every square inch, too."

There was no stopping his innuendo, even though she'd heard his sister Purity say that *double entendres* were crude and a lady ought to ignore them. Alice did exactly that.

"The fact that Mr. Hiram Powers' statue is turning so smoothly," she insisted, "is as spectacular as the figure itself."

"To be sure," Adam agreed. "I'm only looking at it for its clever mechanical aspect."

"Come along," she said. "If you enjoy mechanics, we shall tour the industrial exhibits."

Machines hummed and clanged, powered by a steam generator. And Alice and Adam were genuinely impressed by the hydraulic presses, the large Jacquard loom, and the self-acting spinning mule, which could do the work of many laborer's hands.

Looking at the finer inventions and the best of what had been manufactured, they peered through microscopes, shuddered at surgical instruments, and on the second floor of the main hall—

"Look at the pianos and violins!" After Alice examined them and was given permission to play a violin that caught her eye, Adam immediately ordered one for her.

"Let's go look at the American exhibits," he suggested after giving the man their address.

"I cannot believe you just bought me such a precious gift."

"Why not?" he asked, clearly pleased at her reaction. "You are a fine musician who deserves a fine instrument."

"I cannot take in anything more," she vowed. "Not after the violin."

"Yes, you can. I won't leave until they throw us out," he said.

The American section was a little thin compared to some of the other countries. Alice couldn't keep from laughing at the cornhusk mattress, the jars of Cincinnati pickles, and the double grand piano for four pianists, which she found ugly and unwieldy.

But the hand-cranked contraption that washed dishes, the machine for making ice, and the straight-stitch sewing machine seemed wondrous indeed.

"The Americans have become a pragmatic people, don't you think?" she asked as her husband examined Mr. Goodyear's extensive display.

"Pragmatic, perhaps," Adam agreed, "but there's no accounting for taste." He pointed to the rubber-covered walls and the chairs coated in rubber veneer. There were even paintings done on rubber and rubber clothing.

"Rubber plates and cups, and—*Good God!*—rubber jewelry." He made a face. Then he laughed. "No need to worry about losing your teeth. Here are some rubber ones!"

They were an unnatural looking, dark reddish brown of vulcanized rubber with some type of white bone or ivory stuck into it.

"Please don't let me ever need those," Alice prayed aloud.

They left through the open rubber curtains between the potted rubber plants on either side of the Goodyear display.

"I don't think any of that rubber stuff will ever catch on," Adam mused.

And then they went to a refreshment stand to enjoy some of the Messrs. Schweppes' fizzy drinks and iced syrups before purchasing one of the exhibits most popular food items, the London Bath Bun.

At the same time, Alice and Adam took a bite from the bun, each held wrapped in a piece of wax paper.

"Too sweet," Adam declared.

Alice wrinkled her nose. "Doughy and too small to be a true Sally Lunn." But she finished it, anyway.

"London Bath Bun," Adam muttered, cramming the rest into his mouth before he wadded up the paper and shoved it into his pocket. "Ridiculous name."

They were approaching an exhibit of life-sized Native Americans standing in their colorful costumes before a teepee, when someone touched Alice's arm.

"Lady Fairclough, where on earth have you been?"

CHAPTER EIGHTEEN

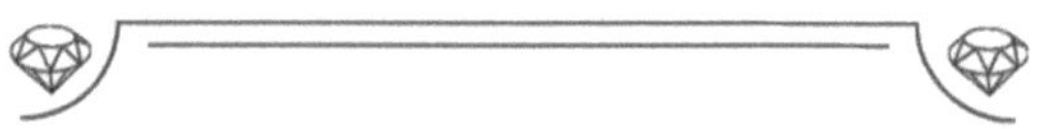

Alice turned to see Lady Devlin, who had been Lady Mary ahead of her in line when they were presented to Queen Victoria. They'd encountered one another many times at balls, and she'd married Lord Devlin a few months after Alice married Richard. Devlin was a tall man, given to squinting, who was constantly pushing spectacles up his nose, but Alice had kissed him, anyway. Only once, if she recalled, next to a fountain at Osterley House.

She didn't think Lady Devlin knew that. In any case, the man was not in evidence. Instead, her old acquaintance was with another familiar face, Miss Kilbey, who Alice didn't think had ever married and who'd been nearly as flirtatious as herself.

"We knew you weren't in mourning to that dog of a husband," Lady Devlin said. "Some of us thought you'd gone abroad."

"And found a new romance," said Miss Kilbey, taking Adam's measure and obviously liking what she saw.

"This is my husband, Lord Diamond," Alice said, not giving them any other explanation. She ought to have allowed Adam to put an announcement in the newspapers regarding their marriage. Hoping to avoid people discussing her return, particularly Gerald, she had begged him not to make a fuss. Yet Alice was sure he didn't appreciate hearing her addressed as "Lady Fairclough" each time they ran into someone who knew her.

To Adam, she said, "This is Lady Devlin and Miss Kilbey."

"A pleasure to meet you, ladies," he offered, sounding as kind as usual.

"*The* Lord Diamond?" asked Lady Devlin.

"There are technically two of us," he responded. "My father and I share the same title as an oddity, since we use our family name for our title, too. Thus, I suppose I am not *the* Lord Diamond, but I am *a* Lord Diamond."

Both the ladies laughed. "What a delight," Miss Kilbey said. "And if your reputation is correct, my lord, then your wife has found a good man the second time around."

"I thank you, ladies," Adam said, appearing calm and confident, while Alice's insides were fluttering. They could say anything about her past behavior, as they'd witnessed some of it. Strangely, they didn't seem to be judging her or holding any of her past against her. Nevertheless, the shorter the conversation, the better.

"We have much yet to see," she said, tugging on his arm. "As I am sure you do, as well."

"Perhaps you will take dinner with my husband and I," Lady Devlin added before moving off. However, over her shoulder, she added, "I'll send you an invitation soon."

Alice stared at Adam. "You are effortlessly charming."

"Thank you. It's easy to be kind, more so now that I have the wife of my dreams and don't have to look twice at any other females."

He was a singular man, indeed. She squeezed his arm, and they continued on their attempt to see all fourteen thousand exhibitors, while knowing it to be unattainable.

They laughed until they cried at a bed with a timer that stood the sleeper up on end when it was time to get up. And Alice declared the hall of stained glass from around the world to be her favorite exhibit.

But when they were leaving, her thoughts lingered on the unexpected encounter.

Unlike her worst fears, the women had seemed nice enough, although she would wager they had walked away still wondering where she'd been for two years and speculating aloud. But when that invitation came, she might tear it up. The alternative, having dinner with a man with whom she'd once flirted and kissed—while her husband and his wife didn't know it—that would feel like a betrayal she couldn't bear.

Unless she simply told Adam.

If an invitation came, she would confess her earlier conduct and let him decide if he wanted to dine with the Devlins.

THRILLED TO HAVE FINALLY got Alice to go out in such a public and crowded place as the Great Exhibition, Adam guessed it would be easier to take his wife to balls and whatnot. Her reserve slightly lessened, but nothing tempted her like a concert.

Thus, their next outing was to see an Italian opera at Covent Garden. A brilliant performance of Rossini's *Semiramide* left them both humming with exhilaration. As they awaited their carriage, Adam spied Fairclough with a well-dressed woman.

Turning away so his back was to his wife's former brother-in-law, he hoped the man hadn't seen him. The last thing he wanted was another tense conversation, especially after an otherwise splendid evening.

"He is coming," Alice said softly, and Adam didn't need to ask who.

Rather, he was shocked by Fairclough's boldness. Here was his wife's former brother-in-law striding directly toward them. Beside him, Alice grew rigid.

"What do you suppose he wants?" he asked her.

"I know not. I wish he had never seen me. Please, may we leave?"

Luckily, their carriage pulled up, and he helped Alice inside before the man was upon them.

"Leave her alone, Fairclough. I am warning you."

With that, Adam climbed in and slammed the door.

"Persistent rotter, isn't he? I can see why you felt the need to disappear if you had to face him at every turn."

"In a city this size," Alice said, sounding dejected, "mayhap I shall never see him again."

Yet the following week, they encountered the blackguard again, this time at a ball thrown by Baron Hermann de Stern at his Gothic Strawberry Hill House in Twickenham. Not too large a gathering, many familiar faces, and some, as Alice predicted, stared at her a little too long before giving Adam a curious glance.

He was becoming used to ignoring those who looked askance, refusing to feel as if there was anything wrong with having married the widow, but he was relieved whenever a genuine well-wisher greeted them.

As usual, Adam thought Alice the most beautiful woman at the party. It was easy to imagine how she had been made vain by the attention she must have garnered as a debutante. Without loving, attentive parents to rein her in, she had been untethered and probably overwhelmed by her first Season. Naturally, she would try to find her own way through the complicated path of high society, and equally understandably, she might stray.

Unfortunately, she'd strayed into Richard Fairclough, and once again, his arse of a brother was intruding upon their evening. This was growing beyond irksome. Outside, in the lovely garden, the man made a beeline for them.

"Diamond," Fairclough said, a bit jovial with drink. "I am exceedingly glad to have run into you and your wife. Once again, I must bring your attention to the matter of a certain large and growing debt to be settled."

"That was your brother's debt," Adam reminded him. "Not my wife's."

"What about the clothing?" Fairclough asked, folding his arms as if he expected a long discussion.

Alice flinched.

"What clothing?" Adam tried to ignore the trickle of uncertainty running through him whenever she had that hunted appearance.

Fairclough sniffed. "There was my brother's debt, and then there was my brother's *wife's* debt. She had a taste for the finest fashion. The modiste still screeches like a banshee if the name of Lady Fairclough is mentioned."

"How would you know that?" Alice spoke for the first time. "Do you frequent Madame Turnbull's establishment?"

"No, but my mistress tried to. When the modiste heard her connection to the name of Fairclough, she couldn't get fitted for a paltry glove never mind a gown."

"But you would have paid for your mistress's clothing, isn't that right?" Adam asked.

"Of course," Fairclough said, lifting of his chin.

"Then shouldn't your brother have afforded the same courtesy to his wife?"

Fairclough looked angry. "Richard had no idea the accounts *she* was opening all over London"—he gave a careless nod in Alice's direction—"nor how much she was spending. Haven't you yet noticed your own coffers dwindling?"

Adam recalled the day he'd received the bill for Alice's new wardrobe. He'd thought little of it. After all, she couldn't dress like a governess any longer, and he was the one who'd asked his mother to take her to the shops. If the cost had made him raise an eyebrow, looking at Alice now, it had been well worth it.

"That is not your business," Adam told him after too long a pause that made Fairclough smile smugly. *Damn the man!*

Alice merely blinked at him. *Was she feeling guilty?*

A stupid thought, which Adam squashed. Fairclough was poisoning their marriage every time he opened his lips.

"The debts of those still claiming against the Fairclough title *are* my business," the man insisted, "and equally, they are your wife's business."

"I don't believe they are," Adam said. "She is protected under the law."

"That's a flimsy sham, and you know it," Fairclough insisted.

"British law is hardly a flimsy sham!" Adam wished he could keep utterly calm, but the notion of that dead reprobate still making Alice's life difficult infuriated him. He wanted her to find contentment and be happy.

"Lady Alice needs to pay *her* debts," the man insisted, "and I see no reason why she shouldn't pay my brother's. They were a partnership, as you are. Don't you agree?"

"You shall refer to her as Lady Diamond, or I will knock your teeth out. Moreover, I would never saddle her with debt, certainly not the expenses of outrageous gambling and keeping a mistress."

Fairclough narrowed his eyes. Perhaps he was considering seeing reason.

"Very well. We'll say those were covered by the meager sticks of furniture and ratty tapestries we found at Stoney Hall."

"Stonely Grange," Alice whispered.

Fairclough ignored her. "That leaves her exorbitant spending all over Mayfair, up and down Bond Street and Oxford Street."

"You sold the London townhouse and reaped the profit," Alice reminded the man. Adam had forgotten that. If Fairclough needed more money, it was probably his own debts he was now trying to cover.

"You are not welcome to speak with us again," Adam reminded him. "The next time we see you, we shall give you the cut direct. If you see us first, I invite you to do the same."

"I want that money," Fairclough said firmly, "for I have no intention of paying it myself."

"Perhaps I could—" Alice began.

"Silence," Adam said to her, more sharply than he intended. "The law is clear, Fairclough."

The man sneered before giving an insolent bow. "I shall see you again," he said, looking only at Alice.

Adam made a fist, never more ready to send out a facer. Lucky for Fairclough, he hurried away.

"What an odious individual," he declared.

Alice also turned away, striding back toward the Strawberry Hill House rear entrance where the party was still going strong. Adam caught up with her in a few strides.

"All my fault," she muttered. "I wanted a new wardrobe as a newly married woman. No longer wishing to wear pastels and demure, high-necked gowns."

"So, you spent quite a bit, I take it."

"An alarming amount," she confessed mirthlessly. "At first, I did it to please Richard, hoping he would look at me the way he had before we were married, and then I did it to make him notice me when the monthly accounts were due. But it wasn't the kind of endearing attention I'd hoped for. His anger was impressive."

"Did he hit you?" Adam asked, wondering how to take vengeance on a dead man.

She hesitated, and he feared the worst.

"Only once. And I shocked him by slapping him back. I said if he ever struck me again, I would retaliate one way or the other. Unfortunately, he told his brother I said that, and the man has always thought me too bold. And then, after Richard's death, Gerald blamed me for that, too."

At last, Alice stopped and faced him, with the lights of the party behind her and the sounds of the musicians and people dancing.

"In any case, it wasn't fun anymore to buy new clothes since my husband stopped escorting me anywhere. I could hardly go alone. I would have felt humiliated, especially when I found out he was taking his mistress to the most exclusive balls and parties."

"What I cannot understand is why," Adam said. "He had a wife who was fair of face and figure. What point was there to having a mistress, especially one who cost him money?"

"I never asked him, but I don't think he liked me very much."

Adam laughed at her quiet admission.

"Whyever not? You are always exceedingly good company, and in all other respects, the most desirable of women. I consider myself fortunate every day I wake up beside you."

Her cheeks turned pink. "Thank you, and I, you. But with him, it was different. He didn't want a woman with opinions. He would have adored the amiable Lady Susanne, although I wouldn't wish him upon my enemy, never mind a sweet girl like her. I was not sweet. When he behaved badly, I had the disagreeable habit of pointing it out, particularly when he drank too much or gambled away an entire month's income from his estate. He most definitely didn't want his faults noted. He said I was a shrew and a scold."

"I am sure his defensiveness made him a joy to live with."

Her short bark of laughter was bitter. "Anyone would have wanted to be free of him," she said, as if talking to herself.

"Indubitably. I don't think you should feel guilty. I only wish you had known someone who could have counseled you on your lack of responsibility for your husband's debts. Then you wouldn't have had to run away after his death."

She nodded but looked unconvinced.

"You don't understand. I had to leave. Everything was such a mess. My parents were… unhelpful. I was humiliated and scared, too. I thought it a perfect solution to disappear. And it was."

She started walking again, up the stone steps and onto the back terrace.

"I suppose you did the best you could under the circumstances," he told her. "Besides, if you hadn't started your new life in Bath, then I wouldn't have found you."

She startled, then glanced at him, her silvery-green eyes alive with thoughts.

"That's true," she said.

He opened the door for her to go inside, and she stepped into the brightly lit ballroom. A waltz was playing, and the ladies and gentlemen were twirling like brightly colored toy tops.

His Alice was a honey-haired goddess in vibrant green silk. Heads turned to gawk at her. Far from appearing the least bit cowed by the people who might have once judged her, she was composed, albeit brittle from the encounter with Fairclough.

He wished he could take her in his arms and bring back the warm, laughing Alice who shared his bed. At that moment, watching her survey the ballroom, chin raised, shoulders back, Adam could imagine the intimidating debutante who'd fended for herself. Men probably flocked to her, a little awed while also seeing her as a challenge. Without guidance, she'd navigated the social waters as best she could, if a little choppily.

As if knowing his gaze was upon her, she suddenly turned and looked at him. He would do anything for her, wondering how he could ever have imagined a tryst with her would have been acceptable, whether she was a lady or a governess.

"Do you wish to stay?" he asked, for he was ready to take her home, cherish her in their bed, and show her how much he loved her.

"That's strange," she said. "A few years ago, all I wanted was this life, but now, it seems tedious at best. If you are ready, I am happy to go home."

CHAPTER NINETEEN

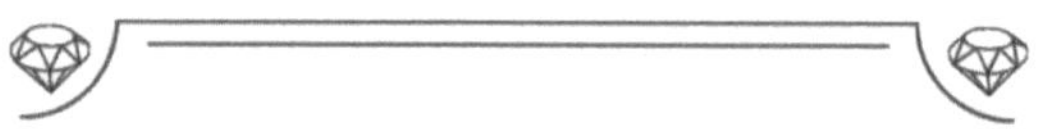

Alice hoped Gerald would cease tormenting her now that she was under Adam's protection, but at his very next chance, the man remained glowering nearby, making her uncomfortable. Moreover, he was reminding everyone of who she used to be.

And everyone who knew her as Lady Fairclough would recall her to be the debutante who had comported herself poorly and was disgraced before having a hasty wedding. Many had thought her with child until that was proved to be untrue.

All she wanted was to be left in peace, to love Adam, and to experience his love in return. Yet as soon as her husband was not by her side, Gerald moved closer.

"I was not surprised by your recent marriage, only that it took you so long, two whole years, to trap another poor sap."

She couldn't believe his gall.

"I did not trap anyone," Alice objected.

"My brother was lured in by your loose lips, and I imagine Diamond was brought into your web with similar enticements."

At the same moment, even as Richard's brother spoke his hateful words, Adam returned.

"I thought I told you to stay away from my wife."

"So territorial," Gerald said. "A good thing you didn't know the old Lady Alice—"

"Lady Diamond!" Adam corrected him. "If I have to tell you again to respect my wife, it will be with my fist."

"Barbaric threats ill-befitting a future earl, but I take your meaning. I shall call her by her correct title when I need to address her at all, but I can tell you this. I do not in any way respect your wife. None of the eligible men from her first Season did. You can ask Dingham, Alton, Nyclyffe, or countless others. They all enjoyed her charms yet married others. I could see through her façade, but I could not stop my brother from pursuing her. And sadly, he was the one who got caught kissing her."

Adam stepped past her, physically pushing Fairclough back a step. "If you dislike her so, then why do I keep finding you bothering her?"

Fairclough shook his head. "After all she put him through before she drove him to drink and an early grave, she ought to pay off his debts or at least her own. If only my brother had stepped aside a minute or two earlier, then the next man would have taken his turn and been snagged by her noose."

Alice screamed as Adam's fist landed on Gerald's nose, knocking the man's head back. As the blood instantly started to flow, her former brother-in-law drew a handkerchief from his pocket.

"You can hit me, but you can't erase her past. I don't hear your wife disavowing my words, do you?"

In fact, no one heard anything more since the room had gone silent.

"Get away from her," Adam spoke into the unnerving quiet, his tone low and menacing.

Around them, Alice saw the shock on the other guests' faces. Adam had been brought low enough to brawl at a private party. The mortified looks were directed at her husband, not at Gerald, who'd been unthinkably wronged in polite society. And it was all her fault.

However, as if being punched in the face was not a dreadful breach of civility in their world, while trying to maintain his dignity, Gerald shrugged and turned away.

His last remark, sounding loud in the still hushed drawing room, resonated in her ears. "You'll find out the truth, Diamond. Mark my words."

Alice realized she was trembling, and it wasn't because of Gerald's threats, nor that every gentleman and lady was openly gawking at her. It was the way Adam looked when he finally faced her.

"I think we should go home and talk." His tone was calm but cool. Polite as a stranger, in fact.

She would have to go further back in her past and tell him everything.

"IS OUR MARRIAGE BASED on untruths?" Adam asked, and for the first time, she saw something in his eyes other than admiration or love.

Thankfully, it wasn't disdain which would be the end, but it was mistrust which might also spell disaster.

Unless she rectified it at once.

"I did withhold the entire truth," she said, licking her lips. If only she'd told him at the outset what a stupid woman he was falling for.

"I cannot say I am now without wariness," he admitted. "You lied about being a governess, about your name, about why you left London. You ran away from me without a goodbye as if you didn't care whether we saw one another again. You withheld details about the current Lord Fairclough's threats. And now, I have to listen to that arse insinuate that you will be unfaithful. Why would he think such a thing?"

Alice was seated on one side of the hearth in his study and Adam on the other. He'd taken her into that room on purpose, she surmised, to keep their bedroom as a sanctuary, a place only of true love and pure passion.

"Richard was not entirely to blame for our dreadful marriage."

"What do you mean?" Adam asked, looking older for his tight-lipped appearance.

She twisted her skirts in her fingers. "I mean to say, it wasn't as if he tricked me into marrying him. The sordid truth is that I was a flirtatious debutante. I enjoyed the power I had over the young men and led them on because I could. I was not like Lady Susanne. Rather, I enjoyed playing games. Despite being smart enough to know better, I did it anyway, lacking all of her sweetness."

"Go on," he said, sounding weary as he watched the coals cooling in the hearth.

"You won't like this," she warned him.

"No, I probably won't, but not knowing is killing me. Also, it is straining our marriage, don't you think? With every new discovery of something to which I am not fully privy, I feel more like we are strangers."

"I understand." She rose to her feet, gestured for him to remain seated, and then Alice began to pace. "I thought Richard Fairclough to be a rum duke the first time I met him. Did you know him?"

"Only *of* him. He was a few years older, and we didn't run in the same circles."

"No, I suppose not, or I would have met you," she agreed.

He sighed. "I would not have been ready for you, nor for marriage, not four or even three years ago."

She nodded. She hadn't been ready either, at least not for what occurred.

"I behaved inappropriately with more than one man during the Season. Escaping the neglectful watch of my mother was easy. I let more than one suitor take me into a dimly lit garden or a discrete alcove or even the dark walk at Vauxhall for a kiss that wasn't stolen but given freely."

Adam stared at her with his deep blue eyes, honest and clever, and her cheeks burned with shame.

"I relished their attention, to be honest."

He nodded. "I think that's understandable. Many a beautiful young lady has toyed with the hearts of the men who pursue her. It has happened to me. However, when we met, you were refreshingly the opposite."

"Because I learned my lesson. Although I admit, I was frightened by how quickly I became captivated with you, and how much I wanted you to kiss me."

He smiled wryly. "After the first time, when you punched me."

"The first kiss was heavenly," she agreed, "but I thought you were playing with me. And I was angry with myself for enjoying it. I thought I was slipping into my old ruinous, immature ways."

"Go on with your story, Alice. You allowed Fairclough to take liberties. Then what?"

"Nothing too appalling," she protested, feeling the need to defend herself. "I'm not a light-skirt!"

"I know that," he said quietly.

"But how do you know? I might've been, yet I vow I wasn't. I let him and the others kiss me more than once because I liked feeling adored. I confess I mistook their advances for love. I had never felt special or cherished at home."

"I can hear in your voice you aren't making a hollow excuse, simply stating the truth as you lived it. I warrant loving parents make a difference."

Alice nodded, appreciating his understanding. "Richard said all the right things to keep me interested. But I don't know whether I would have accepted his proposal if I hadn't been forced to do so by the situation. In fact, I rather think not."

He blinked, and she hoped she wasn't causing her husband undue distress, deciding to hurry to the bitter ending.

"His brother is incorrect, exaggerating terribly. There was certainly not a line of men waiting to kiss me."

"Only one per night?" Adam asked wryly.

She was relieved to hear a more familiar teasing tone.

"Richard monopolized my attention that night. We were caught alone together in a buttery of all places. Given the nature of the room, I was tipsy, and he was well in his cups when we were discovered. I was relieved and grateful when he offered for me the following morning. In retrospect, I believe he didn't care if we got caught, despite his being engaged. He was infatuated with me, probably thought I had a large dowry, as large as Lady Mary's, and he feared I was becoming more interested in another man."

"And were you?" Adam asked.

She shrugged. "Honestly, they were all the same to me. I didn't care greatly for any of them. I craved their attention as a rosebush needs water."

He looked more understanding than she'd expected.

"And thus, you married without love," he said.

"Indeed. I certainly didn't love Richard. Even if I had been inclined to do so, he very quickly changed—"

"Doubtful," Adam interrupted. "More likely, he showed you who he truly was once he had you lawfully wed."

"I suppose," she agreed. "And I didn't care for the man he was. Embarrassing in public, disrespectful and sometimes mean in private, always drunk, and not the least bit interested in me as a person. It was a frightening, lonely year and a half."

Adam stayed silent.

"From the outset, as soon as I entered society, I did not behave in a manner to protect myself. If I had, I never would have ended up with him. Within a month of the wedding, I decided I deserved it."

He still said nothing. While Alice felt rueful and responsible, she had hoped Adam would say it wasn't her fault. "You cannot gainsay me, can you?"

"No, it's not that," Adam promised. "I am trying to think of a way to convince you that it's not a question of whatsoever you deserve. You are not the only person to be tricked or forced into marriage. Nor are you the only person to marry a degenerate through no blame of your own."

"That's the thing. I was to blame. Had I been watched over like Lady Susanne—" She broke off. "No, that's not the issue. Had I cared more about my self-respect than impressing the eligible gentlemen, then I wouldn't have ended up as Richard's wife. Previously, I didn't tell you about my behavior because with the hindsight of marriage and widowhood, I can say I have matured at last. I am also grateful."

Adam leaned back, looking more relaxed than he had when they began the conversation.

"How so?"

Alice had managed to stop pacing, and now, she stood before the man she adored.

"It may be morally wrong, and many including Gerald Fairclough would say so, but I am thankful Richard died. I learned my lesson but was still facing a lifetime of regret and penitence in the form of a dreadful husband from whom I thought I would never be free."

Slowly, Adam rose to his feet and approached. Alice waited until he was toe-to-toe with her.

"I love you, Alice. You have shown me your character, and I don't care if you kissed every man Jack in London in the past, as long as I am the only man you kiss from now on."

She sagged against him, reached up, and pulled his head down to fuse her lips to his.

When they finally drew apart, Alice's relief was intense, causing tears to prick her eyes.

"You are the only man who has ever been in my heart."

"And that's a gift I shall gladly accept," he said. "Is there anything else you should tell me?"

"Only that I love you." She paused and recalled the dinner invitation that had finally come. "And that I once kissed Lord Devlin."

INVITED TO TEA AT THE Countess Diamond's home, along with Adam's four sisters, Alice went unaccompanied. The Diamond women were her new favorite people. She had never met better females. Not a snippy word or sharp tongue among them, at least not directed toward her. The elder ones made her feel welcome with their kindness, and the younger ones wanted to tell her secrets about their older brother, which turned out to be merely funny stories.

Adam's mother generously said she had always hoped for another daughter, which was beyond funny considering her large brood. Alice spent two hours laughing with these women, feeling closer to them than she had ever felt to her mother. Had circumstances been different and Lady Francis Malcolm Jeffrey been a loving, attentive, nurturing mother, Alice could imagine her entrance into society might have been different.

When she left, she hadn't yet reached the safety of her husband's private carriage before Gerald stepped into her path. Undoubtedly, he had been awaiting her outside the Diamond's home on Piccadilly, and she wished she had left when the two older sisters had. The countess had wished to show her some embroidered napkins she'd kept for Adam's bride, and which Alice now carried in a bag.

She could not ignore him since he was standing between her and the carriage door.

"What are you doing here?" she demanded. Perhaps rattling her at Floris perfumery had emboldened Gerald, and knowing Adam wasn't above planting a facer, he'd decided to catch her alone. However, Alice was bolstered by the strength of the women in the house behind her.

"You think you can abandon the Fairclough family," he said, "now that you're married to the heir to an earldom."

"I am beginning to think you are mad," she said. "It is not a question of one family or another. There was no one but you and your brother, and he is gone. You must take up the reins of your title, marry if you wish, and get yourself an heir."

"So much wisdom from the one who was supposed to produce the heir for my brother. Diamond thinks you'll be popping out his brat. Does he know you are barren?"

White-faced, she approached closer. "That's a lie."

"Then why did your previous marriage not beget an heir?"

She couldn't quite believe she was having this conversation. From what she'd already learned from Purity Foxford, Adam's sister who was fond of good manners, this was an appalling breach of polite discussion.

"Maybe it was your brother who was unable to bear fruit."

His eyes narrowed, and his jaw tightened. If Adam's driver hadn't been close by, listening to every word and watching, not to mention her in-laws' home being mere yards away from the vile scene, Gerald might have struck her.

"Is that why you killed him?" he demanded taking a step closer.

Despite growing increasingly frightened, she rolled her eyes and sighed loudly trying to express how ridiculous was his suggestion.

"You are like a dog with a bone. I did nothing of the sort. In all probability, neither your brother nor I have any infertility issues. I never bore him a child because he lost interest in his own wife for the novel amusements of the varied and innumerable whores of London."

"Undoubtedly with good reason."

Gerald was never going to see the darker side of Richard. But that didn't mean she had to accept his vitriol one more minute.

"Enough! You will do as Lord Diamond has told you and leave me alone."

"Not until you repay his debts."

"Even if I wanted to—and believe me, at this point, I would pay any price to end our association—I cannot. You have taken everything of value that I had and sold it."

"Your new husband has enough to pay for my brother's accounts, unfairly gathering interest each month. Diamond won't miss a few gold coins. Isn't that right?"

She shook her head. "My husband has nothing to do with this. Nor shall he!"

"I shall let him know exactly how his predecessor died at your hands."

"That's absurd. He won't believe you, anyway."

"Man to man, he will. I have proof you were with Richard when he died."

She took a step back. "I wasn't," she insisted. "I was nearby, but—"

"You will hang unless you get me the money to pay off those debts. And even if you escape such a well-deserved fate, you will lose your latest conquest. I won't rest until Diamond knows how you lured my brother into your web, and then made his life such a hell he had to drink to stay sane. You will not get away with it."

Without another word, Gerald walked away.

Shaking, Alice climbed into the carriage. Then she thought for a moment and stuck her head out.

"Mr. Heyer," she addressed the driver, "you shall say nothing of this to Lord Diamond. It is a pack of lies that will only worry him for no reason."

"Yes, m'lady," the man agreed.

She had no idea if he would hold his tongue. But she knew she couldn't let Gerald bring Adam into the ugliness of the Faircloughs. With her heart beating like a horse galloping at the Epsom Derby, Alice sat back against the butter-soft squabs and made a decision. Gerald would have no reason to bother any of the Diamonds if she were no longer there. *What choice did she have?*

CHAPTER TWENTY

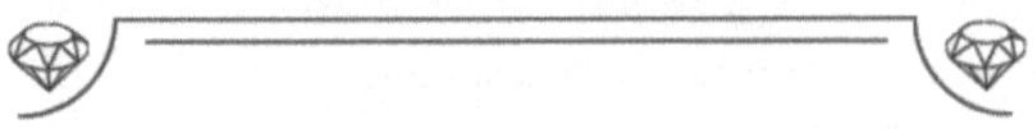

Adam could hardly credit his own ears when his butler told him who was in his foyer. He hadn't seen Alice since breakfast, and he didn't want her to run into this nasty bit of goods in her own home.

"Send Fairclough to me directly. Don't let him linger anywhere, and if you see Lady Diamond, divert her until I get him out of the house."

"Yes, my lord," Mr. Lewis answered and spun about on his heel to do his duty.

In two minutes, Adam was facing Gerald Fairclough across his desk. He didn't sit, nor did he invite the man to do so.

"What do you want?" he demanded.

"Not much of a welcome," Fairclough said. "I hear you Diamonds are known for drinking fine brandy."

"We are, but since you are not welcome here, I won't be offering you any. Let me be frank. I don't like you. I don't want you in my home. I don't want you near my wife. Is there anything else we need to discuss?"

Fairclough simply shrugged, making a face of utter disinterest. Adam hadn't known Richard Fairclough, but he simply couldn't see how his loving wife had ever thought him a rum-duke, nor let him kiss her. He was reputed to be worse than his brother, and this Fairclough was odious enough.

"We do have a matter to discuss. Lady Fairclough—"

Adam felt his blood boil instantly and circled the desk to stand in front of the unwanted visitor.

"Lady Diamond," he corrected. "And you shall speak respectfully of my wife, or I will send you back against the wall with another facer."

"You can try, I suppose. You got lucky last time because you caught me off guard. I couldn't conceive of you behaving like a pugilist in a drawing room. Nevertheless, I didn't come here to fight. I came to warn you."

"About what?" Adam's hand was fisting, ready to punch him.

"Your wife is not what or who she seems."

Since he'd known her first as a governess and secondly, as a lady, Adam believed he knew her as well as anyone.

"You are speaking in riddles. Pointless, petty riddles. Get out."

"There is no way to tell you of her past without speaking disrespectfully since she wasn't respectable when I first knew her. She was flirtatious in the extreme. My brother was vulnerable, having had his heart broken. And then blowsy Lady Alice came along—"

Adam didn't let him say anymore. In a heartbeat, he pressed him against the wall, but instead of a planting a facer, Adam had his arm across the man's throat, making it so Fairclough could barely breathe.

As his adversary turned red, Adam told him, "Your brother took advantage of an innocent young woman who had no protection because of negligent parents. Then he gambled away all he had before he died. The only noble thing Richard Fairclough ever did was die young before he totally ruined her life with the French pox, or worse!"

"She was there. She killed him," Fairclough managed to croak out the words. "I can prove it."

"Liar." Remarkably, Adam wasn't shouting, simply stating what he knew in his heart to be true. He wouldn't dignify the ridiculous accusation with a single request for proof.

Fairclough signaled he couldn't breathe, and Adam finally eased up the pressure.

"I ask again, why are you here?"

Fairclough rubbed his neck before undoing the perfect knot of his cravat.

"My estate is bankrupt. Someone needs to pay my brother's debtors. His widow should have done it sooner. Just because she has married you, it doesn't excuse—"

"Get out," Adam repeated. "Or I shall not be held responsible."

"Very well." Fairclough went to the door and yanked it open. "When you finally regret your marriage with that shrew, when you are wondering why you have no heir because her womb is as empty as her soul, then you won't be able to say I didn't warn you. Man to man. Regardless, I shall discuss this next with a magistrate. Either my brother's debt is repaid, or his murder is avenged. You must choose."

As soon as Alice entered her home on Arlington Street, she sensed something was wrong. Mr. Lewis wore an odd look upon his face, and Adam came to greet her immediately after the butler told him she was home.

"Let's have a cup of tea in the drawing room," he suggested.

"I just had enough cups of tea with your mother to float the Royal Navy." But she accompanied him anyway and took a seat. He sat opposite, rested his elbows on his knees and looked at her.

He didn't immediately speak, so Alice told him something that had struck her that day.

"Your mother and I went for a stroll. We ended up in Regent's Park. Have you seen the sheep there?"

"Yes," he said quietly.

"Have you noticed you can tell which ones have been in London for only a little while and which have been grazing for longer?"

He frowned, shaking his head.

"Their fleece changes color, from natural creamy-white to sooty black. Compared to how I feel at Stonely, I believe London's soot and smoke—or rather, its society and some of its people—can color us as well, even taint us."

"That's a strange way to put it, my lady, but I take your meaning. Perhaps it is true."

She thought he sounded melancholy. "Is something wrong?"

He nodded slowly. "Fairclough showed up today."

Alice couldn't help flinching "Every time you say his name, I think for a moment that you mean Richard. For a horrible instant, I imagine he is still my husband and has the legal right to reclaim me." She shook off the nightmarish thoughts. "What did Lord Fairclough want?"

"Don't you know?"

She glanced at him sharply. "What do you mean? I assume he wants what he always wants—money for his brother's debts."

"He did, but he also said you were with your husband when he died. Were you?"

She gripped the arms of the chair. "Yes."

"Why didn't you tell me?" Adam's tone was harsher than she'd ever heard directed at her. "I thought he was with his mistress."

"He was. I followed him one afternoon."

"Followed him?" Adam repeated. "That's seems risky."

"Does it?" She thought about that day. "It was not yet dark. I had a maid at the time who traveled in the cab with me. I knew on Thursdays Richard went to her home, if that's the correct word for a place where light-skirts entertain men. Sometimes he stayed away until Monday. Anyway, I followed him."

"Why would you do that?" Adam asked. "For what purpose?"

Alice wished she hadn't. "I was half-lunatic at the time. Humiliated and angry, I wanted him to cease his blatant behavior. Have a mistress if he must, but I didn't want him parading her around, going places with her that I wanted to go. Suddenly, she had the life I previously had, attending balls and dinners, and with the man who ought to have been at my side."

"I understand your feelings, but what did you hope to gain by catching him with her?" He was questioning her like a lawyer, and she hated that he doubted her.

"Would you believe me if I said I thought common decency would make him stop if I confronted him?" She couldn't help her bitter tone. "I forgot he didn't have any. Besides, it all went wrong. I sent word through her man-servant who I was and with whom I wished to speak. Not her, by the way. I had no interest in seeing her at all. Then Richard came to the top of the landing and looked down at me in the foyer. He was talking gibberish. *How dare I follow him and ruin his fun!* He would teach me a lesson, he said. And then he took the first step and came tumbling down."

Adam ran a hand through his hair. "He fell down the stairs?"

"He did, like a rag doll." Alice remembered how slowly Richard seemed to fall. She'd watched it, with time to put her hand over her mouth in horror. "He was so limp from the start. I didn't think he would even be injured except for a little blood at his temple. But at the bottom, he broke his neck. I heard a scream and thought it was my own until I looked up and saw his mistress staring down at us."

Adam nodded. "What is her name?"

His cobalt blue eyes were intense, and she knew its importance. The woman was the only witness who could prove without a shadow of a doubt that Alice had nothing to do with Richard's death.

"I don't know."

Adam's jaw clenched while his gaze bore in to hers. Then he sighed. "But the present Lord Fairclough knows, I warrant."

She shrugged. "When Gerald started threatening me, saying I had pushed Richard to his death, I returned to where he died, looking for Richard's mistress to bear witness to my innocence, but she had moved away. It is my word against Gerald's. Thus, I left London."

Under his breath, he emitted what Alice could only describe as a feral growl. Adam was irritated and exasperated because of her, making the pit of her stomach ache.

"I asked you before if there was anything else I should know," he reminded her, "if there was something more you had to tell me."

Alice swallowed the regret. "Since I did not murder Richard, I had nothing else to confess except for being too flirtatious. That was stupid and irresponsible but not a crime."

"Agreed on that point, my lady, but you ought to have confided in me about the strain you were under and the real reason you didn't want to return to London."

She nodded but still defended herself. "I have become used to keeping my own counsel and handling my problems."

Adam leaned back. "Or rather, *not* handling them. Instead, you ran away," he pointed out. "Besides, as my wife, your problems are now mine."

That was what she dreaded. "I don't want my troubles to affect you in any way. But I shall confess something else I have kept from you. Recently, Lord Fairclough accosted me outside your parents' home."

"What?" Adam was on his feet within the span of a heartbeat, towering over her. "And you didn't tell me?"

Alice lowered her head. "He is now demanding I get money from you. Otherwise, he will go to the magistrate with his accusations against me."

"But you didn't come to me asking for money."

"No!" she declared, lifting her gaze to his. "I never would."

Adam crouched down in front of her. "Alice, Alice." He took her hands in his. "We are bound together in matrimony, in the eyes of the Church and Crown. You are mine to look after, and I am yours."

"I know, but I never want any of my past to—"

"It's too late for that," he interrupted. "Don't you understand, Wife? I will do whatever it takes to help you and free you from Fairclough's threats."

Adam meant well, but she knew Gerald, just as she'd known his relentless brother. Whatever they sank their teeth into, they didn't let go, whether it be gaming, whores, or even tormenting her.

"I love you," she whispered. Silently, she added, *Thus, I cannot let you become involved in this.*

She'd seen the type of men Fairclough had sent to throw her out of the Gloucester Street home she'd shared with Richard. They were undoubtedly the same lowly creatures who'd gone to Stonely Grange. If any of the owners of the gaming hells to whom Richard owed money found out Adam was willing to pay a single farthing, those same rough clowes and sneaky dambers would be at his Arlington Street door.

She shuddered. Only she could prevent it and protect her sweet husband and her new family. Only she could keep their snowy fleece untainted by London's soot.

ADAM WANTED TO LOUNGE and appear as relaxed as Alexander Hollidge appeared, but he couldn't. If there was any possibility Alice could be charged with anything, then this was not a brandy-and-cigar moment. Not yet. But after consulting with them the night before, he knew this afternoon, they had good news.

"Fear not, Brother-in-law, your lady wife is safe as a baby bird in a nest," Matthew Foxford quipped. "Once I realized the dead wretch you were speaking of was Fairclough, locating his mistress was easy. Isabelle Janey. Not that I've ever had the pleasure of this particular light-skirt," he added, when Adam gave him a hard stare.

After all, this was Purity's husband. If he'd been tupping the same whores as Fairclough, it had better have been in the long-ago past.

"Foxford is correct," Lord Hollidge said. Clarity's husband had a law degree, although he rarely practiced, preferring to spend his time studying plants and traveling with his wife and two children. "Although I don't think the nest image is entirely accurate."

Purity's husband laughed at Hollidge's more staid manner. Adam didn't feel like laughing any more than he wanted to celebrate with brandy.

"That same mistress saw her in the vicinity," he reminded them. "If Fairclough has her testify that Alice was there at the top of the stairs." He trailed off with a shake of his head.

After finally escaping from a miserable marriage, Alice's husband might reach out from the grave to strike her down with his brother's help.

"Why was Lady Diamond there?" Hollidge asked. Although drinking brandy, he was still jotting down notes.

"She was trying to find Fairclough," Adam explained. "Naively, she hoped confronting him with his courtesan would make him either cease his public affair or divorce her."

"Thanks to Foxford, Miss Janey and her man-servant will testify to Fairclough's inebriated state and that Lady Diamond was at the *bottom* of the staircase when he came tumbling down," Hollidge said, setting down his pen.

"Thus, there is no doubt to her innocence and not a chance anyone will even investigate, never mind bring charges. The current Lord Fairclough has just been blowing smoke before darkened mirrors, trying to scare your wife."

"Trying to wring every last penny because he can't stand that his own brother was such a useless toad. It makes him feel better to blame Alice. But it will stop now," Adam vowed.

"It will," Hollidge agreed. "A letter signed by the mistress should be sufficient. She had been duped by the Faircloughs three times," he added. "For one thing, the deceased brother cheated her out of her regular allowance during the last few months of their association, always with the promise of paying her once he won at the gaming tables or through one of his outrageous wagers."

"Yet he never won. And the second?" Adam asked.

Foxford finally poured Adam a glass of brandy and pushed it toward him. "Unlike us, the man was a grand piss-maker, sucking the monkey from midday till sun up. And that was the only thing that was up. Apparently, Miss Janey grew tired of his whinging about his lobcock."

"Let us drink to Fairclough's lobcock," Adam said, feeling infinitely better about the situation, knowing the man hadn't been able to tup Alice regularly. Thus, he raised his glass, and they all drank. "And what is the third deceit?"

"Gerald Fairclough moved Miss Janey out the following day after his brother died," Hollidge explained. "He said he would pay for her new lodging if she testified against your wife, whom everyone would plainly see was not the grieving widow. Of course, he used every penny he got from selling his brother's London house and from the sale of your lady's country-house inventory to pay not only his brother's debts but a few of his own. When Foxy found Miss Janey, it turned out Fairclough hadn't paid her rent beyond the first month."

Adam chuckled. "And thus, the new Lord Fairclough left the old mistress high and dry, as they say." He imagined the woman was beyond fed up. Knocking back another sip, he asked, "How could my Alice pretend to mourn that fuddled, groggy whore's bird? It would have taken a stellar actress such as Isabella Glyn to convince anyone she felt one whit of grief."

Hollidge refilled his glass. "What is it about that family and their lack of integrity with money?"

"A lack of integrity in general, I warrant," Foxford quipped.

With that last piece of information, Alice was truly out from under Fairclough's lies.

"Here's to the Fairclough's lack of integrity," Adam said. They all drank again. His brothers-in-law had successfully reassured him there was no danger to her anymore, and he couldn't wait to tell her.

When he got home, dashing from room to room, however, Alice was nowhere to be seen. It was already dark out, and she hadn't told him she was going anywhere in particular that afternoon. Besides, where could she be so late in the day?

With each empty chamber, Adam's stomach sank a little more and his anxiety rose. Finally, he called his butler to him in the library, the place he'd thought sure to find her.

"Mr. Lewis, where is Lady Diamond?"

"Lady Diamond has left, my lord. She and Jillian took the train to Reading with the intent of residing at Stonely Grange."

Alice had fled. *Again!* Just as she had done on a whim from Bath, she had hopped the twig to Caversham.

"Dammit!" He nearly sent his fist through the library wall. "How long has she been gone?"

"At least four hours, my lord." Then the man drew his watch out of its small pocket, with its chain dangling from his fingers, and consulted it. "Closer to five actually."

Adam slid his fingers into his hair, making a noise of sheer exasperation before throwing himself down in the high-backed, well cushioned reading chair.

Realizing he was displaying bad behavior in front of his head of household, Adam dismissed his butler. But it didn't stop him from telling the books that surrounded him, "I am going to wrap that woman in a fishing net and tack her to the floor when I get her back."

As soon as the shock wore off, he decided to wait until the morning train. After all, knowing what she would find at her old home, he didn't feel quite so badly about her residing there. If only Alice had learned to trust him and could have let herself depend upon someone besides herself.

The next morning, he sent word to Hollidge to write the lawyerly letter to Fairclough mentioning the sworn testimony of Miss Janey, and then Adam took a hansom cab to Paddington station for the trip to Stonely Grange.

CHAPTER TWENTY-ONE

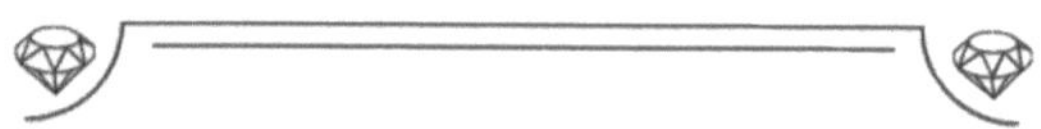

Alice felt calmer as soon as she saw the station, even better when she was able to hire a cab from it to her home. Unlike the last time she arrived at Stonely Grange, she didn't come over the hill on foot, exhausted. Instead, she came in a hired carriage with Jillian by her side.

However, she still held on to the old prevailing fear. Coming face-to-face with Gerald and having him make the same serious threat regarding a murder charge had rocked her to her core. And this time, he thought he could add her husband's wealth to his vengeful plan.

She would not allow him to taint the pure love she had with Adam. Thus, she was eternally grateful when the safe haven appeared before her at the end of the drive.

"Sweet Mary!" Alice exclaimed when she saw the Grange. Nothing about it looked the least bit dilapidated. Every pane of glass was intact, and if she could believe her eyes, there was a fresh coat of gleaming white paint around the casings. Moreover, the yellow stone of its sturdy walls had been scrubbed to a warm sunny gold.

As she got closer, she could see curtains alongside the windows, no longer blank and unwelcoming. There were no fence pieces down or gates hanging askew. The air of shabbiness had been lifted.

How had the unpaid staff done such a thing?

And when she entered, her mouth dropped open. The change to the interior was even more astounding. In the foyer, there was a hall stand. A mirror and sconces once more hung upon the wall.

"It's all lovely, my lady," Jillian said.

Alice could only nod, wandering into the drawing room. Instead of a cavernous space, there was now a sofa upon a plush carpet, as well as a small table with a pillar-base oil lamp perched upon it. Its cheerful ruby glass top would glow beautifully when lit. And as she'd seen from outside, floor-to-ceiling curtains hung at the two front windows and the two side ones as well, ready to keep out the inky black, autumn chill at night.

"It's a tad spartan for a country home," her maid said. "Not that I've been in many, but I've seen a few in my service, like the Diamonds' place in Derby."

Again, Alice nodded. Jillian could not possibly appreciate the astounding difference. While still minimally decorated, it was far beyond what it had been in both comfort and charm.

She passed the dining room on her way to the kitchen, glimpsing in and laughing to herself. While it now had a chandelier, curtains, and sconces, the table was the same home-hewn one she'd eaten at months earlier, and the mismatched chairs were also the same.

Jillian laughed. "That's the oddest grand dining room I've ever laid eyes on, my lady. What sort of place have you brought me to?"

After tapping on the kitchen door, Alice entered. Mrs. Georgie's eyes were like saucers.

"Look who's here!" she exclaimed, jumping up from her kitchen stool. Jenny also rose to her feet with a startled smile.

Within minutes, however, after Mrs. Georgie had hugged Alice ferociously and been introduced to Jillian, the cook began to scold her.

"You abandoned your new husband? Are you mad?"

"I didn't abandon him," Alice insisted, her fingers twisting in the cloth of her skirts. "I came here to save him from having to deal with Lord Fairclough."

"The one who isn't dead?" Mrs. Georgie asked.

"Yes, that one. But please, before you berate me any further, tell me about the miracle that has taken place here at the Grange."

The cook's smile was as broad as the moon. "Lord Diamond has done it all," she said. "Well, I don't mean he came and swept and washed and painted, mind you, but he sent along the blunt so we could do as needed. A right good man, that husband of yours."

"And the furniture?" she asked.

"Enough blunt for that, too. Told me in a letter to buy a few things, but I didn't want to pick out much since he said he would bring you back in the spring to furnish it all as you wished."

Then Mrs. Georgie frowned. "And here you are, thanking him by fleeing your new life. What if he doesn't come after you?"

"I don't want him to come after me," Alice insisted. *Did she?* If he did, he would drag her back to London, and Gerald would continue his demands.

She would have to go back, eventually. After all, she was a wife with an amorous husband, one whom she adored beyond anything. But how else could she keep her former brother-in-law at bay?

Jillian and Jenny listened to every word with interest, and Alice wished she'd sent the younger women out. Even more so when Mrs. Georgie continued to berate her.

"You are a foolish one, m'lady, and I say that with affection. Naturally, you want Lord Diamond to come after you. And if I know him, and I like to think I am as good a judge of character as anyone else, then he will. He's probably worried sick over you."

Alice caught her breath. The last thing she had wanted to do was make Adam worry. By bedtime, he would find the letter she'd left on his pillow under the counterpane. In it, she'd told him of her decision to spend some time at Stonely and how she thought it best to put some distance between her and any trouble.

Naturally, she'd finished with "Love, Alice." He would understand.

Barely twenty-four hours later, she heard carriage wheels and ran to the front door. In truth, she'd had her ears pricked all afternoon. Sure enough, the same horse-drawn fly she'd used from the station the day before came to a halt in the front of the house.

Running out the door, Alice thought it best to meet her husband head on. As he climbed down from his conveyance, his expression told her he most certainly did *not* understand.

"Lady Diamond," he said formally, making her cringe. "I am glad to see you are well."

"Adam, please, don't speak like that, as if we are strangers."

"You behaved like a stranger. I would never have guessed my Alice would let the likes of Fairclough frighten her into leaving her home and her husband."

She bit her lower lip. She had no defense. Running from Gerald had seemed the most natural thing in the world. Right up until the time Mrs. Georgie told her she was a mad fool.

"Won't you come inside? It looks much better now, and I know it is because of you. I am so very grateful."

He merely sighed and nodded to the driver, who had put down a rather small leather bag beside Adam, not the trunk Alice might have expected.

He saw her looking at it. "I am not staying long, only overnight," he said as he picked it up and gestured for her to lead the way.

"We are returning tomorrow?" she asked, not in the least ready to go back to all the strife in London.

"*We* are not. *I* am going home tomorrow. I did not come with the intent of dragging you back to London as if you were medieval chattel."

Suddenly, her fear of Fairclough shrank in comparison to her fear of having damaged her marriage to Adam. When she didn't precede him into the house, he went first, leaving her to trail behind.

Barely glancing at the work that had been done, Adam wandered into the drawing room, dropped his bag, and waited.

Since the only place for her to sit was the single sofa, she sat there. Yet he didn't take the space beside her.

"I need to stand a bit after the journey," he explained. "If you don't mind, we can talk while I remain on my feet."

"I do not mind at all. I had the same feeling yesterday and went for a long walk. If you would rather—"

He shook his head, cutting her off. "This is fine. But I shall ring for a cup of coffee. Do you wish for anything?"

She ought to have offered him a refreshment herself rather than forgetting the most basic of good manners.

"No, I need nothing," she said as he tugged the bell-pull. She simply wanted to begin the discussion for which her husband had come a long way.

All at once, she realized they were both waiting for someone who wasn't coming.

Jumping up, she said, "Stay here, and I'll go get you a cup."

She saw when it dawned upon him, and he nodded.

"Ale will be fine and quicker."

Alice fairly flew down the hallway.

"Mrs. Georgie, he came!" she announced as soon as she entered the kitchen where the cook sat alone reading the paper. "He wants a glass of ale."

Then, without waiting, she dashed to the buttery and took one of the best glasses that remained, uncorked a jug of cool ale from the tile floor, and filled it.

"Is that why the bell went off?" Mrs. Georgie asked, pointing at the line of bells high on the wall.

"Indeed. We forgot momentarily that we don't have staff."

"Oh, but you do. His lordship has been paying us wages to keep the place. But Jenny's not in, and I've never taken food nor drink out to the drawing room before. I should have realized and come a running."

"No matter, don't worry," Alice assured her. "We can manage."

With that, she hurried along with the glass in hand, not even bothering with a tray. When it sloshed over her hand, she swore under her breath but managed to appear calm as she reentered the drawing room.

The sight of him, the handsome man she'd married, not smiling at her entrance shook her and set her heart to pounding. He had always looked pleased to see her until that moment.

After thrusting the glass into his hand and shaking the liquid off her own, she backed away.

"A good thing you chose the ruse of governess and not a tavern wench for you spilled more than remains."

It was said in jest, yet was strangely mirthless. Adam Diamond was angry. Swallowing, she resumed her seat.

"Let me begin," she offered. "I know you are upset that I left."

"Indeed," he said quietly.

"When I agreed to marry you, I vowed never to bring my old troubles to your door, nor let you or your family be affected. Removing myself from London in the same way as I did when I first went to Bath, that was the only way I knew to stop Lord Fairclough."

"It solved nothing," Adam said. "You forget that your troubles became my troubles once we wed. As they should. Meanwhile, I've told my brothers-in-law everything."

Alice felt instantly sick inside to have lost their good opinion of her. Naturally, the husbands would talk to their wives, and then Clarity and Purity would disclose her ugly past to the rest of the family. "What did you tell them?"

"I explained how Fairclough persists in his accusations that you lured your husband into marrying you and then killed him. In fact, the oaf warned me against you while at the same time saying either I should pay up or see you go to jail."

She felt the blood drain from her head. "He is a liar."

"I know that. Thus, there was no reason for you to run away."

"It was the perfect reason to run," she said. "I thought . . . I thought I could protect you by leaving." *What choice did she have?* She was powerless otherwise.

Adam narrowed his eyes. "Why don't you tell me why you fear Fairclough's charges?"

"Richard died at my feet, his forehead bloodied from falling down the stairs and his neck twisted. I told you that. Who would believe I hadn't hit him over the head with a candlestick or pushed him from the landing as his brother likes to believe?"

She rose to her feet again, her hands twisting in her skirts, and began to pace.

"I tell you truthfully, there had been times when I had dreamed of doing precisely that. Not that I ever would, but I could imagine doing nearly anything to be free of him. Yet when he died, with his eyes open and lifeless, staring up at me from the foyer of his mistress's home, I actually felt sorry for him."

"That was a mistake," Adam said in clipped tones. "If there is one thing that has blurred your clarity in this matter, it is emotion."

She sighed. Privately, she thought she had done very well in considering her options and hiding out as a governess. She'd made a plan to do something so foreign to her upbringing, it had taken all her resolve. And yet, she'd accomplished it and could have remained hiding for the rest of her days if Adam hadn't come along and made her love him.

What's more, she was prepared to remain at Stonely Grange for the rest of her life if Gerald would only leave her husband alone.

"At home the night of his death," Alice continued, "I felt utter relief, wicked as that might be, knowing Richard was never again going to stumble through the front door, smelling of other women's cloying perfume and the distinct aromas of swiving and strong liquor. I thought the nightmare of a mistaken marriage and a dreadful husband were behind me. I thought I was free."

"And then his brother showed up," Adam prompted.

"Indeed. Before my hypocritical widow's weeds were even ordered, Gerald came knocking with loud accusations, demands for payments of his brother's debts, and the information that Richard had given his brother permission to sell everything in our London house and to sell off the Grange, too."

She still shivered when recalling Gerald's fearsome rage at being thwarted in the latter, the same way Richard was infuriated by the inability to sell her house and land. She had been exceedingly grateful for the legal trust that kept Stonely Grange in the family.

"When he couldn't sell this place, he emptied it instead. But still it wasn't enough to pay off the debts, or so he said. Even if it had been, I don't think it would have kept Gerald from pestering me. He so desperately wants everything to be my fault, anyone's but his precious older brother's."

"I understand your decision when you were alone two years ago, but as my wife, you should have trusted me." Adam drank down the ale and finally took a seat beside her. Alice wished things were different, and she could simply lean toward him and be assured of a kiss rather than rejection.

ADAM HAD SWALLOWED HIS anger along with the good homemade ale. For obvious reasons, Alice had not felt comfortable going straight to the police as soon as Fairclough started to threaten her. That didn't excuse her running away rather than counting on him, but he could, at the very least, set her mind at ease.

"You were Fairclough's property, and thus, you could not be responsible for his debts, nor even your own in most cases. I thought I made that clear to you before."

She narrowed her eyes and tilted her head. "Is that true? Gerald maintains—"

"Gerald can go to hell," he blurted, then at her wide-eyed look of alarm, he calmed himself. "The laws that restrict you from owning property or signing a business contract also protect you. I know the laws of Great Britain seem to treat you as a child or even an inanimate object at times, but I swear that many of us are trying to change them in Parliament. In the meantime, they protect you from your husband's debts."

"I see."

Accepting his words, applying this information to what she thought was true, Alice looked so adorable, he wanted to relent and kiss her. But his heart ached at her mistrusting him and running as if she could easily bear a life apart.

Then she added, "But he can still have me charged with murder."

"He cannot. Foxford easily located Fairclough's mistress because the man knows that world, which is not a mark of distinction for Purity's husband but useful in this instance. And Hollidge determined the woman is willing to testify on your behalf. Even now, he has composed a letter for her to sign, telling the new Lord Fairclough to scuttle off, except in legal terms. The rat should be receiving it soon."

Her expression came over utterly stunned. "They did all that for me?"

"We are family," he reminded her, wondering how long it would be before she understood what that signified. "I have tried to make you believe that and to trust me. Until you do, we are husband and wife in name only."

Her silvery-green eyes widened, then she looked at her lap and nodded. He could tell the notion of depending upon him still seemed an unfamiliar and dodgy one at best. Moreover, she had proven she preferred to cut stick rather than to stay and fight.

Adam could not change her nature, nor perhaps could she. But he would remain hopeful Alice could change her mind. Inside her was a loving, passionate woman who wanted a family and wanted to trust others—he believed it was so, especially after seeing her blossom under the attention of his parents and sisters. Berating her for leaving him wouldn't help at all.

"I came to tell you all this in person, as a letter seemed insufficient to the importance of the message. But I did not come here to drag you back to London. You must only come when you're ready to return and be my wife, no longer looking back at the past."

He smiled gently and leaned over to tap the side of her head—for it seemed to him she had let her former husband and his brother remain in her thoughts—but he couldn't think of what more to say.

"I don't want to be tangled up with the Faircloughs any longer," she vowed.

With a finger under her chin, Adam turned her to face him.

"May I kiss you, Lady Diamond?"

She nodded.

He took her beloved face in his hands and claimed her lips, hoping she realized she need never feel alone and unsupported again. But it had to come from within her. He'd done all he could. The decision was hers.

CHAPTER TWENTY-TWO

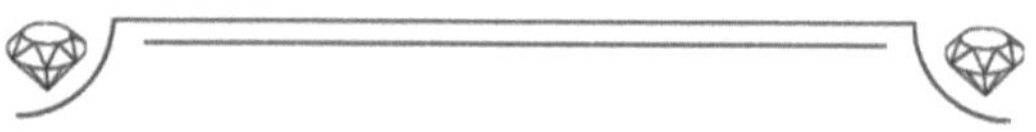

When Adam heard female voices, he thought Alice had returned. Three days had passed since he'd left her. As intended, he'd stayed only the one night and had not invited her into his bed. Nor had she asked him into hers. If she had, he would have resisted. His heart was bruised by how easily his wife had left him behind, and he needed to know she was entirely committed to their marriage.

His hopes were dashed that Alice was in the foyer when he recognized Purity and Clarity's familiar tones and went downstairs to greet them.

"Tell us you came home with her," Clarity said, for they'd heard of Alice's departure through their husbands.

He shook his head.

"I should have known you didn't by the mopey look upon your face," she said. "You are not happy, and I warrant your wife is not happy either."

"If I had dragged her back here, I doubt she would be any happier," he quipped, having the sudden primitive urge to do exactly that, to tangle his fingers in Alice's glorious golden caramel hair and hold on to it like a horse's mane.

"This does *not* look good," Purity said. "It is highly irregular for a new couple to be so quickly separated and living apart. People will wonder and start to talk."

He didn't care too much for gossip, but he knew with Alice's past, she wouldn't like to be whispered about again.

Clarity frowned. "Adam is correct about not bringing her back if she doesn't wish to be here."

"I suppose you are right," Purity said. "And if he knew she was resistant, then he wouldn't enjoy her company to its fullest."

He wished they weren't discussing his marriage as if they were haggling over vegetables at an open-air market. And as if he wasn't even there.

"Sisters, please, don't worry. If Alice doesn't return soon, then I shall fetch her back for I cannot live without her. I merely gave her time to consider her place with me and with us. Moreover, I told her she needn't worry any longer about her former husband's brother."

"But why did she leave?" Clarity asked. "Didn't she know we would help her?"

Purity raised an eyebrow. "Haven't you explained to her about the Diamonds?"

He knew what she meant, and if he hadn't made it clear to Alice before, he certainly had when he saw her last. Even his older sisters' husbands had learned that as much as their wives were now Hollidges and Foxfords, the men were equally members of the Diamond family. They looked after one another, from grandparents on down, whether a Diamond by blood or by marriage.

He'd been a tad harsh though and hoped Alice still understood how much he loved her. *God help him if he'd put her off.* For the first time, he wondered whether she might go farther away instead of coming back. *What if she jarked it by ferry to the Continent?*

"Now what is that distraught expression for?" Clarity asked.

"I told her how close we all are. She hasn't had any experience with familial concern and caring like ours, as her parents were not supportive, and you know she has no brothers or sisters."

Purity sighed. "She has four sisters now."

"We must make it clear," Clarity said, thumping her fist into her other palm. "We shall take the train to Reading station and tell her so."

Adam knew they would do it, too. "I don't think that's wise. Alice needs time to get used to the notion and to decide to trust us." All at once, he realized the utter truth of his own words.

"Even where I am concerned," he added. "I know she loves me, but our courtship was quick and untested by strife. As soon as trouble came, she thought she had to deal with it as she has always done—by herself."

He was feeling better already. Alice was smart, and she would come to believe what he'd told her after she'd mulled it over and let it sink in.

"What are you thinking?" Clarity asked, taking hold of his arm. "I can feel your spirit lightening."

"Because you are all heart," he said.

Purity crossed her arms. "And what am I? A pain in the neck, I suppose."

"Not at all. You are the good sense that keeps us on track. And you are correct about appearances. Alice and I were going to throw a party at week's end to finally welcome everyone into our new life as a couple, and I am going to do it anyway because I trust my wife will come to the correct conclusion."

"Which is?" Purity asked.

"That's it is better to be a Diamond than not."

His sisters looked at one another. "Is that all?" Purity asked.

"No, although that is enough." Adam linked his arms through each of his sister's and took them into the drawing room. "Also, I hope Alice realizes she can depend upon me. That our marriage gives her strength, not weakness. That no one can use her against me or vice versa. If she understands all those things, then she'll come back for the party. Don't you think?"

"Yes!" Clarity said, sounding delighted. "She will. I'll help plan it if there are any loose ends."

"There are plenty to be tied up," he assured her, tugging the bell-pull.

"And I'll make sure Alice knows that you are still hosting it," Purity said. "A pretty invitation from one sister to another, reminding her of her own newlywed party."

"Thank you," Adam said. "I don't know what I would do without you." He couldn't imagine being Alice and having grown up alone. She could have used sisters like his.

"I hope when she returns, she will let you two boss her around." He paused and smiled at them. "I mean, *help* her— as you do me."

ADAM HAD BEEN UTTERLY certain his wife would be back home by the night of the party. Yet there he stood in his fine twill suit, watching his family make sure all was in order before the first guests arrived. And still, no Alice.

So why did he feel so calm?

His mother was suddenly at his side, asking him nearly that same question.

"How can you be so serene when guests shall be descending upon us? I always feel a flutter of nervousness."

"Do you?" he asked. "You always appear as if you have absolutely everything managed to your satisfaction."

"I usually do," Caroline Diamond said. "Regardless, I still have that flutter. By the way, you look so handsome, my love. Nearly as good as your father." She glanced across the room to where Lord Diamond was chatting with Ray, and Adam's gaze followed.

He envisioned his own large family one day, so his wife had better return soon.

"What will you do if—?" She broke off as the voices ascended from the first floor.

He was glad his mother hadn't had a chance to ask him. Because he didn't know the answer.

And then Mr. Lewis began to announce the first guests as they entered the drawing room. Adam caught the butler's eye, giving him a querying look for the hundredth time that day. Again, he received a brief shake of the head. *No Alice.*

For twenty minutes, Adam greeted couples, friends, and family. Each time someone entered, it was the same soaring expectation and then dashing disappointment. Until everyone was there.

No one asked, for they didn't know she was gone. As far as they were concerned, except for his family, the guests thought the lady of the house was somewhere on the premises, maybe taking too long to dress. He wished that were the case.

Drinks were served, the sound of chatter rose and fell, and still, he waited.

The moment Alice entered, he knew, even though his back was to the door. Adam was speaking with Lord and Lady Fenwick when a hush fell, and the hair on the back of his neck rose. He turned.

His Alice! And she looked as if she had truly just come from her dressing room, touching her coiffure with one hand, giving a little wave to some people she knew.

"So happy you all could come," she said. "I am sorry for my tardiness. My dear husband knows I am not the most punctual person."

"Worth the wait," he said, closing the gap between them, not caring if it looked as if they'd been apart for weeks instead of minutes. For they had, and he couldn't keep his hands off her.

Sweeping her into an embrace, Adam hugged her. He wanted to tell her how beautiful she looked, but his throat was choked. Instead, he brushed a chaste kiss across her forehead, breathing in her familiar scent.

After a moment of stillness, feeling her heartbeat and hearing those around them resume their talking, he finally stepped back while still holding her hand.

"A glass of wine, my love?" he offered.

"Yes, thank you." She looked at him with happiness shining from her eyes, and he felt entirely peaceful.

"At last, we can eat," his father said in a loud voice, making everyone laugh.

Alice's cheeks pinkened slightly.

"Don't worry," Lady Diamond said in an equally loud voice. "The earl only teases family."

Nevertheless, Adam felt his wife tremble slightly. And then she nodded, a dazzling smile beaming from her lovely face.

"Then let us go into the dining room," she announced. "I would ask my hungry father-in-law to escort me."

The earl took her arm, and Adam saw them start to chat as they strolled from the drawing room. He took his mother's arm and followed, with the rest of their guests coming behind.

And then Adam knew the frustration of being a host at a long table. He fervently wished he could be alone with Alice for an hour. Maybe two. Instead, he had to look at her down the other end, past the candlesticks and floral centerpieces.

Until he had her in his arms after the guests had departed, she would be too far away.

Finally, the pudding course was served—an array of desserts including a brandy-doused trifle, a sticky toffee pudding, and lavender sponge cake. And then Adam rose to his feet, signifying the meal's end, for he couldn't wait another instant.

Rounding the table, he drew out Alice's chair. Finally, with her arm upon his, they led their guests back to the drawing room for port and sherry.

"Are you surprised?" she asked, her silvery green eyes shining with glee.

Although his heart pounded swift and strong just looking down at her, he shook his head.

"I believed in you. I knew you would think about everything and then return, especially knowing how Purity would chastise you if you didn't show up to host your own party."

She smiled at him. "I would never risk Purity's reprimand."

But Adam wanted her to know something more, something deeper. "You are every inch a lady. I could see it the first moment I laid eyes upon you, and that's why I fell in love with you, even when I thought you to be a governess."

"Even then," she murmured, tilting her head. "Did you marry me to help me out of my lowly status?"

He had never thought of it that way. "After all, the Diamond family motto is *Miseris Succurrere Disco*. Is your Latin up to snuff, or shall I translate?"

His Alice enjoyed a challenge. "I believe I can work it out," she said. "Something along the lines of *I learn to help the wretched*."

"Well done." One woman in a thousand could have translated that. Her intelligence was almost as alluring as her shapely figure.

"And was I the wretched?" she asked.

He considered his life before her. "Not at all. I was until you agreed to be my wife. I married you to help myself. And now, will you do me the honor of a dance, my lady?"

"We don't have a ballroom," she reminded him, starting to laugh.

"Then we shall have to move to a larger house," he quipped.

"No need. We have a serviceable if modest ballroom at Stonely Grange, and it won't take much to restore it to use. Perhaps we could host the next Diamond family Christmas there."

His heart squeezed thinking of enjoying their first Christmas together, and he desperately wanted to kiss her.

"I'm awfully glad you're back. I missed you, Wife."

"I MISSED YOU, HUSBAND," Alice replied. She glanced at the front of his trousers to see if the magical word still worked. He grinned back at her and then did a strange shuffling with his legs.

Leaning over, he whispered in her ear, "Come chase away the spiders, and I'll eat your watercress."

Desire, hot and intense, coursed through her, stronger than any fear. She would never walk away from him again. Despite any threat, she knew she was stronger with him than without him. And how magical to know she was not alone.

After the party, when he scooped her into his arms and carried her upstairs, she understood it was his masculine way of bringing her back despite having allowed her to return in her own time.

When Adam stripped her more swiftly than he ever had before and then sent his own clothing flying hither and yon, Alice knew there wouldn't be any drawn-out sensual play beforehand. Usually, he kissed her skin with the whisper softness of butterfly wings, but this time, he pulled her naked body hard against his own.

Instead of a tender joining, there was a ferocity about their love-making, both knowing what they had nearly lost. Adam barely pressed his lips to hers before she felt herself tumbled backward onto their bed.

Their bed! How she had missed it.

She parted for him at once, not needing anything but the feel of him deep inside. Sensing this, her husband drove into her, making them one.

The rude and naughty term, "the two-backed beast" seemed entirely fitting. Hungry for him, Alice arched, tilting her hips to give him better access. And Adam growled like the beast she'd just imagined before threading his fingers between hers, anchoring her hands to the sheets as he rocked back and surged forward.

"You are so wet," he whispered against her neck.

"I missed you."

"No as much as I missed you," he vowed.

She was about to protest, but the motion, the friction, the pleasure quickly overtook her thoughts. In another moment, they were both soaring toward repletion. He released her hands, so she could drape her arms over his damp back as he finished thrusting.

When her heartbeat calmed, she turned to look at her husband now lying beside her. His eyelids were heavy, but his eyes were open. The love shining from within took her breath.

"Did I mention how happy I am to have you home?" he asked.

"Yes. Did I tell you how much I love you?"

He nodded. "When we swive the next time—"

"In about ten minutes," she interrupted, feeling cheeky.

He barked out a laugh. "Yes, if we can wait that long, it will be slower, I promise."

"We have the rest of our lives, after all," she reminded him.

"Indeed," he said, placing his large palm over her stomach and the secret she suspected was growing within. "Indeed, we do."

CHAPTER TWENTY-THREE

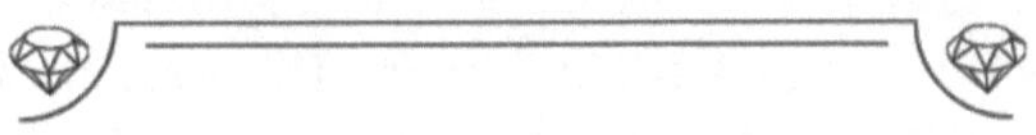

A week later, Alice was pleased to arrive at Clarity's home on Grosvenor square upon Adam's arm. The Hollidges did have a ballroom, and there would be fine musicians. She couldn't wait to dance with Adam again after so long.

Not that she hadn't been in his arms nearly every moment they were alone, but there was something magical about being dressed in fancy clothes. And she had learned that her eldest sister-in-law loved a masquerade, so there would be many opportunities in the years to come.

Dressed as a Roman citizen, Alice entered proudly next to Adam, who was dressed as King Bladud, the supposed founder of Bath. He held a fake stuffed pig under his arm and had a bag of acorns tied to his belt. She thought mayhap they ought to have better coordinated their costumes. Even more so when she saw Clarity dressed as a female *toreador* and her husband, Lord Hollidge, wearing a bull costume.

Having already spent two afternoons with the Diamond women, mother and four daughters, since her return, all bridges had been mended. They'd scolded her gently for leaving them, but also hugged her and told her if anything ever ailed her, she should go to them. She had never felt more treasured and safer.

When the dancing began, Alice thought her slippered feet hardly touched the floor as she sailed around the room with Adam.

"You ought to be a goddess, not a peasant," he said.

"My costume would hardly differ. I would still be draped in fabric. But instead of flowers in my hair, I suppose I would have gold leaves." She wore a crown of delicate blue phlox and white mums.

"Something like that," he agreed. "Can we go to bed now?"

She laughed and couldn't stop. He asked that same question nearly every day, wherever they were, even if they were at home in their own dining room or parlor.

It occurred to her that while his family was nearby, it was as good a time as any to tell him their news. That morning, counting and recounting, she had finally let herself feel certain and had waited for the right moment.

"If you wish to bed me to create an heir, my lord, it is too late. The deed is done."

Adam's affable smile slipped, and his mouth dropped open. Momentarily, he halted in the middle of the dance floor, his blue gaze flickering across her face. And then he grinned. His fingers tightened, both at her waist and where he clasped her hand. Without further comment, they commenced the dance again.

"I believe we missed a few steps," she said as someone almost bumped into her, forcing them to speed up.

"I want to shout it aloud," Adam confessed, "but Purity would descend upon me and quite possibly grab my ear to haul me from the room."

"I wouldn't risk it," Alice agreed. "She is rather fierce." That night, Purity was portraying Catherine of Aragon, who had purportedly ridden with troops in full armor.

"Probably a good thing her husband didn't come as a fox tonight," Alice added, thinking he would be easy prey for his wife. Instead, Lord Foxford was a well-padded King Henry VIII.

Adam shook his head. "My sister is no good at all with archery or a sword. But I would receive a severe tongue-lashing were I to make an embarrassing scene at Clarity's party. Do you think we could at least embrace after we leave the dance floor?"

Alice was, for once, happy when the music stopped. Adam immediately drew her aside. Despite propriety, he pulled her close and kissed her on the lips in front of anyone who might be looking.

"Inappropriate," Purity muttered, coming close as if to intervene. "Save such intimacy for home, please."

"We are celebrating," he retorted. Before he could tell her more, they were surrounded by Bri, Ray, Clarity, and their parents.

Alice thought the family to be like a hive of bees for they seemed to know when to gather and when to spread out across the room.

"What's going on?" Ray asked, her tone already filled with excitement from the party. She was dressed as a shepherd girl, complete with a hook. Bri, beside her, was a white swan with a fabulous headdress.

Alice let Adam tell his family, and soon, congratulations were being repeated.

"Champagne for everyone," Lord Diamond called out to the guests in general. "I have an announcement."

"Go ahead, Father," Purity said, trying to keep the party in order for her sister. Clarity obviously didn't mind the interruption, not even when the earl insisted upon waiting to speak further until servers roamed through the guests with trays of champagne.

Alice received a warm smile from the Countess Diamond, just as Lord Diamond raised his glass high.

"My only son is going to have a child," the earl announced. A cheer went up from the throng. "I wish him and his lovely wife all good health."

Alice thought it a surreal time to announce a baby, with the myriad and fantastical costumes all around her. She already seemed to be in another world, with unfamiliar masks and wigs around her. And now, she was a mother-to-be, an adored wife, and cherished by her in-laws.

After another dance with Adam, a man in a classic Venetian domino costume asked for the next one.

As soon as they were on the dance floor, despite the *bahoo* hood and black mask, she realized it was Gerald Fairclough. A quick and familiar jolt of fear coursed through her, but she let it pass swiftly. She had nothing to be afraid of from this man or his family ever again. Certainly not while in a ballroom in Lady Clarity's home.

"Good evening, Lord Fairclough."

"Good evening, Lady Alice," he said as impertinent as ever. "And congratulations if it's true. I am astounded."

"You shouldn't be, and it is. I told you before that your brother was the problem and not me."

He stiffened. The mask only covered his eyes, but his lower face twisted in a sneer. Regardless, his next words were benign.

"I am glad to see you have returned."

"I cannot imagine my comings and goings could be of any interest to you, certainly not enough to evoke gladness."

"When you are in London, it is easier to remind you of the money you owe," Gerald said, "not to mention easier to direct the good men of the Metropolitan police to your door. Thus, I *am* glad," Fairclough insisted. "We cannot conclude our business if you are not in Town."

Alice didn't even falter in her dance steps. Amazingly, the words that once filled her with dread now barely registered. Just so much nonsense from an inconsequential man.

"On the contrary," she said as calmly as possible, "we have no business. Every connection between us ended the moment my former husband fell down the stairs in a drunken stupor. It was a sad and sorry end to someone who could have had a fine, productive life had he not given himself over to vile drink."

Gerald's face, what she could see of it, grew redder as she spoke.

"No one knows for sure how my brother died," he said.

"Again, you are incorrect. After all, I saw it happen."

Despite how they continued to dance as if they were on amiable terms, Alice had had enough. Where previously, she would have suffered in silence, she glanced around for Adam. Luckily, he wasn't dancing, and he had his gaze upon her.

"Help," she mouthed the word, thrilled to have his dependability and strength on her side.

Quicker than she would have imagined possible, her husband was beside her and simmering with fury. Despite the music continuing, he halted them midturn, and Gerald was forced to release her.

"Is there a problem?" Adam asked, stepping half in front of her.

She nearly sighed with the romantic notion of her personal knight coming to her rescue.

"Lord Fairclough is still mistaken in his assumptions regarding his brother's death," she said into Adam's ear, "and I know I can count on you to help him see the truth."

Gerald crossed his arms. "Your wife thinks she can wish away what she did."

"My wife wishes she had never met your sorry brother," Adam said, "but what is your point? You do know the whore he was with that night backs up everything Lady Diamond says."

Gerald's eyes widened. "You are bluffing. You don't know anything about her."

Adam ignored his retort. "My solicitor thinks we should bring charges against you for stealing the furnishings of Stonely Grange. We could at least get a good accounting of how much was your brother's debt and how much is your own."

Gerald's face shifted to deep purple. "I will have your wife dragged before the magistrate for my brother's murder.

Do you think anyone will believe she went there only to talk to my brother?"

Alice waited to feel alarm and didn't, not with Adam beside her.

And to her amazement her husband laughed in Gerald's face.

"You are like a child trying to blow down a tall oak," Adam said. "Save your breath, Fairclough. We have a solicitor in the family who already sent you a letter on this matter. Did you receive it?"

For the first time, Gerald looked doubtful. "I receive many pieces of correspondence."

"You thought it was another request for money, didn't you?" Adam surmised. "I suggest you go home and read it. You have no case. Miss Janey backs up my wife's every word. Thus, the magistrate says Lady Diamond cannot be charged, nor would they even bother opening an investigation."

Gerald tried to ignore Adam and stare Alice into cowering as he used to, not only since his brother's death but during her marriage, too. He had ever been a bully.

Lifting her chin, she looked Gerald directly in the eyes, empowered not only by her husband, but by the might of all the Diamond family in attendance.

"Lord Diamond is correct. I wish to God I had never met your brother. He was a terrible human being. You ought to try to disassociate yourself with him as I have done. But at the very least, try to behave with a measure of integrity, which he never had."

"And I suggest you start by not showing up at a party to which you weren't invited," Adam said.

"I assumed my invitation had been lost in the post," Gerald said, bristling.

"Impossible," Adam retorted. "Each one was delivered by hand. Thus, not only are you being disrespectful to my wife, you are an unwelcome intruder. Leave before I throw you out myself."

While Alice didn't want violence, she was relieved her husband was a tall, fit man who could easily do as he threatened and shove Gerald out the door.

Indeed, her former brother-in-law took a step back, knowing Adam's was not an empty threat. Moreover, having noticed the quarrel in the middle of the dance floor, the Earl Diamond and his wife, along with Lord Hollidge and Lord Foxford had all approached.

In the next moment, as the music stopped due to the tense gathering on the dance floor, the four sisters also joined them. The entire family remained silent but solidly in support.

And then, Alice saw in Gerald's eyes the exact moment he decided to end his persecution of her. After flaring his nostrils, he simply turned and walked away.

It was finally over. Sagging against Adam who put his arm around her, Alice didn't think she could be any more content than she was that night. He had been entirely correct. She had needed to face her fears and stand up to Gerald, but she couldn't have done it without her husband and her new family.

"Thank you," she said simply.

"Thank you," he returned.

Alice had no idea for what he was expressing gratitude, but when he took her in his arms again, even Purity's *tsking* over public affection didn't stop her from enjoying her husband's kiss.

WHEN THE PARTY WAS near its conclusion, and Alice's gaze scanned the room to take in all the merry partygoers, she realized one person was staring at her. Someone in an adorable honeybee costume, complete with a brown-and-gold dress and artfully crafted wings, was looking in her direction.

What's more, now that Alice had made eye contact, the bee was coming her way.

"It is you, isn't it? The former Lady Fairclough."

Alice peered at the lady, and then it dawned on her—the bee was the former Miss Dumfrey, now Baroness McKennel.

Fearing a scene of epic scorn, Alice nearly didn't respond. But she had suffered enough for her own bad behavior, not only through her horrendous marriage but the harassment of her former brother-in-law. Tonight, she was determined to put it all behind her, and that included making amends.

"I remarried," Alice said, "to Lord Diamond."

"As I learned tonight," Lady McKennel said. "And you have a wee one on the way, so I offer my congratulations twofold."

"Thank you." Alice still waited for the wrathful comments to descend upon her head. The woman who had been Richard's fiancée had every right to her anger and disdain. But Alice also would no longer run from it.

Lady McKennel reached out her gloved hand and touched Alice's.

"I am dreadfully sorry for what you went through with your previous husband."

It was the last thing Alice had expected, and she grew instantly tearful.

"I ought to have told you more of his nature," Lady McKennel continued.

Shaking her head, Alice could barely speak. "I am the one who owes you an apology. I thoughtlessly wronged you. I did many thoughtless things back then."

"If it hadn't been you, it would have been another unfortunate female," the lady said kindly. "I admit, at the time, I was bruised and even foolish enough to blame you. But you weren't the first, and from what I understand, not the last."

"Hardly," Alice agreed. "From what you say, I can only conclude he didn't get us caught on purpose in order to trap me in particular."

"No, I don't think so," Lady McKennel said. "I believe he wanted to marry me for my fortune, but you are so lovely, he couldn't keep his gaze from wandering."

"In that case, our being caught by the party's host was equally unfortunate for Richard as for me. He certainly burned through a great deal of money and needed quite a bit more, money which I couldn't provide."

"The incident was extremely lucky for me," Lady McKennel agreed, "to have escaped him. But I should not have let you marry him, either. I ought to have warned you that he had a streak of irresponsibility and disrepute which my father had lately noticed. At the least, I could have gone to your parents to tell them my fears."

Alice shook her head. "That wouldn't have done any good." She wouldn't bother explaining her parents' disinterest in the details, with their only thought being one of gratitude that Alice would be married and off their hands.

"It is all of no matter any longer. Everything worked out as it should have. And in the end, you have your fine Lord McKennel"—she nodded to the handsome Scot who stood nearby—"and I have my Lord Diamond, who was worth going through hell and back for."

"I am glad you came back from it," Lady McKennel said, again squeezing Alice's hand.

Alice decided then and there she would make an effort to have a friendship with this gentle woman, even if it was long-distance through letters.

When she again found Adam, who welcomed her to his side with a wink as he held out his hand, her heart was lighter than it had been in years.

CHAPTER TWENTY-FOUR

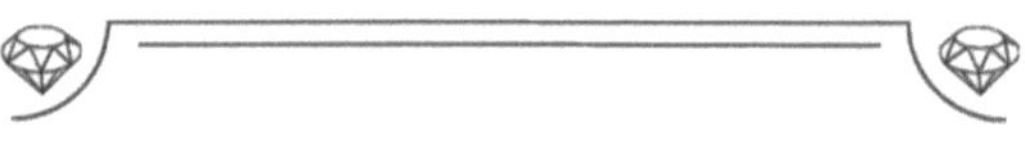

Derby, December 1851

Christmas in Caversham was not possible that year. After settling into their townhouse on Arlington Street as a newly wedded couple, Adam and Alice watched the year come swiftly to an end. They had no time to make an extended trip to Stonely Grange and choose furnishings, wallpaper, and paint.

In short, the Grange was in no condition to host a massive Diamond Christmas.

Thus, Adam had the pleasure of taking his pregnant wife to Oak Grove Hall in Derby for her first extended-family house party.

He thought, perhaps, Alice was relieved not to be in charge during her first year as his wife. Not only did growing a babe sap her energy, but she was still not as comfortable hosting gatherings as his mother and sisters were.

Besides, it gave him more time simply to coddle and cherish her. Thus, while merry, familial chaos reigned all around them, they took walks in the crisp air, skated on the frozen pond, and sat drinking mugs of hot milk punch or an apple toddy. Naturally, there was also plenty of beef tea and, when one needed a cool beverage, frothy eggnog.

Alongside the daily air of merriment, there were also platters of sugar cookies and ginger biscuits, toffee cakes, and pear tarts on every table and sideboard. Adam would swear he had put on a stone's weight at least in the week they'd been there, and they had another week to go.

"Happy?" he asked his wife, who had never looked more relaxed since he'd met her.

"Yes," she hissed out the last letter as she smiled. "And after another half hour of doing nothing, I shall find some paper from your mother's study and pen a letter to Lady Beasley and her daughters."

"Whyever for?" he asked. "Do they owe you back wages?"

They both laughed at that.

"They asked after me in Lady Beasley's recent missive to your mother. Wasn't that kind? They are all ever so happy for us."

"Are they?" Adam was a little surprised after his final conversation with Lady Beasley.

"Indeed, yes," she said. "When next we go to Bath, we are invited to visit them."

Since they had decided to keep his maternal grandparents' Royal Crescent home, it was a real possibility they would be back in Bath the following summer. First, they intended to spend the spring at Stonely Grange, preparing it to be lived in. His family was champing at the bit to descend upon Alice's home and explore where new little Diamonds would be raised for some part of each year.

"If you wish to visit Lord and Lady Beasley or the Queen herself, I shall be pleased to go with you."

That night, they helped decorate the tree in the main drawing room, and Adam had never enjoyed a Christmas eve more than that one.

He even won at Snap-Dragon, although he considered it a waste of good brandy seeing it going up in blue flames for the sake of a few raisins and a party game. Much later, in the room he'd always been assigned since he was born, Adam snuggled under extra blankets with Alice, her back to his front, with him curled around her.

Swiving had been as intense as ever, despite her slightly rounded stomach. Now, as they drifted off to sleep, he happily played with her full breasts, stroking her curves while she sighed happily.

"Merry Christmas, Husband," she said, and although his desire roared to life again at her sultry, drowsy tone, he didn't act upon it. Alice needed more sleep than she used to.

"Merry Christmas, Wife." And soon after, he heard her gentle snoring.

Caversham, Spring 1852

ALICE DIDN'T MIND IF they ever returned to London. Stonely Grange wasn't merely restored to its former grandeur, it was much improved.

One thing she'd learned in the interim between when the Grange had been ravaged and when she'd walked room-by-room with Adam to plan its refurbishing was she preferred less to more. She liked the open spaces. Instead of minimal furniture and fewer bric-a-brac making the Grange seem empty, it felt freeing.

Especially since Alice liked to pace, either when happy and thinking or distraught and worrying, not that she could recall the last time she was either of the latter.

"No one in London would consider this finished," Adam said as they sat with their feet up on the same ottoman, leaning back on a velvet couch in their upstairs private salon.

"Don't you think so?" Alice asked, glancing around at this, one of the last rooms they'd completed since it was unimportant to the daily life of the manor.

Now that it was done, they were enjoying it. "But it is so peaceful and functional. A sofa for sitting, a place for our feet, a table at either end for our drinks and lamps. We have a mirror to add light and space, a painting for beauty and to engage the mind, and plenty of books to capture the imagination."

Why was Adam laughing at her?

"You sound like one of those long-winded, zealous advertisements in the newspaper or a theatre bill. But you are selling the joy of *not* buying."

"I am," she agreed. "Maybe we could add another sideboard and put a lace doily in the center and, upon that, a red glass. Mr. Henry has plenty of flowers we could pinch. Would that help?"

Adam was laughing at her again. "Let's keep it as it is," he said. "All of it. We'll live with the Viking raid style until we tire of it."

She smacked his thigh resting against her own. "It is not a Viking raid style. It is uncluttered—"

"Stark," he interjected.

"Tastefully understated," she retorted.

"Unusually austere," he shot back.

"Discreet."

"Spartan as if we have lost all our money," he said, before laughing again at her wide-eyed expression.

Alice shook her head. "Now I see the issue. It reflects badly upon the Diamond name if every wall isn't filled with gilded mirrors and oil paintings. We ought to buy a few dozen framed ocean scenes and bowls of fruit. If we can actually see the pattern on the soft wool rug, then we ought to add a few dozen chairs and tables to cover every square inch."

He turned his whole body to face her, giving himself better access, and started to tickle her. Her husband had discovered her vulnerability only a month ago and used it to his advantage.

"No," she squealed, leaning away from his probing fingers, a hand at each side of her rib cage. Still, she teased, "Maybe two more sofas in this room alone."

Against the armrest, Alice couldn't squirm away. Grabbing his hands, she tried to hold them still. Breathlessly, she added, "Maybe we need to put a pink glass fountain in the middle of the house."

Instantly, Adam ceased his torment and rested those same large hands upon each of her breasts. "I would rather have an alabaster statue of you."

"For any guests to see?" she asked. Her husband wasn't a dreadfully jealous man, but he was possessive. "What about our staff? You don't mind the footmen dusting my marble thighs."

He put his head back and laughed. "You are a minx. I would keep it covered except for when we were alone. For my eyes only. Both would add a certain polish to the Grange, a ten-foot statue and an indoor fountain."

"Like the perfect panache of feathers upon a lady's hat," she said.

"Indeed," he answered, and his thumbs started teasing her nipples through the soft combed cotton of her gown.

"Snout-nose," Alice muttered in an attempt to win the debate before she was overcome with desire for him and lost her ability to speak. For her husband knew precisely how to stroke her body, playing her like a musician of the highest caliber, until she was unable to think.

Adam froze. "I vow I am not." He appeared uncertain. "I promise you I don't need to flaunt my wealth."

Rolling her eyes, she assured him, "I was speaking in jest. I know who you are, Lord Diamond. Now, touch me again."

He relaxed. "We don't need anything more to make Stonely perfect," he added, cradling her face in his hands. Then he leaned over her to kiss her.

"There is one thing more," she said before his mouth fitted to hers. "Mrs. Georgie would like one of those hand-cranked, dish-washing machines."

They started to make love even as Alice could feel her husband's body shaking with laughter.

Bath, Late Summer 1852

THE ROYAL CRESCENT townhouse rang out with his wife's cries, and Adam poured himself a glass of brandy. Since none of his family were nearby, Alice was being attended by Lady Beasley and Lady Susanne, along with the best midwife in Bath.

"All shall be fine, my lord," Lady Beasley had assured him, looking cool as ever despite the heat. Then she had shut his bedroom door in his face. He thought she'd appeared satisfied to do so.

Still, the birthing room was no place for a man. He would only get in the way, show worry on his face, perhaps even faint if things got dodgy. He couldn't even bear to think of Alice in pain. And it was all his fault.

But his father had been through this five times successfully. He wished the earl was there instead of in London, at least to drink brandy with him, slap him on the back, and—*for God's sake*—tell him everything was going to be fine.

In any case, word had been sent to Piccadilly of the impending babe, and some or all of his family would arrive as soon as they could get themselves loaded into a train carriage.

A sudden rapping at the front door caused him to jump up from the chair he'd dragged into the hallway outside the bedroom door. Although spilling his drink down his shirt, he managed to set the glass down rather than dropping it to shatter.

Of all the emotions he was expecting when this moment came, he hadn't thought he would be as nervous as a cat in a rocking chair emporium.

Not bothering to put on his jacket, Adam dashed downstairs to answer the knock himself since he was entirely useless to do anything helpful for Alice. Besides, Mr. Lewis was back in London, and their skeleton staff in Bath were not as quick.

"Lord Beasley!" Adam exclaimed, seeing the man on the doorstep. Then he reached out, took hold of his arm, and yanked him inside.

"My, my," Lord Beasley said. But instead of freeing his arm, he patted Adam's shoulder. "I thought I might be needed, what with you being a first-time father."

"Indeed, my lord. I am exceedingly grateful for company. I thought I might go mad left to my own counsel. Would you care for some brandy? I know I would. In fact, I was just drinking some and then spilled it."

Looking down at his shirtfront, he could see the damage and gave it a futile wipe.

"I have a decanter upstairs," Adam added. "Please, come this way."

The Beasleys had become their friends after he and Alice returned to Bath upon finishing their first round of refurbishing Stonely Grange. Privately, Adam still thought his wife would want to add a few more oddments and trinkets to clutter the place up a bit in the current fashion, especially when they went back there with the baby.

Ever since they'd arrived in Bath, she had been feathering their nest with more stuff in the nursery than it seemed they'd put in all of the Grange.

"Does the wee one really need—?" Adam would begin to ask when she arrived home with another blanket, a painted miniature chair, or even a whip-and-top toy. *But Alice, it's a baby!*

A jump rope appeared in the nursery recently, along with a hoop that could be sent flying along the street with the right stick, a miniature sailboat, and a doll. She was ready for any eventuality of sex or interest.

Whatever he asked about, Alice held up her hand, and he let it go with a smile. After all, since they planned for a large family, it was money well spent. Even if the first child barely used the new rocking horse, the next one surely would.

"Thank you for coming," Adam said once they were seated in the upstairs salon beside the room where Alice labored. Adam kept the door open so he could still hear what was going on and poured Lord Beasley a drink.

Alice had sent over a calling card to The Paragon residence as soon as they'd returned to the spa city, determined to make amends. Invited to dinner forthwith, Adam had been relieved when his mother's friend forgave them before the first glass of wine.

"While we haven't found a governess nearly as good as you," Lady Beasley had said, "I am pleased you found your happiness, and to think I had something to do with bringing my good friend's son together with the perfect wife."

Losing her best governess, with a lack of notice given before departure, and Alice marrying Susanne's suitor—it was all water under the bridge once the Beasleys learned her true identity.

"Two years in hiding!" Lord Beasley had said in wonder over the roast chicken. "I vow you could have confided in us, Lady Diamond, and we would have done our utmost to assist."

"We would have," Lady Beasley confirmed his words, "although I would have been loath for our girls to miss out on your excellent tutelage."

Adam and Alice exchanged more than one glance that night. Lady Beasley hadn't quite understood the severity of the situation.

At the beef and vegetables course, Adam had mused, "My parents looked kindly upon your assistance in allowing us to keep company when you could have easily not allowed it, given the circumstances."

Lady Beasley appreciated such a statement.

Lady Susanne had been quiet at first. She'd eyed her former governess's blossoming stomach, draped in the finest satin gown. Eventually, over the pudding course, she said, "When I saw you two kissing, it was not really improper, for you were destined to be married."

Awkward silence had reigned for a very long moment, and then the two younger girls giggled.

Finally, Alice had said, "That's exactly correct." No one made mention of the impropriety again.

In any case, Lady Beasley had offered assistance when the time came for his wife's labor. As promised, her ladyship had come as soon as Adam sent word, despite it being the middle of the night. But he hadn't expected the support of Lord Beasley.

"No reason you should punish yourself and sit in a hallway," his lordship said. Then he tapped his glass to Adam's, and they drank down a long sip of brandy. "By the way, it becomes easier with each birth."

"I believe my mother said that." At least, Adam thought she had. His brain felt a little like warm mush.

Lord Beasley laughed. "I meant for *you*. I don't know anything about how—"

Alice cried out again, and Adam was glad he was seated. But then he heard the unmistakable squall of a baby. Jumping to his feet and spilling his brandy for the second time that night, he set his glass down and raced out to the closed door of his bedroom.

Pounding on it, he couldn't help shouting, "Alice, are you well? The babe is it healthy?"

The door opened, and Lady Susanne blocked his view. Her hair was unusually mussed and her cheeks pale. Apparently, she'd received an education of sorts from his wife after all. It had been a long night and an even longer day.

"Both are fine, my lord," Lady Susanne promised. "The midwife is just . . . *uh* . . . cleaning everyone up."

She looked over her shoulder, and Adam peered past, seeing a scene of tangled sheets and Alice leaning back on many pillows—perhaps all the pillows they owned in the entire house—to keep her sitting up.

Their eyes locked.

"Let him in, Susanne," Alice ordered, her voice strong but hoarse.

In three steps, he was beside her, ignoring the mess at the foot of the bed, for his baby was cradled in his wife's arms.

"You are marvelous," he said, meaning Alice but equally referring to the infant. Reaching out to touch its head, he stopped just short of the tuft of black fluffy hair. "May I?"

"I think so," Alice said. She looked spent, her face as pale as Lady Susanne's but with a bruised look around her eyes. "He's a boy," she added, looking down at the bundle in her arms, her face breaking out in a tired smile.

"A boy," Adam repeated. Finally, he let the tips of his fingers touch his son, stroking his hair, then his cheek. The babe's eyes were closed, his face red, and he appeared already to be sleeping.

"Peaceful chap," Adam said.

Alice's gaze shot to his, her silver-green eyes looking in disbelief. "After what he's just put me through," she quipped, "peaceful is the last thing I think of him."

Then she chuckled. "He does look like a little lamb though, doesn't he?"

"Indeed."

Lady Beasley rose from the chair on the other side of the bed. He hadn't even noticed her for the past few minutes, nor the midwife.

"Congratulations," her ladyship said. "Your wife handled her first labor superbly," she said to Adam. "See that she gets some broth or whatever her stomach yearns to eat, but make sure she drinks plenty. It helps with the milk production," she added when he knew he looked baffled.

"Yes, of course," he said. "Thank you."

"Susanne and I will leave you two alone now, but I will return later to make sure you have everything you need." She nodded to Alice and went to the door. "Do feel at liberty to name the baby after my husband, my lord, since he kept you company. I think it's a tradition. I'll collect him on my way out." With that, she disappeared with Lady Susanne following.

Adam turned to Alice, whose eyes had grown round as saucers.

"Dear God, do we have to?" he asked her. "Just because they were here? Is that a custom?"

Alice shrugged. "I cannot even recall Lord Beasley's given name."

However, the midwife was chuckling as she gathered up her things. "Her ladyship is only teasing you, I'm sure," the woman said. "There's no such custom to naming that I've ever heard."

"Thank goodness," Adam said, "for we did have a few ideas of our own."

The woman left, and it was finally only the three of them.

"Sit, please," Alice said.

He took the spot beside her on the mattress, and before he realized what she was doing, she handed him their boy.

"Now I can stretch." Which she did, wincing before reaching over to take the glass of water from beside the bed. "Lady Beasley is correct. I am famished *and* thirsty. Broth would be lovely, but also some bread and cheese, a cup of tea, and . . . oddly, I would adore a cup of cocoa."

Adam drew the swaddled baby up higher against his chest before leaning down and kissing his forehead.

"You be good," he told the infant. "I am going to go make sure your mother has all she desires, and then I shall return directly." He would run to the kitchen as fast as he could to place the order for his hungry wife.

She held her arms out, and he gave her back their son. Placing a kiss on her forehead, too, Adam went to the door.

"I will make sure to fend off any watercress Cook tries to give you."

He heard Alice's answering laugh as he left the room. A father now in his own right, Adam asked himself if he felt any different going out the door as to when he had entered the room. *Was he more mature, perhaps, and responsible?*

No, was his answer. *But was it possible for his heart to have grown?* For he felt impossibly full of love, choked on it, in fact, making him clear his throat while tears sprang to his eyes.

A brand-new Diamond had entered the world, and by God, the little gem was his!

EPILOGUE

Derby, May 1853

"You planned your life very well, my love," Alice said to Adam. "Having four sisters, with two not yet married, has made it extremely easy for us to start our family. We never lack assistance."

They were enjoying a Diamond gathering at Oak Grove Hall, celebrating his mother's birthday and another child's entrance to the family, belonging to Clarity.

"If only our boy would grow up a bit," Adam said, flat on his back and idly putting his hands behind his head, staring at the sky through the branches of an apple tree. "I want to start teaching him to fish and ride."

Under the tree, reclining out of the noon sun on a blanket, she looked over at young William, lying between them. He was thriving under the love of his parents, aunts, uncles, cousins, and grandparents. At least, those on the Diamond side.

Alice had received a brief note of congratulations upon writing to her parents when she'd married Adam. And when she sent them word of the birth of her first baby, in their usual fashion, their felicitations reached her months later. Her parents welcomed their only grandchild, although they didn't say when or if they would return to meet him.

If she were honest with herself, her parents' absence didn't impact her life at all, beyond being a little embarrassed to call them family. Adam assured her it was *their* loss. Moreover, she had become as much a daughter of the Earl and Countess Diamond as the other four females were by blood. Alice was entirely comfortable going to her mother-in-law or sisters-in-law with any questions, even of the most personal nature or anything to do with child-rearing.

And the two younger sisters behaved as loving, practiced nannies to their nephew, making it easy for her and Adam to have time alone occasionally.

She couldn't imagine her life being any richer.

"Do not wish a minute of our boy's life away," she said. "Nor try to hurry him along. I adore Will at this age." Their son was on his back, looking up into the tree branches like his father, while kicking his legs and stretching up his still-pudgy arms as if preparing to pick the apples that would appear in another few months.

"I was only speaking in jest," Adam said. "Besides, I can strap him securely to a horse tomorrow."

"Adam!" she warned.

He laughed, and she joined in. Life was ridiculously grand.

She'd been thrilled to know she could have children, even happier to continue making love to her husband, often and soundly in order to bring their young son a brother or a sister. Adam wanted a large family, and Alice was pleased to oblige for she could think of nothing more worthy for her to do than make more Diamonds. And hopefully, at least one would take up the violin, for she would dearly love to play a duet with her own child.

When she considered where she had been not that long ago, her present life seemed truly astonishing. She'd been given a Diamond which, as she'd once told Adam, was far more precious than the Koh-i-Noor given to the Queen.

ADAM ENJOYED TEASING his wife, although he did intend to at least mount up and have William on his lap. Not today, nor tomorrow, but soon. It wouldn't hurt the boy to become used to sitting in a saddle.

Regardless, they couldn't hold back the wheels of time. Nor did Adam want to. As they turned, so did their lives become increasingly improved. Alice thought she was the one who'd been blessed by the many miracles that had changed her life—from hiding out as a governess to being Lady Diamond, a wife, mother, and sister.

Yet Adam felt equally changed for the better. He hadn't even realized what a complacent snout-nose he'd become until he'd been forced to set aside his prejudices. Letting his heart reign and rule had been the best thing he had ever done.

Turning his head to look at Alice, his warm and wonderful wife, he mused aloud, "Some people say lovers are fools. That one should always use one's brain over one's heart."

She hummed, thinking a moment. "Shakespeare said, 'So true a fool is love.' But he also said, 'Love looks not with the eyes, but with the mind.' I suppose you can consider love either way—and all-encompassing—in any case."

"Indeed. But can you imagine if we had missed out upon knowing one another?"

Alice shook her head, appearing momentarily alarmed.

"Truly, I cannot. It seems as if everything happened the way it was meant to, right down to my package of rosin falling onto the street when you were behind me."

"Watching your delightful arse," Adam said, because it was fun to be crude with his own wife once in a while. As usual, he made her laugh.

"It almost makes me believe in destiny," Alice continued, "as Lady Susanne so gracelessly mentioned at dinner that night."

They both groaned, recalling their utter mortification at the Beasleys' dining table.

Plucking some cool green grass, his wife trailed it over Will's arm, bringing forth his wonderful giggle. Then she sighed.

"There are times when I wonder how I can accept another moment of your kindness and generosity, not to mention the extraordinary way you love me. It is almost too wondrous."

Adam closed his eyes and took a deep breath. The air at Oak Grove in the apple orchard smelled familiar, evoking his childhood and his home, and now, it would forever remind him of this special time with his new family.

When he opened his eyes again, he had to lighten the mood. If they ventured further into the serious territory of how much they cherished what they had, futile fear would creep in over how much they had to lose. Thus, he pushed himself up to sitting.

"I am entirely mercenary, Wife. Think of all the money I shall save by not needing to hire a governess. Why, I believe we still have your frumpy clothing, with buttons up to the chin all in grays and browns, in a trunk in the attic. I'll have Mr. Lewis bring it down as soon as we return to London." He chuckled at the notion.

But Alice simply smiled with satisfaction. "I would do it all again to end up right here with you, *Husband*."

The way she said that word in her particular fashion, with a little whispering emphasis upon the "s" before it rolled off her sweet tongue, caused his body's typical, potent reaction.

Swallowing, his mouth suddenly dry, he didn't feel like laughing any longer. Adam wanted to roll her under him and tup her till she arched and spent while crying out his name like the primordial Eve.

Glancing back the way they'd come, he considered how much privacy they had in the orchard, the comfort of the blanket, the willingness of his wife, and the cooperation of their babe.

To his delight, Alice lifted Will, already languid from food and sunshine, and moved him to the edge of the blanket. Then she brushed her fingertips across his forehead. It was a trick she used to make their little one nod off. Sure enough, Will yawned broadly and closed his eyes, letting his thick dark lashes rest upon his cheeks.

Then she lay down again, closer, and started to draw up her light cotton skirt and petticoat.

"Husband," Alice repeated, drawing out the syllables, knowing exactly what she was doing.

Adam unfastened his trousers and proceeded to make love to his perfect lady until she did exactly as he'd imagined. Hearing his name called in her throaty fashion, he followed her pleasure by pumping his seed into Alice's fertile womb. Their passion was as old as his namesake, yet as fresh and new as their babe.

When they returned to the house half an hour later, he carried the basket of vegetables they'd been sent hours earlier to pick from the fruitful garden at Oak Hall—spring onions, radishes, and asparagus, having made sure to leave the watercress behind—and Alice carried William.

They walked in peaceful silence, both of the same mind, knowing each other without speaking, wrapped in intimacy, and protected by love.

Finis

ABOUT THE AUTHOR

USA Today bestselling author Sydney Jane Baily writes historical romance set in Victorian England, late 19th-century America, the Middle Ages, the Georgian era, and the Regency period. She creates happily-ever-after stories, engaging characters, and passionate romance with a touch of intrigue.

Born and raised in California, she has traveled the world, spending a lot of exceedingly happy time in the U.K. where her extended family resides, eating fish and chips, drinking shandy, and snacking on Maltesers and Cadbury bars. Sydney currently lives in New England with her family—human, canine, and feline.

At her website, SydneyJaneBaily.com, you can learn more about her books, sign up for her newsletter (and get a free book), and contact her. She loves to hear from her readers.